PENGUIN B

A Ship of the Line

In 1793, at the tender age of just seventeen, Horatio Hornblower was forced to find his sea legs as a midshipman. After suffering his first bout of seasickness, the hapless doctor's son quickly rose through the ranks to become Admiral of the Fleet Lord Hornblower. In between, Hornblower must sail back and forth along the coasts of Europe and the Americas, repeatedly engaging or eluding the mighty ships of Napoleon and Spain. His heroic exploits in the French revolutionary war and his many other adventures in service of his country have made the name Horatio Hornblower into legend.

C. S. Forester was born in Cairo in 1899, where his father was stationed as a government official. He studied medicine at Guy's Hospital, and after leaving Guy's without a degree he turned to writing as a career. His first success was *Payment Deferred*, a novel written at the age of twenty-four and later dramatized and filmed with Charles Laughton in the leading role. In 1932 Forester was offered a Hollywood contract, and from then until 1939 he spent thirteen weeks of every year in America. On the outbreak of war he entered the Ministry of Information and later he sailed with the Royal Navy to collect material for *The Ship*. He then made a voyage to the Bering Sea to gather material for a similar book on the United States Navy, and it was during this trip that he was stricken with arteriosclerosis, a disease which left him crippled. However, he continued to write and in the Hornblower novels created the most renowned sailor in twentieth-century fiction. He died in 1966.

Bernar‹   ›rpe
series o

523 469 59 7

A Ship of the Line

C. S. FORESTER

Introduction by Bernard Cornwell

PENGUIN BOOKS

PENGUIN BOOKS

Published by the Penguin Group
Penguin Books Ltd, 80 Strand, London WC2R ORL, England
Penguin Group (USA) Inc., 375 Hudson Street, New York, New York 10014, USA
Penguin Group (Canada), 90 Eglinton Avenue East, Suite 700, Toronto, Ontario, Canada M4P 2Y3
(a division of Pearson Penguin Canada Inc.)
Penguin Ireland, 25 St Stephen's Green, Dublin 2, Ireland (a division of Penguin Books Ltd)
Penguin Group (Australia), 250 Camberwell Road, Camberwell, Victoria 3124, Australia
(a division of Pearson Australia Group Pty Ltd)
Penguin Books India Pvt Ltd, 11 Community Centre, Panchsheel Park,
New Delhi – 110 017, India
Penguin Group (NZ), 67 Apollo Drive, Rosedale, Auckland 0632, New Zealand
(a division of Pearson New Zealand Ltd)
Penguin Books (South Africa) (Pty) Ltd, 24 Sturdee Avenue, Rosebank, Johannesburg 2196, South Africa

Penguin Books Ltd, Registered Offices: 80 Strand, London WC2R ORL, England

www.penguin.com

First published by Michael Joseph 1938
Published in Penguin Books 1956
Reissued in this edition 2011

002

Copyright © the Estate of C. S. Forester, 1938
Introduction copyright © Bernard Cornwell, 2006
All rights reserved

The moral right of the author has been asserted

Typeset in 11/13pt Monotype Dante
by Palimpsest Book Production Limited, Falkirk, Stirlingshire
Printed in England by Clays Ltd, St Ives plc

ISBN: 978-0-241-95558-1

www.greenpenguin.co.uk

Introduction

This is the second book in the series (but the sixth in the chronological order of the tales) and it was published in 1938, a year after the first. Forester claims its inspiration was, of all things, a shish kebab. He was eating one and, as he pushed the pieces of lamb, onion and peppers off their skewer onto his plate, he was suddenly struck by the idea that each piece of food was a miniature story, an episode, and to hold them all together he just needed a skewer, and the skewer would be a ship. Instead of one long story he would use smaller episodes of 'cutting-out expeditions, convoy battles and shore raids' and would trust in the reader's fascination with the ship and its renowned captain to keep the interest going. It was a technique he frequently used for his Hornblower novels, and he made it work extraordinarily well, though nowadays it is out of fashion.

The skewer is HMS *Sutherland*, a ship of the line captured from the Dutch. The normal practice was to keep the names of captured foreign ships unless they were entirely unsuitable. At the Battle of the Nile the *Tonnant* was captured and she fought at Trafalgar as HMS *Tonnant*, but the *Franklin*, another French ship taken at the Nile, was renamed HMS *Canopus*, presumably on the grounds that no British ship could possibly carry the name of an American rebel. Hornblower's new command had originally been named the *Eendracht*, but that was probably too tortuous for British tongues so she becomes the *Sutherland*.

HMS *Sutherland* is a ship of the line, a phrase that indicates she was heavy enough to take her place in the line of battle. Ships with fewer than sixty-four guns would never be willingly exposed to the horrors of battleship broadsides, and most of those broadsides came from seventy-fours; the workhorses of the Napoleonic navies. Seventy-four merely signifies the number of guns carried. In British ships eighteen of those cannon would have been small nine-pounder guns on the forecastle and quarterdeck, though the real power lay on the gundecks. The upper usually had twenty-eight eighteen pounders (sometimes twenty-four pounders), while the lower gundeck carried twenty-eight thirty-two pounders. This gave a seventy-four a broadside (which was just half the ship's guns firing) of around three quarters of a ton of metal, though in truth it was heavier for a seventy-four would inevitably have carried a half-dozen short-range carronades. For comparison the eighty field guns of the French Grand Battery at Waterloo, which hammered the centre of Wellington's line, fired only a quarter of a ton of metal with each discharge. A ship of the line was a floating artillery platform, and a formidable one, and the passage in this book where Forester describes the *Sutherland* attacking a column of troops on a coastal road is a chilling reminder of the sheer killing power of such a warship.

The story of *A Ship of the Line* carries on from *The Happy Return*, and it continues the distant relationship between Hornblower and Lady Barbara Wellesley, a relationship made even more difficult by Lady Barbara's marriage to Admiral Sir Percy Leighton, who now commands the squadron in which the *Sutherland* sails. Sir Percy is irritating, though Forester resisted the temptation to make him into a fool. Yet, throughout the book and, indeed, through much of the series, Hornblower is presented as the one competent man in a sea of ineptitude. There are exceptions; Bush is one, as is the wonderful character of Coxswain Brown who accompanies Hornblower through much of his subsequent career. We also learn in this book, though no explanation is given, that Hornblower hated parsons! Why? One suspects it was a prejudice of the author.

Cecil Scott Forester was born in Egypt to British parents in 1899. His real name was Cecil Lewis Troughton Smith and he was raised in Britain where, as a child, he was an avid reader, usually the first step in the making of a writer. In 1917, before his eighteenth birthday, he volunteered for the British army, fully expecting to fight on the Western Front, but he was rejected as medically unfit. He was a skinny, short-sighted six-footer who enjoyed sports, but the army's physical examination revealed a dangerously weak heart. So instead of serving as a soldier, Forester entered Guy's Hospital as a medical student, an experience as unhappy as it was unsuccessful, but Forester's ambitions were already fixed on writing. His first efforts failed, but he persevered and in 1924, with *Payment Deferred*, enjoyed his first success. The filming of that novel introduced Forester to Hollywood and, more crucially, California. During the Second World War he moved to the United States at the request of the British government, who wanted him to produce articles and stories that would encourage American support for the British war effort. He discovered he liked living in the States and most of the Hornblower books were written in California, where, with his second wife, he remained until his death in 1966. By then he had become one of the world's most popular authors with almost sixty novels to his name and, even if he had never dreamed up Hornblower, he would be famous as the author of *The African Queen*, *The Gun*, *Brown on Resolution* and *Hunting the Bismarck*.

The first three Hornblower books are all short, and this second book ends in disaster, so it was obvious to readers that a follow-up novel must come. So it did, and that third novel, together with the first two, were the joint basis for the Hollywood movie which starred the incomparable Gregory Peck. Not bad for a tale partially inspired by a shish kebab! 'And to this day,' Forester wrote, 'the sight of shish kebab on a skewer calls up to my mind's eye a three-dimensional picture of a blue sea and a hot sun and HMS *Sutherland* standing in under easy sail to her rendezvous off Palamos Point.' A ship of the line, Horatio Hornblower and French enemies; a recipe for pure pleasure.

I

Captain Horatio Hornblower was reading a smudgy proof which the printers had just sent round to his lodgings.

'To all Young men of *Spirit*,' he said. 'Seamen, Landsmen, and Boys, who wish to strike a Blow for Freedom and to cause the Corsican Tyrant to wish that he had never dared the Wrath of these British Isles. His Majesty's Ship *Sutherland* of two decks and seventy-four guns is at present commissioning at Plymouth, and a few *Vacancies* still exist to complete her Crew. Captain *Horatio Hornblower* in command has lately returned from a Cruize in the *South Sea* during which in command of the Frigate *Lydia* of thirty-six guns, he engaged and *sank* the Spanish vessel *Natividad* of two decks and more than *twice the force*. The Officers, Petty Officers, and men of the *Lydia* have all joined him in the *Sutherland*. What Heart of Oak can resist this Appeal to Join this Band of Heroes and Share with them the new Glories which await them? Who will teach Monsieur *Jean Crapaud* that the Seas are *Britannia's* where no Frog-eating *Frenchman* can show his Face? Who wishes for a Hatful of Golden Louis d'or for *Prize Money*? There will be *Fiddlers* and *Dancing* every evening, and Provisions at *sixteen* ounces to the Pound, the Best of Beef, and Best of Bread, and *Grog* at midday every Day of the Week and *Sundays*, all in addition to the *Pay* under the *Warrant* of His Most

Gracious Majesty King *George*! In the *Place* where this notice is read can be found an Officer of His Majesty's Ship *Sutherland* who will enlist any *Willing Hearts* who Thirst for Glory.'

Captain Hornblower struggled against hopelessness as he read the proof. Appeals of this sort were to be read in dozens in every market town. It hardly seemed likely that he could attract recruits to a humdrum ship of the line when dashing frigate captains of twice his reputation were scouring the country and able to produce figures of prize money actually won in previous voyages. To send four lieutenants, each with half a dozen men, round the southern counties to gather recruits in accordance with this poster was going to cost him practically all the pay he had accumulated last commission, and he feared lest it should be money thrown away.

Yet something had to be done. The *Lydia* had supplied him with two hundred able-bodied seamen (his placard said nothing of the fact that they had been compulsorily transferred without a chance of setting foot on English soil after a commission of two years' duration) but to complete his crew he needed another fifty seamen and two hundred landsmen and boys. The guardship had found him none at all. Failure to complete his crew might mean the loss of his command, and from that would result unemployment and half pay – eight shillings a day – for the rest of his life. He could form no estimate at all of how much favour he was regarded with at the Admiralty, and in the absence of data it was natural to him to believe that his employment hung precariously in the balance.

Anxiety and strain brought oaths to his lips as he tapped on the proof with his pencil – silly blasphemies of whose senselessness he was quite well aware even as he mouthed them. But he was careful to speak softly; Maria was resting in the bedroom through the double doors behind him, and he did not want to rouse her. Maria (although it was too early to be certain) believed herself to be pregnant, and Hornblower was sated with her cloying tenderness. His irritation increased at the thought of it; he hated the land, the necessity of recruiting, the stuffy sitting room, the loss of the independence he had enjoyed during the months of his last commission. Irritably he took his hat and stole quietly out. The printer's messenger was waiting, hat in hand, in the hall. To him Hornblower abruptly handed back the proof with a curt order for one gross of placards to be struck off, and then he made his way into the noisy streets.

The tollkeeper at the Halfpenny Gate Bridge at sight of his uniform let him through without payment; a dozen watermen at the ferry knew him as the captain of the *Sutherland* and competed to catch his eye – they could expect an ample fee for rowing a Captain to his ship up the long length of the Hamoaze. Hornblower took his seat in a pair-oared wherry; it gave him some satisfaction to say no word at all as they shoved off and began the long pull through the tangle of shipping. Stroke oar shifted his quid and was about to utter some commonplace or other to his passenger, but at sight of his black brow and ill-tempered frown he thought better of it and changed his opening word to a self-conscious cough – Hornblower, acutely aware of the by-play although he had spared the man no open glance, lost some of his ill-temper as a result. He noticed the play of muscles in the brown forearms as the man strained at his oar; there was tattooing on the wrist, and a thin gold ring gleamed in the man's left ear. He must have been a seaman before he became a waterman – Hornblower longed inexpressibly to have him haled on board when they should reach the *Sutherland*; if he could only lay his hands on a few dozen prime seamen his anxiety would be at an end. But the fellow of course would have a certificate of exemption, else he would never be able to ply his trade here in a part where a quarter of the British Navy came seeking for men.

The victualling yard and the dockyard as they rowed past were swarming with men, too, all of them able bodied, and half of them seamen – shipwrights and riggers – at whom Hornblower stared as longingly and as helplessly as a cat at goldfish in a bowl. The rope walk and the mast house, the sheer hulk and the smoking chimneys of the biscuit bakery went slowly by. There was the *Sutherland*, riding to her moorings off Bull Point; Hornblower, as he gazed at her across the choppy water, was conscious of a queer admixture of conservative dislike in the natural pride which he felt in his new command. Her round bow looked odd at a time when every British-built ship of the line had the beakhead to which his eye had long grown accustomed; her lines were ungainly and told their tale (as Hornblower noticed every time he looked at her) of more desirable qualities sacrificed for shallow draught. Everything about her – save for the lower masts which were of English origin – proved that she was Dutch built, planned to negotiate the mudbanks and shallow estuaries of the Dutch coast. The *Sutherland*, in fact, had once been the Dutch 74 *Eendracht*, captured off the Texel and, now re-armed, the ugliest and least desirable two-decker in the Navy List.

God help him, thought Hornblower, eyeing her with a distaste accentuated by his lack of men to man her, if ever he should find himself trying to claw off a lee shore in her. She would drift off to leeward like a cocked-hat paper boat. And at the subsequent court-martial nobody would believe a word of the evidence regarding her unweatherly qualities.

'Easy!' he snapped at the wherrymen, and the oars ceased to grind in the rowlocks as the men rested; the sound of the waves slapping the side of the boat became suddenly more apparent.

As they drifted over the dancing water Hornblower continued his discontented examination. She was newly painted, but in as niggardly a fashion as the dockyard authorities could manage – the dull yellow and black was unrelieved by any white or red. A wealthy captain and first lieutenant would have supplied the deficiency out of their own pockets, and would have shown a lick of gold leaf here and there, but Hornblower had no money to spare for gold leaf, and he knew that Bush, who kept four sisters and a mother on his pay, had none either – not even though his professional future depended in some part on the appearance of the *Sutherland*. Some captains would by hook or by crook have cozened more paint – gold leaf, too, for that matter – out of the dockyard, as Hornblower ruefully told himself. But he was not good at cozening; not the prospect of all the gold leaf in the world could lead him to slap a dockyard clerk on the back and win his favour with flattery and false bonhomie; not that his conscience would stop him, but his self-consciousness would.

Someone on deck spied him now. He could hear the pipes twittering as preparations were made to receive him. Let 'em wait a bit longer; he was not going to be hurried today. The *Sutherland*, riding high without her stores in her, was showing a wide streak of her copper. That copper was new, thank God. Before the wind the ugly old ship might show a pretty turn of speed. As the wind swung her across the tide she revealed her run to him. Looking over her lines, Hornblower occupied his mind with estimates of how to get the best perform-ance out of her. Twenty-two years of sea-going experience helped him. Before his mind's eye he called up a composite diagram of all the forces that would be at work on her at sea – the pressure of the wind on her sails, the rudder balancing the headsails, the lateral resistance of the keel, the friction of the skin, the impact of waves against her bows. Hornblower sketched out a preliminary trial arrangement, deciding just how (until practical tests gave him more data) he would have the masts raked and the ship trimmed. But next moment he remembered bitterly that at present he had no crew to man her, and that unless he could find one all these plans would be useless.

'Give way,' he growled to the wherrymen, and they threw their weight on the oars again.

'Easy, Jake,' said bow oar to stroke, looking over his shoulder.

The wherry swung round under the *Sutherland*'s stern

– trust those men to know how a boat should be laid alongside a ship of war – giving Hornblower a sight of the stern gallery which constituted to Hornblower one of the most attractive points about the ship. He was glad that the dockyard had not done away with it, as they had done in so many ships of the line. Up in that gallery he would be able to enjoy wind and sea and sun, in a privacy unattainable on deck. He would have a hammock chair made for use there. He could even take his exercise there, with no man's eye upon him – the gallery was eighteen feet long, and he would only have to stoop a little under the overhanging cove. Hornblower yearned inexpressibly for the time when he would be out at sea, away from all the harassing troubles of the land, walking his stern gallery in the solitude in which alone he could relax nowadays. Yet without a crew all this blissful prospect was withheld from him indefinitely. He must find men somewhere.

He felt in his pockets for silver to pay the boatmen, and although silver was woefully short his self-consciousness drove him into overpaying the men in the fashion he attributed to his fellow captains of ships of the line.

'Thank 'ee, sir. Thank 'ee,' said the stroke oar, knuckling his forehead.

Hornblower went up the ladder and came in through the entry port with its drab paint where in the Dutchmen's time gilding had blazed bravely. The pipes of the boatswain's mates twittered wildly, the marine guard presented arms, the sideboys stood rigidly at attention. Gray, master's mate – lieutenants kept no watch in harbour – was officer of the watch and saluted

7

as Hornblower touched his hat to the quarterdeck. Hornblower did not condescend to speak to him, although Gray was a favourite of his; the rigid guard he kept on himself for fear of unnecessary loquacity forbade. Instead he looked round him silently.

The decks were tangled with gear as the work of rigging the ship proceeded, but the tangle, as Hornblower was careful to note, carried under its surface the framework of orderliness. The coils of rope, the groups at work on the deck, the sail-maker's party sewing at a topsail on the forecastle, gave an impression of confusion, but it was disciplined confusion. The severe orders which he had issued to his officers had borne fruit. The crew of the *Lydia* when they had heard that they were to be transferred bodily to the *Sutherland* without even a day on shore, had nearly mutinied. They were in hand again now.

'Master-at-arms wishes to report, sir,' said Gray.

'Send for him, then,' answered Hornblower.

The master-at-arms was the warrant officer responsible for enforcing discipline, and was a man new to Hornblower, named Price. Hornblower concluded that he had allegations of indiscipline to lodge, and he sighed even while he set his face in an expression of merciless rigidity. Probably it would be a matter of flogging, and he hated the thought of the blood and the agony. But, at the beginning of a commission like this, with a restive crew under his orders, he must not hesitate to flog if necessary – to have the skin and flesh stripped from the offenders' backbones.

Price was coming along the gangway now at the head of the strangest procession. Two by two behind him came a column of thirty men, each one handcuffed to his neighbour, save for the last two who clanked drearily along with leg-irons at their ankles. Nearly all of them were in rags, and the rags had no sort of nautical flavour about them at all. The rags of a great many of them were sacking, some had corduroy, and Hornblower, peering closer, saw that one wore the wrecks of a pair of moleskin breeches. Yet another wore the remains of what had once been a respectable black broadcloth suit – white skin showed through a rent in the shoulder. All of them had stubbly beards, black, brown, golden, and grey, and those who were not bald had great mops of tangled hair. The two ship's corporals brought up the rear.

''Alt,' ordered Price. 'Orf 'ats.'

The procession shuffled to a halt, and the men stood sullenly on the quarterdeck. Some of them kept their eyes on the deck, while the others gaped sheepishly round them.

'What the devil's all this?' demanded Hornblower sharply.

'New 'ands, sir,' said Price. 'I signed a receipt to the sodgers what brought 'em, sir.'

'Where did they bring them from?' rasped Hornblower.

'Exeter assizes, sir,' said Price, producing a list. 'Poachers, four of 'em. Waites, that's 'im in the moleskin breeches, sir, 'e was found guilty of sheepstealing. That 'un in black, 'is crime's bigamy, sir – 'e was a brewer's manager before this 'appened to 'im. The others is larceny mostly, sir, 'cept for them two in front what's in for rick-burning and t'other two in irons. Robbery with violence is what they done.'

'Ha – h'm', said Hornblower, wordless for the moment. The new hands blinked at him, some with hope in their eyes, some with hatred, some with indifference. They had chosen service at sea rather than the gallows, or transportation, or the gaol. Months in prison awaiting trial accounted for their dilapidated appearance. Here was a fine addition to the ship's company, thought Hornblower, bitterly – budding mutineers, sullen skulkers, half-witted yokels. But hands they were and he must make the best of them. They were frightened, sullen, resentful. It would be worth trying to win their affection. His naturally humanitarian instincts dictated the course he decided to pursue after a moment's quick thinking.

'Why are they still handcuffed?' he demanded, loud enough for them all to hear 'Release them at once.'

'Begging your pardon, sir,' apologized Price. 'I didn't want to without orders, sir, seeing what they are and 'ow they come 'ere.'

'That's nothing to do with it', snapped Hornblower. 'They're enlisted in the King's service now. And I'll have no man in irons in *my* ship unless he's given *me* cause to order it.'

Hornblower kept his gaze from wavering towards the new hands, and steadily addressed his declamation to Price – it was more effective delivered that way, he knew, even while he despised himself for using such rhetorical tricks.

'I never want to see new hands in charge of the master-at-arms again,' he continued, hotly. 'They are recruits in an honourable service, with an honourable future before them. I'll thank you to see to it another time. Now find one of the purser's mates and see that each of these men is properly dressed in accordance with my orders.'

Normally it might be harmful to discipline to rate a subordinate officer in front of the men, but in the case of the master-at-arms Hornblower knew that little damage was being done. The men would come to hate the master-at-arms anyway sooner or later – his privileges of rank and pay were given him so that he might be a whipping boy for the crew's discontent. Hornblower could drop the rasp in his voice and address the hands directly, now.

'A man who does his duty as best he can,' he said, kindly, 'has nothing to fear in this ship, and everything to hope for. Now I want to see how smart you can look in your new clothes, and with the dirt of the place you have come from washed off you. Dismiss.'

He had won over some of the poor fools, at least, he told himself. Some of the faces which had been sullen with despair were shining with hope now, after this experience of being treated as men and not as brutes – for the first time for months, if not the first time in their lives. He watched them off the gangway. Poor devils; in Hornblower's opinion they had made a bad bargain in exchanging the gaol for the navy. But at least they represented thirty out of the two hundred and fifty additional human bodies which he needed to drag at ropes and to heave at capstan bars so as to take this old *Sutherland* out to sea.

Lieutenant Bush came hastening on to the quarterdeck, and touched his hat to his captain. The stern swarthy face with its incongruous blue eyes broke into a smile just as incongruous. It gave Hornblower a queer twinge, almost of conscience, to see the evident pleasure which Bush experienced at sight of him. It was odd to know that he was admired – it might even be said that he was loved – by this very capable sailor, this splendid disciplinarian and fearless fighter who boasted so many of the good qualities in which Hornblower felt himself to be lacking.

'Good morning, Bush,' he said. 'Have you seen the new draft?'

'No, sir. I was rowing guard for the middle watch and I've only just turned out. Where do they hail from, sir?'

Hornblower told him, and Bush rubbed his hands with pleasure.

'Thirty!' he said. 'That's rare. I never hoped for more than a dozen from Exeter assizes. And Bodmin assizes open today. Please God we get another thirty there.'

'We won't get topmen from Bodmin assizes,' said Hornblower, comforted beyond measure at the equanimity with which Bush regarded the introduction of gaolbirds into the *Sutherland*'s crew.

'No, sir. But the West India convoy's due this week. The guards ought to nab two hundred there. We'll get twenty if we get our rights.'

'M'm,' said Hornblower, and turned away uneasily. He was not the sort of captain – neither the distinguished kind nor the wheedling kind – who could be sure of favours from the Port Admiral. 'I must look round below.'

That changed the subject effectively enough.

'The women are restless,' said Bush. 'I'd better come, too, sir, if you don't object.'

The lower gun deck offered a strange spectacle, lit vaguely by the light which came through half-a-dozen open gun ports. There were fifty women there. Three or four were still in their hammocks, lying on their sides looking out on the others. Some were sitting in groups on the deck, chattering loud-voiced. One or two were chaffering for food through the gun ports with the occupants of shore boats floating just outside; the netting which impeded desertion had a broad enough mesh to allow a hand to pass through. Two more, each backed by a supporting group, were quarrelling violently. They were in odd contrast – one was tall and dark, so tall as to have to crouch round-shouldered under the five-foot deck-beams, while the other, short, broad, and fair, was standing up boldly before her menacing advance.

'That's what I said,' she maintained stoutly. 'And I'll say it again. I ain't afeared o' *you*, Mrs Dawson, as you call yourself.'

'A-ah,' screamed the dark one at this crowning insult. She swooped forward, and with greedy hands she seized the other by the hair, shaking her head from side to side as if she would soon shake it off. In return her face was scratched and her shins were kicked by her stout-hearted opponent. They whirled round in a flurry of petticoats, when one of the women in the hammocks screamed a warning to them.

'Stop it, you mad bitches! 'Ere's the cap'n.'

They fell apart, panting and tousled. Every eye was turned towards Hornblower as he walked forward in the patchy light, his head bowed under the deck above.

'The next woman fighting will be put ashore instantly,' growled Hornblower.

13

The dark woman swept her hair from her eyes and sniffed with disdain.

'You needn't put *me* ashore, Cap'n,' she said. 'I'm goin'. There ain't a farden to be had out o' this starvation ship.'

She was apparently expressing a sentiment which was shared by a good many of the women, for the speech was followed by a little buzz of approval.

'Ain't the men *never* goin' to get their pay notes?' piped up the woman in the hammock.

'Enough o' that,' roared Bush, suddenly. He pushed forward anxious to save his captain from the insults to which he was exposed, thanks to a government which left its men still unpaid after a month in port. 'You there, what are you doing in your hammock after eight bells?'

But this attempt to assume a counter-offensive met with disaster.

'I'll come out if you like, Mr Lieutenant,' she said, flicking off her blanket and sliding to the deck. 'I parted with my gown to buy my Tom a sausage, and my petticoat's bought him a soop o' West Country ale. Would you have me on deck in my shift, Mr Lieutenant?'

A titter went round the deck.

'Get back and be decent,' spluttered Bush, on fire with embarrassment.

Hornblower was laughing, too – perhaps it was because he was married that the sight of a half-naked woman alarmed him not nearly as much as it did his first lieutenant.

'Never will I be decent now,' said the woman, swinging her legs up into the hammock and composedly draping the blanket over her, 'until my Tom gets his pay warrant.'

'An' when he gets it,' sneered the fair woman. 'What can he do with it without shore leave? Sell it to a bumboat shark for a quarter!'

'Fi' pound for twenty-three months' pay!' added another. 'An' me a month gone a'ready.'

'Avast there,' said Bush.

Hornblower beat a retreat, abandoning – forgetting, rather – the object of his visit of inspection below. He could not face those women when the question of pay came up again. The men had been scandalously badly treated, imprisoned in the ship within sight of land, and their wives (some of them certainly were wives, although by Admiralty regulations a simple verbal declaration of the existence of a marriage was sufficient to allow them on board) had just cause of complaint. No one, not even Bush, knew that the few guineas which had been doled out among the crew represented a large part of Hornblower's accumulated pay – all he could spare, in fact, except for the necessary money to pay his officers' expenses when they should start on their recruiting journeys.

His vivid imagination and absurd sensitiveness between them perhaps exaggerated part of the men's hardships. The thought of the promiscuity of life below decks, where a man was allotted eighteen inches' width in which to swing his hammock, while his wife was allowed eighteen inches next to him, all in a long row, husbands, wives, and single men, appalled him. So did the thought of women having to live on the revolting lower-deck food. Possibly he made insufficient allowance for the hardening effect of long habit.

He emerged through the fore hatchway on to the maindeck a little unexpectedly. Thompson, one of the captains of the forecastle, was dealing with the new hands.

'P'raps we'll make sailors of you,' he was saying, 'and p'raps we won't. Overside with a shot at your feet, more likely, before we sight Ushant. And a waste o' good shot, too. Come on wi' that pump, there. Let's see the colour o' your hides, gaolbirds. When the cat gets at you we'll see the colour o' your backbones, too, you –'

'Enough of that, Thompson,' roared Hornblower, furious.

In accordance with his standing orders the new hands were being treated to rid them of vermin. Naked and shivering, they were grouped about the deck. Two of them were having their heads shorn down to the bare skin; a dozen of them, who had already submitted to this treatment (and looking strangely sickly and out of place with the prison pallor still on them), were being herded by Thompson towards the washdeck pump which a couple of grinning hands were working. Fright was making them shiver as much as cold – not one of them, probably, had ever had a bath before, and what with the prospect, and Thompson's bloodcurdling remarks and the strange surroundings, they were pitiful to see.

It enraged Hornblower, who somehow or other had never forgotten the misery of his early days at sea. Bullying was abhorrent to him like any other sort of wanton cruelty, and he had no sympathy whatever with the aim of so many of his brother officers, to break the spirit of the men under him. One of these days his professional reputation and his future might depend on these very men risking their lives cheerfully and willingly – sacrificing them, if need be – and he could not imagine cowed and broken-spirited men doing that. The shearing and the bath were necessary, if the ship was to be kept clear of the fleas and bugs and lice which could make life a misery on board, but he was not going to have his precious men cowed more than was unavoidable. It was curious that Hornblower, who never could believe himself to be a leader of men, would always lead rather than drive.

'Under the pump with you, men,' he said kindly, and when they still hesitated – 'When we get to sea you'll see *me* under that pump, every morning at seven bells. Isn't that so, there?'

'Aye, aye, sir,' chorused the hands at the pump – their captain's strange habit of having cold seawater pumped over him every morning had been a source of much discussion on board the *Lydia*.

'So under with you, and perhaps you'll all be captains one of these days. You, there, Waites, show these others you're not afraid.'

It was blessed good fortune that Hornblower was able not only to remember the name, but to recognize in his new guise Waites, the sheepstealer with the moleskin breeches. They blinked at this resplendent captain in his gold lace, whose tone was cheerful and whose dignity still admitted taking a daily bath. Waites steeled himself to dive under the spouting hose, and, gasping, rotated heroically under the cold water. Someone threw him a lump of holystone with which to scrub himself, while the others jostled for their turn – the poor fools were like sheep; it was only necessary to set one moving to make all the rest eager to follow.

Hornblower caught sight of a red angry welt across one white shoulder. He beckoned Thompson out of earshot.

'You've been free with that starter of yours, Thompson,' he said.

Thompson grinned uneasily, fingering the two-foot length of rope knotted at the end, with which petty officers were universally accustomed to stimulate the activity of the men under them.

'I won't have a petty officer in my ship,' said Hornblower, 'who doesn't know when to use a starter and when not to. These men haven't got their wits about 'em yet, and hitting 'em won't remedy it. Make another mistake like that, Thompson, and I'll disrate you. And then you'll clean out the heads of this ship every day of this commission. That'll do.'

Thompson shrank away, abashed by the genuine anger which Hornblower displayed.

'Keep your eye on him, Mr Bush, if you please,' added Hornblower. 'Sometimes a reprimand makes a petty officer take it out of the men more than ever to pay himself back. And I won't have it.'

'Aye aye, sir,' said Bush, philosophically.

Hornblower was the only captain he had ever heard of who bothered his head about the use of starters. Starters were as much part of Navy life as bad food and eighteen inches per hammock and peril at sea. Bush could never understand Hornblower's disciplinary methods. He had been positively horrified when he had heard his captain's public admission that he, too, had baths under the washdeck pump – it seemed madness for a captain to allow his men to guess that they were of the same flesh as his. But two years under Hornblower's command had taught him that Hornblower's strange ways sometimes attained surprising results. He was ready to obey him, loyally though blindly, resigned and yet admiring.

2

'The boy from the Angel has brought a note, sir,' said the landlady, when Hornblower called her in in reply to her knock at the sitting room door. 'He waits an answer.'

Hornblower felt a shock as he read the address – the clear feminine handwriting, which he recognized although it was months since he saw it last, meant so much to him. He tried to disguise his feelings as he spoke to his wife.

'It is addressed to both of us, my dear,' he said. 'Shall I open it?'

'As you please,' said Maria.

Hornblower broke the wafer and unfolded the note.

> *The Angel Inn,*
> *Plymouth.*
> *Fourth May, 1810.*
> *Rear Admiral Sir Percy and Lady Barbara Leighton*
> *would esteem it an Honour if Captain and Mrs Horatio*
> *Hornblower would dine with them at this address*
> *Tomorrow, the Fifth, at four o'clock.*

'The Admiral is at the Angel. He wants us to dine with him tomorrow,' said Hornblower, as casually as his beating heart would allow. 'Lady Barbara is with him. I think we must accept, my dear.'

He passed the note over to his wife.

'I have only my blue sack gown,' said Maria, looking up from reading it.

The first thing a woman ever thought about on receiving an invitation was what she should wear. Hornblower tried to bend his mind to the consideration of the blue sack gown, when all the time his heart was singing songs at the knowledge that Lady Barbara was only two hundred yards away.

'It looks perfect on you, my dear,' he said. 'You know how much I have always liked it.'

It would call for a far better gown to look well on Maria's dumpy figure. But Hornblower knew that they must – they *must* – accept the invitation, and it would be a kindness to reassure Maria. It did not matter what clothes Maria wore as long as she thought she looked well in them. Maria smiled happily at the compliment, giving Hornblower a prick of conscience. He felt like Judas. Maria would look coarse and badly dressed and stupid beside Lady Barbara, and yet he knew that as long as he pretended to be in love with her she would be happy and unconscious.

He wrote a careful acceptance, and rang the bell for it to be given to the messenger. Then he buttoned his uniform coat.

'I must go down to the ship,' he said.

Maria's reproachful look hurt him. He knew that she had been looking forward to spending the afternoon with him, and indeed he had not intended to visit the ship that day. It was only an excuse to gain privacy for himself. He could not bear the thought of being mewed up in that sitting room with Maria and her platitudes. He wanted to be alone to hug to himself the thought

21

that Lady Barbara was in the same town, that he was going to see her tomorrow. He could not sit still with those thoughts bubbling within him. He could have sung for joy as he walked briskly down to the ferry, thrusting aside all remembrance of Maria's dutiful acquiescence in his departure – well she knew how great were the demands made upon a captain by the commissioning of a ship of the line.

In his yearning for solitude he urged the rowers of his boat until they sweated. On deck he gave the briefest of salutes to the quarterdeck and to the officer of the watch, before plunging below to the security and peace for which he had been yearning. There were a hundred matters to which he could have devoted his attention but he would not stay for one of them. He strode across his cabin – littered with the preparations made for when he should come on board – and out through the stern window into the great stern gallery. There, sheltered from all interruption, he could lean against the rail, and stare across the water.

The ebb was running, and with the wind light from the north-east the *Sutherland*'s stern gallery looked southward down the length of the Hamoaze. To his left lay the dockyard, as busy as a beehive. Before him the glittering water was studded with shipping, with shore boats rowing hither and thither. In the distance beyond the roofs of the victualling yard he could see Mount Edgcumbe – Plymouth was out of his sight, round the corner from the Devil's Point; he would not have the satisfaction of gazing upon the roof that sheltered Lady Barbara.

Still, she was there, and he would see her tomorrow.

He gripped the rail in his ecstasy until his fingers hurt him. He turned away and began to walk up and down the gallery, his hands behind his back to counterbalance the stoop necessitated by the cove above. The pain he had felt at first, three weeks back, when he had heard of Lady Barbara's marriage to Admiral Leighton was gone by now. There was only the joy in the thought that she still remembered him. Hornblower dallied with the idea that she might have travelled down to Plymouth with her husband in the expectation of seeing him. It was possible – Hornblower would not stop to think that she might have been influenced by the desire to spend a few more days with her new husband. She must have cajoled Sir Percy into sending this invitation on the moment of his arrival; Hornblower would not make allowance for the fact that any admiral must be anxious for an early opportunity to study an unknown captain placed under his command. She must have made Sir Percy ask at the Admiralty for his services – that would explain why they had found for him a new ship and a new command without a single month's interval of half pay. It was to Lady Barbara that he owed the very comforting addition of ten shillings a day to his pay which went into the command of a ship of the line.

He was a quarter of the way up the captains' list now. In less than twenty years' time – long before he was sixty – if he continued to obtain commands in this fashion he would hoist his flag as an admiral. Then they might yellow him if they wanted to; he would be satisfied with admiral's rank. On admiral's half pay he could live in London, find a patron who would nominate him to a seat in Parliament. He would know power, and dignity, and security. All this was possible – and Lady Barbara still remembered him, cherished a kindly thought of him, was anxious to see him again despite the ludicrous way in which he had behaved towards her. High spirits bubbled within him again.

A seagull, wheeling motionless up wind, suddenly flapped its wings until it hovered stationary, and screamed raucously in his face. It flapped and screamed aimlessly along the gallery, and then, equally aimlessly, wheeled away again. Hornblower followed it with his eyes, and when he resumed his walk the thread of his thoughts was broken. Instantly there loomed up again into his consciousness the knowledge of the frightful need of men under which he laboured. Tomorrow he would have to confess miserably to his admiral that the *Sutherland* was still a hundred and fifty men short of complement; he would be found wanting in the very first of a captain's duties. An officer might be the finest possible seaman, the most fearless fighter (and Hornblower did not think himself either), and yet his talents were useless if he could not man his ship.

Probably Leighton had never asked for his services at all, and he had been allotted to Leighton's squadron by some trick of fate. Leighton would suspect him of having been his wife's lover, would be consumed with jealousy, and would watch for every opportunity to achieve his ruin. He would make his life a misery to him, would plague him to madness, and would finally have him broken and dismissed the service – any admiral could break any captain if he set his mind to it. Perhaps Lady Barbara had planned to put him thus in Leighton's power, and was working his ruin in revenge for his treatment of her. That seemed much more likely than his earlier wild imaginings, thought Hornblower, the cold fit working on him.

She must have guessed just what Maria was like, and must have sent the invitation so as to have the pleasure of gloating over her weaknesses. The dinner tomorrow would be one long humiliation for him. He could not venture to draw on his next quarter's pay for another ten days at least; otherwise he would have taken Maria out to buy her the finest gown in Plymouth – although what would a Plymouth gown avail in the sight of an earl's daughter who would undoubtedly buy all her clothes from Paris? He had not twenty pounds in the whole world now, having sent Bush and Gerard and Rayner and Hooker, his four lieutenants, out to drum-up recruits. They had taken thirty men with them, the only trustworthy men in the whole ship, too. Probably there would be trouble on the lower deck in consequence – probably reaching a head tomorrow while he was dining with his admiral.

Gloomy anticipation could go no further than that. He jerked his head up with irritation, and hit it hard against one of the beams of the cove above. Then he clenched his fists and cursed the service, as he had cursed it a thousand times before. That made him laugh at himself – if Hornblower had never been able to laugh at himself he would have been, long ago, another of the mad captains in the Navy List. He took a firmer grip on his emotions and set himself to thinking seriously about the future.

The orders which had attached him to Admiral Leighton's squadron had stated briefly that he was destined for service in the Western Mediterranean, and it was an uncovenanted mercy on the part of the lords of the Admiralty to give him that much warning. He had known of captains who had laid in personal stores in the expectation of service in the West Indies only to find that they had been allotted to the Baltic convoy. The Western Mediterranean meant the Toulon blockade, the protection of Sicily, harassing the Genoese coasters, and, presumably, taking a hand in the war in Spain. It meant a more variegated life than the blockade of Brest, at least, although now that Spain was England's ally there would be far less chance of prize money.

His ability to speak Spanish seemed to make it certain that the *Sutherland* would be employed on the coast of Catalonia in concert with the Spanish army. Lord Cochrane had distinguished himself there, but Cochrane was under a cloud now. The courts martial which had followed the action in the Basque Roads were still echoing through the service, and Cochrane would be lucky if he ever got another ship – he was the standing example of the folly of an officer on the active list taking part in politics. Perhaps, thought Hornblower, trying to combat both optimism and pessimism simultaneously, he was intended by the Admiralty to supply Cochrane's place. If that were the case, it meant that his professional reputation was far higher than he dared believe. Hornblower had to battle sternly with his feelings at that thought; he found himself grinning when he warned himself that excess of emotion only resulted in his hitting his head on the beams above.

That quieted him, and he began to tell himself, philosophically, that all this anticipation was merely waste of effort; he would know sooner or later anyway, and all the worrying in the world would not alter his destiny a ha'porth. There were a hundred and twenty British ships of the line at sea, and nearly two hundred frigates, and in every one of these three hundred and twenty ships there was a post captain, each one a god to his crew, and presumably each one a puppet to the Admiralty. He must act like a sensible man, empty his mind of all these imaginings, and go home and spend a quiet evening with his wife untroubled by thoughts of the future.

Yet even as he left the stern gallery to pass the word for his gig to take him back a new wave of delirious anticipation surged through him at the thought of seeing Lady Barbara tomorrow.

3

'Do I look well?' asked Maria, her toilet completed.

Hornblower was buttoning his full dress coat as he stood and looked at her; he made himself smile admiringly at her.

'Admirable, my dear,' he said. 'The gown sets off your figure better than any you have ever worn.'

His tact was rewarded by a smile. It was no use speaking the truth to Maria, telling her that that particular shade of blue revolted against the heavy red of her cheeks. With her thick figure and coarse black hair and bad complexion Maria could never appear well dressed. At best she looked like a shopkeeper's wife; at worst like some scrub woman dressed in finery cast off by her mistress. Those stubby red hands of hers, thought Hornblower, looking at them, were very like a scrub woman's.

'I have my Paris gloves,' said Maria, noting the direction of his glance. It was the very devil, the way in which she was eager to anticipate every wish of his. It was in his power to hurt her horribly, and the knowledge made him uncomfortable.

'Better and better,' he said gallantly. He stood before the mirror and twitched his coat into position.

'Full dress suits you well,' said Maria, admiringly.

Hornblower's first act when he had returned to England in the *Lydia* had been to buy himself new uniforms – there had been humiliating incidents last commission as a result of the poverty of his wardrobe. He eyed himself tolerantly in the glass. This coat was of the finest blue broadcloth. The heavy epaulettes that hung at the shoulders were of real bullion, and so was the broad gold lace round the edges and the button-holes. Buttons and cuffs flashed as he moved; it was pleasant to see the heavy gold stripes on his cuffs that marked him as a captain with more than three years' seniority. His cravat was of thick China silk. He approved the cut of his white kerseymere breeches. The thick white silk stockings were the best that he could find – he remembered with a twinge of conscience as he gloated over them that Maria wore concealed under her skirt only cheap cotton stockings at four shillings a pair. From the crown of his head to his ankles he was dressed as a gentleman should be dressed; only about his shoes was he doubtful. Their buckles were merely pinchbeck, and he feared lest their brassiness should be accentuated by contrast with the genuine gold every-where else – funds had begun to run low when he bought them, and he had not dared spend twenty guineas on gold buckles. He must take care this evening to do nothing to call attention to his feet. It was a pity that the sword of one hundred guineas' value voted him by the Patriotic Fund for his fight with the *Natividad* had not yet reached him. He still had to wear the fifty-guinea sword which had been awarded him eight years ago after the capture of the *Castilla* as a mere lieutenant.

He took up his cocked hat – the button and lace on it were real gold, too – and his gloves.

'Are you ready, my dear?' he asked.

'Quite ready, Horatio,' said Maria. She had early learned how he hated unpunctuality, and dutifully took care never to offend in this respect.

The afternoon sunlight in the street sparkled on his gold; a militia subaltern whom they passed saluted him respectfully. Hornblower noted that the lady who hung on the subaltern's arm looked more keenly at Maria than at him, and he thought he read in her glance the pitying amusement he expected. Maria was undoubtedly not the sort of wife one would expect to see on the arm of a distinguished officer. But she was his wife all the same, the friend of his childhood, and the self-indulgent soft-heartedness which had moved him to marry her had to be paid for now. Little Horatio and little Maria had died of the smallpox in a Southsea lodging – he owed her his devotion on account of that if for nothing else. And she thought she was carrying another child of his own. That had been madness, of course, but madness excusable in a man whose heart was torn with jealousy at the news that Lady Barbara was married. Still, it had to be paid for in more devotion to Maria; all his decent instincts as well as his soft-heartedness and irresolution compelled him to remain faithful to her, to give her pleasure, to act as if he were her truly devoted husband.

Nor was that all. His pride would never permit him to make public acknowledgement that he had made a mistake, a silly blunder worthy of any foolish boy. On that account alone, even if he could steel himself to break Maria's heart, he would never come to an open breach with her. Hornblower could remember the lewd comments of the navy over Nelson's matrimonial affairs, and there were Bowen's and Samson's after that. As long as he held loyally to his wife that kind of thing would never be said about him. People were tolerant of eccentricity while they laughed at weakness. They might marvel at his devotion, but that was all. While he carried himself as if Maria was the only woman in the world for him people would be forced to assume that there was more in her constitution than was apparent to an onlooker.

'It is the Angel to which we were bidden, is it not, my dear?' asked Maria, breaking in on his thoughts.

'Why, yes.'

'We have walked straight past it. You did not hear me when I spoke before.'

They retraced their steps, and a jolly Devon servant-maid led them through into the cool dark depths at the back of the inn. There were several persons in the oak-panelled room into which they were ushered, but for Hornblower there was only one. Lady Barbara was there in a blue dress, blue-grey, the exact colour of her eyes. From a gold chain round her neck hung a sapphire pendant, but the sapphires seemed lifeless compared with her glance. Hornblower made his bow, and mumbled as he presented Maria. The fringes of the room seemed to be deep in mist; only Lady Barbara could be clearly seen. The golden sunburn which Hornblower had last seen in her cheeks had disappeared now; her complexion was as creamy white as any great lady's should be.

Hornblower became aware that someone else was speaking to him – had been speaking for some time.

'A most pleasurable occasion, Captain Hornblower,'

he was saying. 'May I present you? Captain Hornblower, Mrs Elliott. Captain Hornblower, Mrs Bolton. My Flag-captain, Captain Elliott, of the *Pluto*. And Captain Bolton of the *Caligula*, who tells me he was shipmates with you in the old *Indefatigable*.'

The mists were clearing from Hornblower's eyes a little. He was able to stammer a few words, but fortunately the entrance of the innkeeper with the announcement of dinner gave him a little longer in which to collect himself. It was a circular table at which they were seated. Opposite him sat Bolton, with his ruddy cheeks and open, honest face. Hornblower still felt Bolton's grip lingering on his palm and remembered the horniness of his hand. There was nothing of the elegant world about Bolton, then. Nor was there about Mrs Bolton, who sat on Hornblower's right, between him and the Admiral. She was as plain and dowdy as Maria herself – to Hornblower's infinite relief.

'I must congratulate you, Captain, on your appointment to the *Sutherland*,' said Lady Barbara on his left. A breath of perfume was wafted from her as she spoke, and Hornblower's head swam. To smell the scent of her, and to hear her voice again, was still some romantic drug to him. He did not know what he said in reply.

'The innkeeper here,' announced the Admiral to the table at large, dipping a ladle into the silver tureen before him, 'swore to me that he knew the art of turtle soup, and I entrusted a turtle to his care. God send he spoke the truth. The sherry wine – George, the sherry – I trust you will find tolerable.'

Hornblower incautiously took a mouthful of soup far too hot, and the pain he experienced while swallowing it down helped to bring him back to reality. He turned his head to study the Admiral to whom he would owe obedience for the next two or three years, who had won Lady Barbara's hand in marriage after a courtship that could not have endured more than three weeks. He was tall and heavily built and darkly handsome. The star of the Bath and the red ribbon set off his glittering uniform. In age he could hardly be much over forty – only a year or two older than Hornblower – so that he must have attained to post rank at the earliest age family influence could contrive it. But the perceptible fullness about his jowl indicated to Hornblower's mind either self-indulgence or stupidity; both, perhaps.

So much Hornblower saw in a few seconds' inspection. Then he forced himself to think of his manners, although between Lady Barbara and the Admiral it was hard to think clearly.

'I trust you are enjoying the best of health, Lady Barbara?' he said. A quaint quarter-deck rasp of formality crept into his voice as he tried to hit the exact tone he thought the complicated situation demanded. He saw Maria, on the other side of Captain Elliott beyond Lady Barbara, raise her eyebrows a little – Maria was always sensitive to his reactions.

'Indeed, yes,' said Lady Barbara, lightly. 'And you, Captain?'

'I have never known Horatio better,' said Maria interposing.

'That is good news,' said Lady Barbara, turning towards her. 'Poor Captain Elliott here is still shaken sometimes with the ague he acquired at Flushing.'

It was deftly done; Maria and Lady Barbara and Elliott

were at once engaged in a conversation which left no room for Hornblower. He listened for a moment, and then forced himself to turn to Mrs Bolton. She had no fund of small talk. 'Yes' and 'No' were all she could say, seemingly, and the Admiral on her other side was deep in talk with Mrs Elliott. Hornblower lapsed into gloomy silence. Maria and Lady Barbara continued a conversation from which Elliott soon dropped out, and which was continued across his unresisting body with a constancy which not even the arrival of the next course could interrupt.

'Can I carve you some of this beef, Mrs Elliott?' asked the Admiral. 'Hornblower, perhaps you will be good enough to attend to those ducks before you. Those are neats' tongues, Bolton, a local delicacy – as you know, of course. Will you try them, unless this beef claims your allegiance? Elliott, tempt the ladies with that ragout. They may be partial to foreign kickshaws – made dishes are not to my taste. On the sideboard there is a cold beefsteak pie which the landlord assures me is exactly like those on which his reputation is founded, and a mutton ham such as one only finds in Devonshire. Mrs Hornblower? Barbara, my dear?'

Hornblower, carving the ducks, felt a real pain in his breast at this casual use of the Christian name which was sacred to him. For a moment it impeded his neat dissection of long strips from the ducks' breasts. With an effort he completed his task, and, as no one else at the table seemed to want roast duck, he took for himself the plateful he had carved. It saved him from having to meet anyone's eyes. Lady Barbara and Maria were still talking together. It seemed to his heated imagination as if there was something specially pointed about the way Lady Barbara turned her shoulder to him. Perhaps Lady Barbara had decided that it was a poor compliment to her that he should have loved her, now that she had discovered the crudity of his taste from his choice of a wife. He hoped Maria was not being too stupid and gauche – he could overhear very little of their conversation. He could eat little of the food with which the table was covered – his appetite, always finicking, had quite disappeared. He drank thirstily of the wine which was poured for him until he realized what he was doing, and he checked himself; he disliked being drunk even more than overeating. Then he sat and fiddled with his food on his plate, making a pretence at eating; fortunately Mrs Bolton beside him had a good appetite and was content to be silent while indulging it, as otherwise they would have made a dull pair.

Then the table was swept clear to make room for cheese and dessert.

'Pineapples not as good as we enjoyed at Panama, Captain Hornblower,' said Lady Barbara, turning back to him unexpectedly. 'But perhaps you will make a trial of them?'

He was almost too flustered to cut the thing with the silver knife, so much was he taken off his guard. He helped her eventually, awkwardly. Now that he had her attention again he longed to talk to her, but the words would not come – or rather, seeing that what he found he wanted to ask her was whether she liked married life, and, while he just had enough sense not to blurt out that question, he did not have enough to substitute another for it.

'Captain Elliott and Captain Bolton,' she said, 'have been plying me incessantly with questions about the battle between the *Lydia* and the *Natividad*. Most of them were of too technical a nature for me to answer, especially, as I told them, since you kept me immured in the orlop where I could see nothing of the fight. But everyone seems to envy me even that experience.'

'Her ladyship's right,' roared Bolton, across the table – his voice was even louder than when Hornblower had known him as a young lieutenant. 'Tell us about it, Hornblower.'

Hornblower flushed and fingered his neckcloth, conscious of every eye upon him.

'Spit it out, man,' persisted Bolton; no lady's man, and oppressed by the company, he had said hardly a word so far, but the prospect of having the battle described found his tongue for him.

'The Dons put up a better fight than usual?' asked Elliott.

'Well –' began Hornblower, lured into explaining the conditions in which he had fought. Everybody listened; apt questions from one or other of the men drew him on, bit by bit. Gradually the story unfolded itself, and the loquaciousness against which Hornblower was usually on his guard led him into eloquence. He told of the long duel in the lonely Pacific, the labour and slaughter and agony, up to the moment when, leaning weakly against the quarterdeck rail, he had known triumph at the sight of his beaten enemy sinking in the darkness.

He stopped self-consciously there, hot with the realization that he had been guilty of the unforgivable sin of boasting of his own achievements. He looked round the table from face to face expecting to read in them awkwardness or downright disapproval, pity or contempt. It was with amazement that instead he saw expressions which he could only consider admiring. Bolton, over there, who was at least five years his senior as a captain and ten in age, was eyeing him with something like hero-worship. Elliott, who had commanded a ship of the line under Nelson, was nodding his massive head with intense appreciation. The admiral, when Hornblower could bring himself to steal a glance at him, was still sitting transfixed. There might possibly be a shade of regret in his dark handsome face that his life-time in the navy had brought him no similar opportunity for glory. But the simple heroism of Hornblower's tale had fascinated him, too; he stirred himself and met Hornblower's gaze admiringly.

'Here's a toast for us,' he said, lifting his glass. 'May the captain of the *Sutherland* rival the exploits of the captain of the *Lydia*.'

The toast was drunk with a murmur of approval while Hornblower blushed and stammered. The admiration of men whose approval he valued was overwhelming; more especially as now he was beginning to realize that he had won it under false pretences. Only now was the memory returning to him of the sick fear with which he had waited the *Natividad*'s broadsides, the horror of mutilation which had haunted him during the battle. He was one of the contemptible few, not like Leighton and Elliott and Bolton, who had never known fear in their lives. If he had told the whole truth, told of his emotions as well as of the mere manoeuvres and incidents of the fight, they would be sorry for him, as for a cripple, and the glory of the *Lydia*'s victory would evaporate. His embarrassment was relieved by Lady Barbara's arising from the table and the other women following her example.

'Do not sit too long over your wine,' said Lady Barbara, as the men stood for them. 'Captain Hornblower is a whist player of renown, and there are cards waiting for us.'

4

When they walked away from the Angel through the pitch-dark street Maria clung eagerly to Hornblower's arm.

'A delightful evening, my dear,' she said. 'Lady Barbara seems to be a very genteel person.'

'I'm glad you have enjoyed yourself,' said Hornblower. He knew only too well that Maria after any party to which he accompanied her delighted in discussing the others who had been present. He shrank from the inevitable dissection of Lady Barbara which was bound to come.

'She had breeding,' said Maria, inexorably, 'far beyond what I was led to expect by what you told me about her.'

Searching back in his memory Hornblower realized that he had only laid stress on her fine courage and her ability to mix with men without embarrassment. At that time it had pleased Maria to think of an earl's daughter as a masculine hoyden; now she was just as pleased to revert to the traditional attitude, admiring her for her breeding, and being gratified at her condescension.

'She is a very charming woman,' he said, cautiously falling in with Maria's mood.

'She asked me if I were going to accompany you on your approaching voyage, and I explained that with the hopes of the future which we were beginning to cherish it was inadvisable.'

'You told her *that*?' asked Hornblower sharply. At the last moment he was able to keep the anguish out of his voice.

'She wished me joy,' said Maria, 'and asked me to give you her fe-felicitations.'

It irked Hornblower inexpressibly to think of Maria's discussing her pregnancy with Lady Barbara. He would not allow himself to think why. But the thought of Lady Barbara's knowledge was one more complexity in the whirl of thoughts in his mind, and there was no chance of straightening anything out in the course of the short walk to their lodgings.

'Oh,' said Maria when they were in their bedroom. 'How tight those shoes were!'

She chafed her feet in the white cotton stockings as she sat in the low chair; from the candle on the dressing table her shadow danced on the opposite wall. The shadow of the bed tester lay in a grim black rectangle on the ceiling.

'Hang up that best coat of yours carefully,' said Maria, beginning to take the pins out of her hair.

'I'm not ready for sleep,' said Hornblower, despairingly.

He felt that no price would be too great to pay at the moment to be able to slip away to the solitude of his ship. But he certainly could not do that; the hour would make such a thing odd and the full dress uniform he wore would make it preposterous.

'Not ready for sleep!' It was so like Maria to repeat his words. 'How strange, after this tiring evening! Did you eat too much roast duck?'

'No,' said Hornblower. It was hopeless to try to

explain a too rapidly working mind to Maria, hopeless to try to escape. Any attempt to do so would only hurt her feelings, and he knew by experience he could never make himself do that. With a sigh he began to unbuckle his sword.

'You have only to compose yourself in bed and you will sleep,' said Maria, from her own constant experience. 'We have few enough nights together left to us now, darling.'

That was so; Admiral Leighton had told them that the *Pluto*, *Caligula*, and *Sutherland* were ordered to escort as far as the Tagus an East India convoy which was even then assembling. And that raised once more the cursed question of the shortage of men – how the devil was he to complete his crew in time? Bodmin Assizes might send him a few more criminals. His lieutenants, due to return any day now, might bring in a few volunteers. But he needed fifty more topmen, and topmen could not be picked up in gaols, nor in the market squares.

'It is a hard service,' said Maria, thinking of the approaching separation.

'Better than counters at eightpence a week,' replied Hornblower, forcing himself to speak lightly.

Before their marriage Maria had taught in a school with graduated fees – readers paid fourpence, writers sixpence, and counters eightpence.

'Indeed yes,' said Maria. 'I owe much to you, Horatio. Here's your nightshirt, ready for you. The torment I went through when Miss Wentworth found I had taught Alice Stone the multiplication table although her parents only paid fourpence! And then the ungrateful minx egged that little Hopper boy to let those mice loose in

41

the schoolroom. But I'd suffer it all again, darling, if – if that would keep you near me.'

'Not while duty calls, my dear,' said Hornblower, diving into his nightshirt. 'But I'll be back with a bagful of guineas for prize money before two years are up. Mark my words.'

'Two years!' said Maria pitifully.

Hornblower yawned elaborately, and Maria rose to the bait thus deftly cast, just as Hornblower had been sure she would.

'And you said you were not ready for sleep!' she said.

'It has come upon me now,' said Hornblower. 'Perhaps the admiral's port is beginning to take effect. I can hardly keep my eyes open. I shall say "good night" now, my love.'

He kissed her as she sat before the dressing table, and, turning hastily away, he climbed up into the big bed. There, lying on the farthest edge, keeping rigidly still, he lay until Maria had blown out the candle and climbed up beside him, until her breathing grew quiet and regular. Only then could he relax and change position and give rein to the galloping thoughts coursing through his mind.

He remembered what Bolton had said to him with a wink and a nod when they found themselves together at one time during the evening in a corner where they could not be overheard.

'He means six votes to the Government,' said Bolton, jerking his head towards the Admiral.

Bolton was as stupid as a good seaman could be, but he had been in London recently and attended a levee and had heard the gossip. The poor old king was going mad again, a Regency was imminent, and with the Regency the Tories might go out and the Whigs might come in – the six votes of the Leighton interests were valuable. With the Marquis Wellesley as Foreign Secretary, and Henry Wellesley as Ambassador in Spain, and Sir Arthur Wellesley – what was his new title? Lord Wellington of course – as Commander in Chief in the Peninsula it was not surprising to find Lady Barbara Wellesley married to Sir Percy Leighton, and still less to find the latter given a command in the Mediterranean. The virulence of the Opposition was growing day by day, and the history of the world hung in the balance.

Hornblower shifted restlessly in bed at the thought, but a slight movement by Maria in reply fixed him rigid again. It was only a small party of men – the Wellesleys chief among them – who still had the resolution to continue the struggle against the Corsican's dominion. The smallest check, on land, at sea, or in Parliament, might pull them from their high positions, bring their heads perilously near the block, and tumble all Europe into ruin.

Sometime during the evening Lady Barbara had been pouring tea, and Hornblower had found himself standing alone beside her, waiting for his refilled cup.

'It gave me pleasure,' she had murmured, 'when my husband told me you had been given the *Sutherland*. England needs all her best captains at present.'

She must have meant more than she said then. Probably she was hinting at the necessity for maintaining Leighton in his command. It had been no indication, all the same, that she had exerted herself to obtain the appointment for Hornblower. But it was satisfactory to be able to think that she had married Sir Percy for some other reason than love. Hornblower hated the thought of Lady Barbara being in love with anyone. He began to remember every word she had said to her husband, every look she had given him. Certainly she did not seem in the least like an adoring bride. But the fact remained that she was Leighton's wife – that she was in bed with him at this very minute. Hornblower writhed in fresh anguish at the thought.

Then he checked himself. He told himself very sensibly that only misery and madness lay before him if he allowed himself to think about that, and, grasping resolutely at the tail of the first train of thought which recurred to him, he began to analyse the whist he had been playing. If he had not taken that unsuccessful finesse against that lead of Elliott's he would have saved the rubber. His play had been correct – the chances were three to two – but a gambler would not have stopped to consider that. He would have gone baldheaded for results and in this case would have achieved them. But only a gambler could risk a king being unguarded. He prided himself on the precision and science of his play. Nevertheless, he was two guineas the poorer as the result of this evening, and the loss of two guineas was a devilish serious matter at present.

He wanted to buy a litter of pigs, and two dozen fowls – a couple of sheep as well, for that matter – before weighing anchor in the *Sutherland*. There was the wine he needed, too. Some he could buy later and more advantageously in the Mediterranean, but it would be well to have five or six dozen on board at the start. The effect on the officers and men might be bad for discipline if he were not provided with every luxury as a captain should be; and if the voyage out were long and lazy he would have to entertain his brother captains – the admiral, too, most likely – and they would look at him askance if he offered them the ship's fare on which he was content to live. The list of things he needed stretched longer and longer in his imagination. Port, sherry, and madeira. Apples and cigars. Raisins and cheeses. A dozen at least of shirts. Four more pairs of silk stockings if there was to be much shore-going formality, as seemed likely. A chest of tea. Pepper and cloves and allspice. Prunes and figs. Wax candles. All these things were necessary to his dignity as captain – and to his own pride, for he hated the idea of people thinking him poor.

He could spend all the next quarter's pay on these things and still not have bought too much. Maria would feel the pinch during the next three months, but Maria, fortunately, was used to poverty and to staving off creditors. It was hard on Maria, but if ever he became an admiral he would repay her loyalty with luxury. There were books which he wanted to buy as well; not for entertainment – he had a chest of books, including Gibbon's *Decline and Fall of the Roman Empire* for bedside reading, all old friends – but to fit him for the coming campaign. In the *Morning Chronicle* yesterday there had been a notice of *An Account of the Present War in Spain* which he would like to have, and there were half-a-dozen others. The more he knew about the peninsula on whose coast he was going to fight, and of the leaders of the nation he was to help, the better. But books cost money, and he did not know where to turn for money.

He rolled over again and thought of the ill-fortune which had always dogged him in the matter of prize money. The Admiralty had refused to pay out a penny on account of the sunk *Natividad*. Since the capture of the *Castilla* when he was a young lieutenant he had never had a windfall, while frigate captains whom he knew had made thousands of pounds. It was maddening – especially as in his present poverty-stricken condition he was hampered in his exertions to complete the *Sutherland*'s crew. That shortage of men was the most harassing of all his worries – that and the thought of Lady Barbara in Leighton's arms. Hornblower's thoughts had gone a full circle now, and were starting all over again. There was plenty to keep him restless and wakeful all through the weary night, until the dawn began to creep through the curtains; fantastic theories about Lady Barbara's state of mind, and hard-headed plans for making the *Sutherland* efficient for sea.

5

Captain Hornblower was walking up and down his quarterdeck amid all the last-minute bustle of getting ready for sea. He was raging to himself at the length of time necessary for these final preparations although he knew quite well that every factor causing delay was susceptible to a reasonable explanation. Two-thirds of the men scurrying about the decks, urged on by the cane of Harrison the boatswain and the rope's ends of the petty officers, were landsmen most of whom until lately had never seen the sea, let alone been in a ship. The simplest order left them merely bewildered, and they had to be led to their tasks and the ropes actually put into their hands; even then they were far more inefficient than trained seamen, because they had not learned the knack of throwing all their weight simultaneously on the rope and walking away with it. And having once set them heaving, it was hard for a petty officer to remember that a shout of 'Avast' or 'Belay' meant nothing to them. More than once the few trained seamen among them, obeying promptly, were thrown off their feet and trampled upon by the rush of landsmen still heaving away. On one occasion of this sort a water butt while being hove up by a whip to the main yardarm had simply gone away with a run again, and only the mercy of providence had saved it from going clean through the bottom of the longboat overside.

It was owing to Hornblower's own orders that the water was so late in being brought aboard. Water left months in cask became so foul and so alive with living things that he had put off bringing it aboard until the last possible moment. Even a gain of a day or two was desirable. That twelve tons of biscuit had also been delayed was the result of the usual incompetence of the victualling yard, whose officials seemed incapable of reading or writing or figuring. The complication due to the fact that a shore boat with captain's stores was having to be unloaded at the same time, and its precious cargo passed carefully down the after hatchway, was due to the Patriotic Fund's delay in sending down to him the sword value one hundred guineas which he had been awarded for his fight with the *Natividad*. No shopkeeper or ship chandler would give credit to a captain about to sail on a new commission. The sword had only arrived yesterday, barely in time for him to pledge it with Duddingstone the chandler, and Duddingstone had only grudgingly given him credit on it, forcing him to promise faithfully to redeem it at the earliest opportunity.

'A sight too much writing on this for me,' said Duddingstone, pointing with a stubby forefinger at the wordy legend which the Patriotic Fund had had engraved, at vast expense, upon the blue steel of the blade.

Only the gold on the hilt and scabbard, and the seed pearls on the pommel, had any intrinsic value. Duddingstone, to give him his due, had been quite right in saying that it was hardly worth forty guineas' credit at his shop, even allowing for his profit and the chance of its being redeemed. But he had kept his word and had sent off the stores at dawn next morning – one more complication in the business of preparing for sea.

Along the gangway Wood the purser was dancing with rage and anxiety.

'God damn and blast all you hamfisted yokels!' he was saying. 'And you, sir, down there. Take that grin off your face and be more careful, or I'll have you clapped under hatches to sail with us today. Easy, there, easy! Christ, rum at seven guineas an anker isn't meant to be dropped like pig iron!'

Wood was supervising the loading of the rum. The old hands were doing their best to make sure that the clumsiness of the new ones would result in the staving of a keg or two, so as to swill from the leaks, and the grinning lightermen overside were abetting them. Hornblower could see by the red faces and uncontrollable hilarity that some of the men had succeeded in getting at the spirits, despite Wood's eagle eye and the marine sentries on guard; but he had no intention of interfering. It would merely compromise his dignity to try and keep sailors from stealing rum if they had the barest opportunity – no one had ever yet succeeded in that task.

From this position of vantage beside the quarterdeck rail he looked down upon a curious bit of by-play on the main deck. A bewildered young giant – a tin miner, Hornblower guessed, from his biceps – had rounded upon Harrison, apparently driven frantic by the volley of orders and blasphemy hurled at him. But Harrison at forty-five had fought his way up to the boatswain's rank through hundreds of such encounters, and in his prime might have contested the highest honours of the prize ring. He slipped the Cornishman's clumsy punch and felled him with a crashing blow on the jaw. Then without ceremony he seized him by the scruff of the neck and kicked him across the deck to the tackle which was waiting. Dazed, the Cornishman took hold with the others and heaved with them, while Hornblower nodded approvingly.

The Cornishman had made himself liable to 'death, or such less penalty' – as the Articles of War said – by raising his hand to his superior officer. But it was not the moment to invoke the Articles of War, even though they had been read over to the Cornishman last night on his compulsory enlistment. Gerard had sailed round with the longboat and had raided Redruth and Camborne and St Ives, taking each place by surprise and returning with fifty stout Cornishmen who could hardly be expected yet to appreciate the administrative machinery of the service which they had joined. In a month's time, perhaps, when everyone on board would have learnt the heinousness of such an offence, a court martial might be needed, and a flogging – death, perhaps – but at the present time it was best to do what Harrison had just done, and crack the man on the jaw and set him to work again. Hornblower found time to thank God he was a captain and out of the hurly burly, for any attempt on his part of cracking men on the jaw would be a lamentable failure, he knew.

He shifted his weight from one leg to the other, and was reminded of the fact that he was horribly tired. Night after night now he had not slept, and his days had been spent in all the numerous activities necessitated by commissioning a ship of the line. The nervous tension induced by his worrying about Lady Barbara and Maria, by money troubles and manning troubles, had prevented him from leaving the details to Bush and Gerard, even though he knew they were perfectly capable of dealing with everything. Worry and anxiety would not allow him to rest, and had goaded him into activity. He felt sick and stupid and weary. Day after day he had longed for the moment when he should get to sea, and could settle down into the comfortable solitude which surrounds a ship's captain, leaving all shore worries behind him, even leaving Lady Barbara behind him.

He had the sense to realize that this new meeting with her had thoroughly upset him. He had given up as insoluble the problem of whether or not she had secured his nomination to the *Sutherland*; he had tried his hardest to combat his consuming jealousy of her husband. He had persuaded himself in the end that what he had wanted more than anything else was to escape from her, just as he wanted to escape from Maria's cloying sweetness and lovable stupidity, from all the complex misery of life on land. He had yearned for the sea as a castaway yearns for a drink of water. Two days ago the prospect of thus standing on the deck in the final bustle of departure seemed marvellously desirable to him. Now, he realized with a gulp, he was not quite so sure. It was like having a limb torn out by the roots to be leaving Lady Barbara like this. And, oddly enough, he was distressed at leaving Maria, too. There would be a child born before he could be home again, a child well over a year old, running about, perhaps even saying its first few words. Maria would have to go through her pregnancy and confinement without his moral support; and he knew, despite the brave way in which she had dismissed the subject, and despite her stout-hearted goodbye, how much she would miss him. It was that which made it so painful to leave her.

With all her courage her lips had trembled and her eyes had been wet when she lifted her face to him, in the sitting room of their lodgings; they had agreed long ago that it was foolish to prolong the pangs of parting by her accompanying him on board. Even then the urge to be off had still been strong enough to take him from her arms without a pang, but it was different now. Hornblower mentally spurned himself as a sentimental fool, and glanced impatiently up at the masthead vane. Without a doubt the wind was backing northerly. If it should come round to north or nor'east the admiral would be anxious to start. The convoy, and the *Pluto* and *Caligula*, were assembled now, or pretty nearly, in Cawsand Bay; if the admiral decided not to wait for the stragglers he would be irritated at the *Sutherland*'s delay, be it never so unavoidable.

'Keep the men to it, Mr Bush,' shouted Hornblower.

'Aye aye, sir,' answered Bush, patiently.

That patience in his voice irritated Hornblower further. It implied a slight rebuke, a rebuke only apparent to Bush and Hornblower. Hornblower knew that Bush was working as hard as he could, and that he was working the men as hard as he could, too. Hornblower's order had been a mere manifestation of impatience, and Bush knew it. Hornblower was annoyed with himself for having so unguardedly broken his rule of never saying an unnecessary word to his officers, and by way of advancing a reason for having spoken he went down below to his cabin, as he had not intended to do.

The sentry stood aside for him as he entered the door of his sleeping cabin on the half deck. There was plenty of room here; even the presence of a twelve pounder left ample space for his cot and his desk and his chest. Polwheal had set everything to rights here already; Hornblower passed through into the main cabin. Here there was ample room, too; the Dutchmen who designed the *Sutherland* had lofty ideas regarding the comfort of the captain. The cabin extended across the whole width of the stern, and the great stern windows gave plenty of light. The stone-coloured paint made the cabin sunny and cheerful, and the black bulks of a twelve pounder on each side made an effective colour scheme. A couple of hands were standing by Polwheal in here while he lay on his stomach packing away cases of wine into the lockers. Hornblower glared at them, realizing that he could not yet retire to the solitude of the stern gallery while he should be under their observation through the stern windows.

He went back to the sleeping cabin and threw himself with a sigh on his cot, but his restlessness brought him to his feet again and across to his desk. He took out a crackling document and sat down to look through it again.

Orders to the Inshore Squadron, Western Mediterranean, by Sir Percy Gilbert Leighton, K.B., Rear Admiral of the Red, Commanding.

There was nothing unusual about them at all – night signals, private signals, British, Spanish, and Portuguese; rendezvous in case of separation; a line or two regarding the tactics to be adopted in the event of encountering while with the convoy a hostile squadron of any force. The flagship would accompany the Lisbon convoy of transports into the Tagus – calling for orders, presumably; the *Caligula* was to take the storeships *Harriet* and *Nancy* to Port Mahon; the *Sutherland* was to escort the East Indiamen as far as Latitude 35° before heading for the Straits, to the final rendezvous off Palamos Point. Captains of His Britannic Majesty's Ships were informed that the coast of Andalusia, with the exception of Cadiz and Tarifa, was in the hands of the French, and so also was the coast of Catalonia from the frontier to Tarragona. At the same time captains entering any Spanish port whatever must take the most careful precautions lest the French should be in occupation there. The attached schedule of instructions to masters of ships in the convoy was mostly repetition of all this.

But to Hornblower, musing over these orders, they told a very full and complicated story. They told how, although Trafalgar had been fought five years back, and although England was maintaining at sea the greatest fleet the world had ever seen, she was still having to strain every nerve in the struggle. The Corsican was still building fleets in nearly every port in Europe, Hamburg, Antwerp, Brest, Toulon, Venice, Trieste, and a score of places in between, so that outside every port storm-beaten squadrons of English battleships had to maintain an unceasing watch – a hundred and twenty ships of the line could be found employment, if they could have been spared, on the blockade alone, without regard to the other duties. And at the same time every creek and fishing harbour along half the coasts of Europe maintained privateers, even if hardly better than big rowboats full of men, always ready to dash out and capture the helpless British merchant ships to be found in every sea. To guard against these depredations British frigates had to maintain unceasing patrol, and no King's ship could be dispatched on any mission whatever without taking advantage of the opportunity given to convoy merchant shipping on part of their journey at least. In this war against the world only the most careful and scientific distribution of force could prevail, and now, mustering all her strength, England was taking the offensive. Her armies were on the march in Spain, and three ships of the line, scraped together from other duties from which they might just be spared, were being sent to attack the vulnerable flank which Bonaparte had incautiously exposed by his advance into the Peninsula. The *Sutherland* was destined to be the point of the spearhead which was making the thrust against the tyranny which dominated all Europe.

All very well, said Hornblower to himself. Automatically he was pacing up and down again, his head bent under the deck beams, and his walk limited to four strides between the twelve pounder and the door. It was an honourable and responsible position, and yet he had not the men to man his ship. To make or set sail in the way it should be done in a King's ship – or rather, with the rapidity and facility which might make the difference between defeat and victory – called for two hundred and fifty trained seamen. And if all the trained men were aloft at once there would be none at the guns. To serve the guns, if both broadsides were in action at once, called for four hundred and fifty men – two hundred of them, he admitted, might be untrained – and nearly a hundred more carrying powder and engaged upon necessary duties about the ship.

He had a hundred and ninety trained men from the *Lydia* and a hundred and ninety raw landsmen. During the commissioning of the *Sutherland* only twenty old *Lydias* had deserted, abandoning two years' pay and risking the penalty of a thousand lashes, and he knew he was lucky at that. Some captains would have lost two-thirds of their crews during as long a stay as this in a home port. But those twenty missing men would have been desperately useful now. He was a hundred and seventy men – a hundred and seventy *trained* men – short of complement. In six weeks he might drill his landsmen, all except that proportion of hopeless ones, diseased, crippled, or idiotic whom he could expect to find among them, into passable seamen and gunners. But in less than six weeks, possibly in less than three, he would be in action on the coast of Spain. By tomorrow night, even, he might be at grips with the enemy – the wind was backing towards the east and might bring out a French squadron of ships of the line from Brest, evading the blockading squadron, and crammed with men, to fall upon such a tempting prize as the East India convoy. What chance would the *Sutherland* stand, yardarm to yardarm with a French first rate, with only two-thirds of her proper crew, and half of them seasick?

Hornblower clenched his fists again, boiling with exasperation at the thought. It was he who would be held responsible for any disaster, who would have to sustain the contempt or the pity – either alternative horrible to contemplate – of his brother captains. He yearned and hungered for men, more passionately than ever a miser desired gold, or a lover his mistress. And now he had no more chance of finding any. Gerard's raid upon St Ives and Redruth had been his last effort; he knew that he had been fortunate to get as many as fifty men from there. There would be no chance of obtaining any from the convoy. Government transports to Lisbon, government storeships to Port Mahon, East India Company's ships – he could not take a man from any of those. He felt like a man in a cage.

He went across to his desk again and took out his private duplicate of the ship's watch bill, which he and Bush had sat up through most of the night to draw up. It was largely upon that watch bill that the efficiency of the ship would depend in her short-handed condition; the trained men had to be distributed evenly over every strategic point, with just the right proportion of landsmen to facilitate training and yet not to impede the working of the ship. Foretop, maintop, and mizzen top; forecastle and afterguard; every man had to be assigned a duty, so that whatever evolution out of the thousand possible was being carried out, in fair weather or foul, in daylight or darkness, he would go to his position without confusion or waste of time, knowing exactly what he had to do. He had to have his place at the guns allotted him under the command of the officer of his division.

Hornblower looked through the watch bill again. It was satisfactory as far as it went. It had a kind of card-castle stability – adequate enough at first sight, but incapable of standing any strain or alteration. Casualties or disease would bring the whole thing down in ruins. He flung the watch bill down as he remembered that, if the cruise were a healthy one, he might expect one death every ten days from accident or natural causes without regard to hostile action. Fortunately it was the unseasoned men who were the more likely to die.

Hornblower cocked his ear at the din on the main deck. The hoarse orders, the pipes of the boatswain's mates, and the stamp-and-go of many feet told him that they were heaving up the longboat from overside. A strange squeaking, unlike that of the sheaves in the blocks, which had reached him for some time and which he had been unable to identify so far, he suddenly realized was the noise of the various families of pigs – captain's stores and wardroom stores – at last come on board. He heard a sheep bleating and then a cock crowing to the accompaniment of a roar of laughter. He had brought no cock along with his hens; it must belong to someone in the wardroom or the midshipmen's berth.

Someone thumped on the cabin door, and Hornblower snatched up his papers and dropped into his chair. Not for worlds would he be seen standing up and obviously awaiting the hour of departure with discomposure.

'Come in!' he roared.

A scared young midshipman put his head round the door – it was Longley, Gerard's nephew, newly come to sea.

'Mr Bush says the last of the stores are just coming on board, sir,' he piped.

Hornblower eyed him with a stony indifference

which was the only alternative to grinning at the frightened little imp.

'Very good,' he growled, and busied himself with his papers.

'Yes, sir,' said the boy, after a moment's hesitation, withdrawing.

'Mr Longley!' roared Hornblower.

The child's face, more terrified than ever, reappeared round the door.

'Come inside, boy,' said Hornblower, testily. 'Come in and stand still. What was it you said last?'

'Er – sir – I said – Mr Bush –'

'No, nothing of the sort. What was it you said *last*?'

The child's face wrinkled into the extreme of puzzlement, and then cleared as he realized the point of the question.

'I said "Yes, sir",' he piped.

'And what ought you to have said?'

'Aye aye, sir.'

'Right. Very good.'

'Aye aye sir.'

That boy had a certain amount of quickness of wit, and did not allow fright to bereave him entirely of his senses. If he learned quickly how to handle the men he would make a useful warrant officer. Hornblower put away his papers and locked his desk; he took a few more turns up and down his cabin, and then, a sufficient interval having elapsed to conserve his dignity, he went up to the quarterdeck.

'Make sail when you're ready, Mr Bush,' he said.

'Aye aye, sir. Easy with those falls there, you – you –'

Even Bush had reached the condition when there

was no more savour in oaths. The ship was in a horrible state of muddle, the decks were filthy, the crew exhausted. Hornblower stood with his hands behind him in a careful attitude of Olympian detachment as the order was given for all hands to make sail, and the petty officers drove the crew, stupid with weariness, to their stations. Savage, the senior midshipman, whom Hornblower had seen grow from boyhood to manhood under his eye, came shouting for the afterguard to man the main topsail halliards. Savage was wan and his eyes were bloodshot; a night of debauchery in some foul haunt in Plymouth had not left him in the best of conditions. As he shouted he put his hand to his temple, where clearly the din he was making was causing him agony. Hornblower smiled to himself at the sight – the next few days would sweat him clean again.

'Captain of the afterguard!' yelled Savage, his voice cracking. 'I don't see the afterguard coming aft! Quicker than that, you men! Clap on to the main topsail halliards, there! I say, you master-at-arms. Send the idlers aft. D'ye hear, there!'

A boatswain's mate headed a rush to the mizzen rigging at Hornblower's elbow. Hornblower saw young Longley standing, hesitating, for a second, looking up at the men preceding him, and then, with a grimace of determination, the boy leaped for the ratlines and scrambled up after them. Hornblower appreciated the influences at work upon him – his fear of the towering height above him, and then his stoical decision that he could follow wherever the other men could venture. Something might be made of that boy.

Bush was looking at his watch and fuming to the master.

'Nine minutes already! God, look at them! The marines are more like sailors!'

The marines were farther aft, at the mizzen topsail halliards. Their booted feet went clump-clump-clump on the deck. They did their work like soldiers, with soldierly rigidity, as if at drill. Sailors always laughed at that, but there was no denying that at the present moment it was the marines who were the more efficient.

The hands scurried from halliards to braces. A roar from Harrison forward told that the mooring was slipped, and Hornblower, casting a final glance up at the windvane, saw that the wind had backed so far easterly that rounding Devil's Point was not going to be simple. With the yards braced round the *Sutherland* turned on her keel and slowly gathered way. Women's screeches and a fluttering of handkerchiefs from the shore boats told how some of the wives whom Hornblower had turned out twenty-four hours ago had put off to say goodbye. Close overside he saw a woman in the stern-sheets of a boat blubbering unashamed, her mouth wide open and the tears running like rivers. It was no more than an even chance that she would ever see her man again.

'Keep your eyes inboard, there!' yelled Harrison, who had detected some member of the crew waving farewell. Every man's attention must be kept strictly to the business in hand now.

Hornblower felt the ship heel as Bush directed her course as near to the wind as she would lie; with Devil's Point ahead, and an unfamiliar ship to handle, it was clearly as well to get as far to windward as possible. That heeling of the ship awakened a storm of memories. It was not until one was in a ship under sail, with the deck unstable under one's feet, and the familiar rattle of the blocks and piping of the rigging in one's ears, that the thousand and one details of life at sea became vivid and recognizable again. Hornblower found himself swallowing hard with excitement.

They were shaving the Dockyard Point as closely as possible. Most of the dockyard hands left their work to stare at them, stolidly, but not a soul among them raised a cheer. In seventeen years of warfare they had seen too many King's ships putting out to sea to be excited about this one. Hornblower knew that he ought to have a band on board, to strike up 'Britons, Strike Home' or 'Come cheer up, my lads, 'tis to glory we steer', but he had no band; he had not the money for one, and he was not going to call on the marine fifer or the ship's fiddler to make a tinny little noise at this moment. Stonehouse Pool was opening up before them now, and beyond it lay the roofs of Plymouth. Maria was there somewhere; perhaps she could see the white topsails, closehauled to the wind. Perhaps Lady Barbara was there, looking out at the *Sutherland*. Hornblower gulped again.

A little flaw of wind, blowing down Stonehouse Pool, took the ship nearly aback. She staggered until the helmsman allowed her to pay off. Hornblower looked round to starboard. They were coming dangerously close in to Cremyll – he had been correct in his surmise that the *Sutherland* would make plenty of leeway. He watched the wind, and the set of the tide off the point.

He looked ahead at Devil's Point on the starboard bow. It might be necessary at any moment to put the ship about and beat up to the northward again before breasting the tide once more. At the very moment when he saw that they would weather the point he saw Bush raise his head to bark the orders to go about.

'Keep her steady as she goes, Mr Bush,' he said; the quiet order was an announcement that he had taken charge, and Bush closed the mouth which had opened to give the order.

They cleared the buoy a bare fifty yards from any danger, with the water creaming under the lee now as she lay over to the fresh breeze. Hornblower had not interfered to demonstrate the superiority of his seamanship and judgement, but merely because he could not stand by and watch something being done a little less artistically than was possible. In the cold-blooded calculation of chances he was superior to his lieutenant, as his ability at whist proved. Hornblower stood sublimely unconscious of his motives; in fact he hardly realized what he had done – he never gave a thought to his good seamanship.

They were heading straight for the Devil's Point now; Hornblower kept his eye on it as they opened up the Sound.

'You can put the helm aport now,' he said. 'And set the t'gallant sails, Mr Bush.'

With the wind abeam they headed into the Sound, the rugged Staddon Heights to port and Mount Edgcumbe to starboard. At every yard they advanced towards the open sea the wind blew fresher, calling a keener note from the rigging. The *Sutherland* was feeling the sea a little now, heaving perceptibly to the waves under her bows. With the motion, the creaking of the wooden hull became audible – noticeable on deck, loud below until the ear grew indifferent to the noise.

'God blast these bloody farmers!' groaned Bush, watching the way in which the topgallant sails were being set.

Drake's Island passed away to windward; the *Sutherland* turned her stern to it as with the wind on her port quarter she headed down the Sound. Before the topgallant sails were set they were abreast of Picklecomb Point and opening up Cawsand Bay. There was the convoy – six East Indiamen with their painted ports like men of war, all flying the gridiron flag of the Honourable Company and one sporting a broad pendant for all the world like a king's commodore; the two naval storeships and the four transports destined for Lisbon. The three-decker *Pluto* and the *Caligula* were rolling to their anchors to seaward of them.

'Flagship's signalling, sir,' said Bush, his glass to his eye. 'You ought to have reported it a minute ago, Mr Vincent.'

The *Pluto* had not been in sight more than thirty seconds, but there was need for promptness in acknowledging this, the first signal made by the admiral.

'*Sutherland*'s pendant, sir,' said the unfortunate signal midshipman, staring through his glass. 'Negative. No. Seven. Number Seven is "Anchor", sir.'

'Acknowledge,' snapped Hornblower. 'Get those t'gallants in again and back the main topsail, Mr Bush.'

With his telescope Hornblower could see men racing

up the rigging of the ships. In five minutes both the *Pluto* and the *Caligula* had a cloud of canvas set.

'They commissioned at the Nore, blast 'em,' growled Bush.

At the Nore, the gateway of the busiest port in the world, ships of the Royal Navy had the best opportunity of completing their crews with prime seamen taken from incoming merchant vessels, in which it was not necessary to leave more than half a dozen hands to navigate their ships up to London river. In addition, the *Pluto* and *Caligula* had enjoyed the advantage of having been able to drill their crews during the voyage down channel. Already they were standing out of the bay. Signals were soaring up the flagship's halliards.

'To the convoy, sir,' said Vincent. 'Make haste. Up anchor. Make all sail con-conformable with the weather, sir. Jesus, there's a gun.'

An angry report and a puff of smoke indicated that the admiral was calling pointed attention to his signals. The Indiamen, with their heavy crews and man o' war routine, were already under way. The storeships and transports were slower, as was only to be expected. The other ships were backing and filling outside for what seemed an interminable time before the last of them came creeping out.

''Nother signal from the flagship, sir,' said Vincent, reading the flags and then hurriedly referring to the signal book. 'Take up stations as previously ordered.'

That would be to windward of the convoy, and, with the wind abaft as it was, in the rear. Then the ships of war could always dash down to the rescue if a Frenchman tried to cut off one of the convoy under their noses. Hornblower felt the freshening breeze on his cheek. The flagship's topgallants were set, and as he looked, he saw her royals being spread as well. He would have to conform, but with the wind increasing as it was he fancied that it would not be long before they would have to come in again. Before nightfall they would be reefing topsails. He gave the order to Bush, and watched while the crew gathered at Harrison's bellow of 'All hands make sail'. He could see the landsmen flinch, not unnaturally – the *Sutherland*'s main royal yard was a hundred and ninety feet above the deck and swaying in a dizzy circle now that the ship was beginning to pitch to the Channel rollers.

Hornblower turned his attention to the flagship and the convoy; he could not bear the sight of frightened men being hounded up the rigging by petty officers with ropes' ends. It was necessary, he knew. The Navy did not – of necessity could not – admit the existence of the sentences 'I cannot' and 'I am afraid'. No exceptions could be made, and this was the right moment to grain it into the men, who had never known compulsion before, that every order must be obeyed. If his officers were to start with leniency, leniency would always be expected, and leniency, in a service which might at any moment demand of a man the willing sacrifice of his life, could only be employed in a disciplined crew which had had time to acquire understanding. But Hornblower knew, and sympathized with, the sick terror of a man driven up to the masthead of a ship of the line when previously he had never been higher than the top of a haystack. It was a pitiless, cruel service.

'Peace'll be signed,' grumbled Bush to Crystal, the

master, 'before we make sailors out of these clod-hoppers.'

A good many of the clodhoppers in question had three days before been living peacefully in their cottages with never a thought of going to sea. And here they were under a grey sky, pitching over a grey sea, with a keener breeze than ever they had known blowing round them, overhead the terrifying heights of the rigging, and underfoot the groaning timbers of a reeling ship.

They were well out to sea now, with the Eddystone in sight from the deck, and under the pressure of the increased sail the *Sutherland* was growing lively. She met her first big roller, and heaved as it reached her bow, rolled corkscrew fashion, as it passed under her, and then pitched dizzily as it went away astern. There was a wail of despair from the waist.

'Off the decks, there, blast you!' raved Harrison. 'Keep it off the decks!'

Men were being seasick already, with the freedom of men taken completely by surprise. Hornblower saw a dozen pale forms staggering and lurching towards the lee rails. One or two men had sat down abruptly on the deck, their hands to their temples. The ship heaved and corkscrewed again, soaring up and then sinking down again as if she would never stop, and the shuddering wail from the waist was repeated. With fixed and fascinated eyes Hornblower watched a wretched yokel vomiting into the scuppers. His stomach heaved in sympathy, and he found himself swallowing hard. There was sweat on his face although he suddenly felt bitterly cold.

He was going to be sick, too, and that very soon. He

wanted to be alone, to vomit in discreet privacy, away from the amused glances of the crowd on the quarter-deck. He braced himself to speak with his usual stern indifference, but his ear told him that he was only achieving an unsuccessful perkiness.

'Carry on, Mr Bush,' he said. 'Call me if necessary.'

He had lost his sea legs, too, during this stay in harbour – he reeled as he crossed the deck, and he had to cling with both hands to the rail of the companion. He reached the half-deck safely and lurched to the after cabin door, stumbling over the coaming. Polwheal was laying dinner at the table.

'Get out!' snarled Hornblower, breathlessly. 'Get out!'

Polwheal vanished, and Hornblower reeled out into the stern gallery, fetching up against the rail, leaning his head over towards the foaming wake. He hated the indignity of seasickness as much as he hated the misery of it. It was of no avail to tell himself, as he did, despair-ingly, while he clutched the rail, that Nelson was always seasick, too, at the beginning of a voyage. Nor was it any help to point out to himself the unfortunate co-incidence that voyages always began when he was so tired with excitement and mental and physical exertion that he was ready to be sick anyway. It was, true, but he found no comfort in it as he leaned groaning against the rail with the wind whipping round him.

He was shivering with cold now as the nor'easter blew; his heavy jacket was in his sleeping cabin, but he felt he could neither face the effort of going to fetch it, nor could he call Polwheal to bring it. And this, he told himself with bitter irony, was the calm solitude for which he had been yearning while entangled in the complications of the shore. Beneath him the pintles of the rudder were groaning in the gudgeons, and the sea was seething yeastily in white foam under the counter. The glass had been falling since yesterday, he remembered, and the weather was obviously working up into a nor'easterly gale. Hounded before it across the Bay of Biscay he could see no respite before him for days, at this moment when he felt he could give everything he had in the world for the calm of the Hamoaze again.

His officers were never sick, he thought resentfully, or if they were they were just sick and did not experience this agonizing misery. And forward two hundred seasick landsmen were being driven pitilessly to their tasks by overbearing petty officers. It did a man good to be driven to work despite his seasickness, always provided that discipline was not imperilled thereby as it would be in his case. And he was quite, quite sure that not a soul on board felt as miserable as he did, or even half as miserable. He leaned against the rail again, moaning and blaspheming. Experience told him that in three days he would be over all this and feeling as well as ever in his life, but at the moment the prospect of three days of this was just the same as the prospect of an eternity of it. And the timbers creaked and the rudder groaned and the wind whistled and the sea hissed, everything blending into an inferno of noise as he clung shuddering to the rail.

6

When the first paroxysm was over Hornblower was able
to note that the breeze was undoubtedly freshening. It
was gusty, too, sudden squalls bringing flurries of rain
which beat into the stern gallery where he was standing.
He was suddenly consumed with anxiety as to what
would happen aloft if the *Sutherland* were caught in a
wilder squall than usual with a crew unhandy at getting
in sail. The thought of the disgrace involved in losing
spars or canvas in sight of the whole convoy drove all
thought of seasickness out of his head. Quite automatically he went forward to his cabin, put on his pilot
coat, and ran up on deck. Gerard had taken over from
Bush.

'Flagship's shortening sail, sir,' he said, touching his
hat.

'Very good. Get the royals in,' said Hornblower,
turning to look round the horizon through his glass.

The convoy was behaving exactly as convoys always
did, scattering before the wind as if they really wanted
to be snapped up by a privateer. The Indiamen were in
a fairly regular group a mile ahead to leeward, but the
six other ships were hull down and spread out far beyond
them.

'Flagship's been signalling to the convoy, sir,' said
Gerard.

Hornblower nearly replied 'I expect she has' but

restrained himself in time and limited himself to the single word 'Yes'. As he spoke a fresh series of flaghoists soared up the *Pluto*'s halliards.

'*Caligula*'s pendant,' read off the signal midshipman. 'Make more sail. Take station ahead of convoy.'

So Bolton was being sent ahead to enforce the orders which the transports had disregarded. Hornblower watched the *Caligula* re-set her royals and go plunging forward over the grey sea in pursuit of the transports. She would have to run down within hailing distance and possibly have to fire a gun or two before she could achieve anything; masters of merchant ships invariably paid no attention at all to flag signals even if they could read them. The Indiamen were getting in their top-gallants as well – they had the comfortable habit of shortening sail at nightfall. Happy in the possession of a monopoly of the Eastern trade, and with passengers on board who demanded every luxury, they had no need to worry about slow passages and could take care that their passengers ran no risk of being disturbed in their sleep by the stamping and bustle of taking off sail if the weather changed. But from all apperances it might have been deliberately planned to spread the convoy out still farther. Hornblower wondered how the admiral would respond, and he turned his glass upon the *Pluto*.

Sure enough, she burst into hoist after hoist of signals, hurling frantic instructions at the Indiamen.

'I'll lay he wishes he could court martial 'em,' chuckled one midshipman to the other.

'Five thousand pounds, those India captains make out of a round voyage,' was the reply. 'What do they care about admirals? God, who'd be in the Navy?'

With night approaching and the wind freshening there was every chance of the convoy being scattered right at the very start of its voyage. Hornblower began to feel that his admiral was not showing to the best advantage. The convoy should have been kept together; in a service which accepted no excuses Sir Percy Leighton stood already condemned. He wondered what he would have done in the admiral's place, and left the question unanswered, vaguely telling himself the profound truth that discipline did not depend on the power to send before a court martial; he did not think that he could have done better.

'*Sutherland*'s pendant,' said the signal midshipman, breaking in on his reverie. 'Take – night – station.'

'Acknowledge,' said Hornblower.

That was an order easy to obey. His night station was a quarter of a mile to windward of the convoy. Here he was drawing up fast upon the Indiamen to his correct position. He watched the *Pluto* go down past the Indiamen in the wake of the *Caligula*; apparently the admiral had decided to make use of his flagship as a connecting link between the halves of the convoy. Night was coming down fast and the wind was still freshening.

He tried to walk up and down the reeling deck so as to get some warmth back into his shivering body; his stomach was causing him terrible misgivings again now with this period of waiting. He fetched up against the rail, hanging on while he fought down his weakness. Of all his officers, Gerard, handsome, sarcastic, and able, was the one before whom he was least desirous of vomiting. His head was spinning with sickness and fatigue, and he thought that if he could only lie down he might perhaps sleep, and in sleep he could forget the heaving misery of his interior. The prospect of being warm and snug in his cot grew more and more urgent and appealing. Hornblower held on grimly until his eyes told him, in the fast fading light, that he was in his correct station. Then he turned to Gerard.

'Get the t'gallants in, Mr Gerard.'

He took the signal slate, and wrote on it, painfully, while warring with his insurgent stomach, the strictest orders his mind could devise to the officer of the watch with regard to keeping in sight, and to windward, of the convoy.

'There are your orders, Mr Gerard,' he said. He quavered on the last word, and he did not hear Gerard's 'Aye aye, sir' as he fled below.

This time it was agony to vomit, for his stomach was completely empty. Polwheal showed up in the cabin as he came staggering back, and Hornblower cursed him savagely and sent him away again. In his sleeping cabin he fell across his cot, and lay there for twenty minutes before he could rouse himself to sit up. Then he dragged off his two coats, and, still wearing his shirt and waistcoat and breeches, he got under the blankets with a groan. The ship was pitching remorselessly as she ran before the wind, and all the timbers complained in spasmodic chorus. Hornblower set his teeth at every heave, while the cot in which he lay soared upward twenty feet or more and then sank hideously downward under the influence of each successive wave. Nevertheless, with no possibility of consecutive thinking, it was easy for exhaustion to step in. He was so tired that with his mind empty he fell asleep in a few minutes, motion and noise and seasickness notwithstanding.

So deeply did he sleep that when he awoke he had to think for a moment before he realized where he was. The heaving and tossing, of which he first became conscious, was familiar and yet unexpected. The door into the after cabin, hooked open, admitted a tiny amount of grey light, in which he blinked round him. Then, simultaneously with the return of recollection, his stomach heaved again. He got precariously to his feet, staggered across the after cabin, to the rail of the stern gallery, and then peered miserably across the grey sea in the first faint light of dawn, with the wind whipping round him. There was no sail in sight from there, and the consequent apprehension helped him to recover himself. Putting on coat and greatcoat again, he walked up to the quarterdeck.

Gerard was in charge of the deck, so the middle watch was not yet ended. Hornblower gave a surly nod in reply to Gerard's salute, and stood looking forward over the grey sea, flecked with white. The breeze was shrilling in the rigging, just strong enough for it to be unnecessary to reef topsails, and right aft, blowing round Hornblower's ears as he stood with his hands on the carved rail. Ahead lay four of the Indiamen, in a straggling line ahead, and then he saw the fifth and sixth not more than a mile beyond them. Of the flagship, of the transports, of the store ships, of the *Caligula*, there was nothing to be seen at all. Hornblower picked up the speaking trumpet.

'Masthead, there! What do you see of the flagship?'

'Northin', sir. Northin' in sight nowhere, sir, 'cepting for the Indiamen, sir.'

And that was that, thought Hornblower, replacing the speaking trumpet. A rare beginning to a voyage. The traverse board showed that the *Sutherland* had held steadily on her course through the night, and the deck log on the slate showed speeds of eight and nine knots. Before long Ushant should be in sight in this clear weather; he had done all his duty in keeping the Indiamen under his eye, on their course, and under canvas conformable with the weather. He only wished that the queasiness of his stomach would permit him to be quite confident about it, for the gloomy depression of seasickness filled him with foreboding. If a victim had to be found, it would be he, he felt sure. He gauged the strength of the wind and decided that it would be inadvisable to set more sail in the hope of overtaking the rest of the convoy. And with that, having reached the satisfactory conclusion that he could do nothing to avert blame if blame were coming to him, he felt more cheerful. Life at sea had taught him to accept the inevitable philosophically.

Eight bells sounded, and he heard the call for the watch below. Bush arrived on the quarterdeck to relieve Gerard. Hornblower felt Bush's keen glance directed at him, and ignored it in surly silence. He had made it a rule never to speak unnecessarily, and he found so much satisfaction in it that he was never going to break it. There was satisfaction to be found now, in paying no attention to Bush, who kept stealing anxious glances at him, ready to respond the moment he was spoken to, like a dog with his master. Then it occurred to Hornblower that he must be cutting a very undignified figure; unshaved and tousled, and probably pale green with seasickness. He went off below in a pet again.

In the cabin where he sat with his head in his hands, all the hanging fitments were swaying in the slow time set by the creaking of timbers. But as long as he did not look at them he was not uncontrollably sick. When Ushant had been sighted he would lie down and close his eyes. Then Polwheal came in, balancing a tray like a conjurer.

'Breakfast, sir,' said Polwheal in a flood of garrulity. 'I didn't know you was up, sir, not till the port watch told me when they came below. Coffee, sir. Soft bread, sir. Galley fire's bright an' I could have it toasted for you in two twos, sir, if you 'uld like it that way.'

Hornblower looked at Polwheal in a sudden flood of suspicion. Polwheal was making no attempt to offer him any of the fresh food, except for bread, which he had sent on board; not a chop or a steak nor rashers of bacon, nor any other of the other delicacies he had bought so recklessly. Yet Polwheal knew he had eaten no dinner yesterday, and Polwheal was usually insistent that he should eat and overeat. He wondered why, therefore, Polwheal should be offering him a Frenchman's breakfast like this. Polwheal's stony composure wavered a little under Hornblower's stare, confirming Hornblower's suspicions. Polwheal had guessed the secret of his captain's seasickness.

'Put it down,' he rasped, quite unable to say more at the moment. Polwheal put the tray on the table and still lingered.

'I'll pass the word when I want you,' said Hornblower sternly.

With his head between his hands he reviewed all of

what he could remember of yesterday. Not merely Polwheal, he realized now, but Bush and Gerard – the whole ship's company, for that matter – knew that he suffered from seasickness. Subtle hints in their bearing proved it, now that he came to think about it. At first the thought merely depressed him, so that he groaned again. Then it irritated him. And finally his sense of humour asserted itself and he smiled. While he smiled, the pleasant aroma of the coffee reached his nostrils, and he sniffed at it wondering, reacting to the scent in two opposite ways at once, conscious both of the urge of hunger and thirst and of the revulsion of his stomach. Hunger and thirst won in the end. He poured coffee for himself and sipped it, keeping his eyes rigidly from the swaying of the cabin fitments. With the blessed warmth of the strong sweet coffee inside him he instinctively began to eat the bread, and it was only when he had cleared the tray that he began to feel qualms of doubts as to the wisdom of what he had done. Even then his luck held, for before the waves of seasickness could overcome him a knock on the cabin door heralded the news that land was in sight, and he could forget them in the activity the news demanded of him.

Ushant was not in sight from the deck, but only from the masthead, and Hornblower made no attempt to climb the rigging to see it. But as he stood with the wind whipping round him and the rigging harping over his head he looked over the grey sea eastward to where France lay beyond the horizon. Of all landfalls perhaps this one loomed largest in English naval history. Drake and Blake, Shovel and Rooke, Hawke and Boscawen, Rodney and Jervis and Nelson had all of them stood as he was standing, looking eastward as he was doing. Three-quarters of the British mercantile marine rounded Ushant, outward and homeward. As a lieutenant under Pellew in the *Indefatigable* he had beaten about in sight of Ushant for many weary days during the blockade of Brest. It was in these very waters that the *Indefatigable* and the *Amazon* had driven the *Droits de l'Homme* into the breakers, and a thousand men to their deaths. The details of that wild fight thirteen years ago were as distinct in his memory as those of the battle with the *Natividad* only nine months back; that was a symptom of approaching old age.

Hornblower shook off the meditative gloom which was descending on him, and applied himself to the business of laying a fresh course for Finisterre and directing the Indiamen upon it – the first was a far easier task than the second. It called for an hour of signalling and gunfire before every one of his flock had satisfactorily repeated his signals; it appeared to Hornblower as if the masters of the convoy took pleasure in misunderstanding him, in ignoring him, in repeating incorrectly. The *Lord Mornington* flew the signal for ten minutes at the dip, as if to indicate that it was not understood; it was only when the *Sutherland* had borne down almost within hail of her, with Hornblower boiling with fury, that she was able to clear the jammed signal halliards and hoist the signal properly.

Bush chuckled sardonically at the sight, and began some remark to his captain to the effect that even Indiamen were as inefficient as men of war at the beginning of a commission, but Hornblower stamped away angrily out of earshot, leaving Bush staring after him.

The ridiculous incident had annoyed Hornblower on account of his fear lest he himself should appear ridiculous; but it had its effect in prolonging his forgetfulness of his seasickness. It was only after a spell of standing solitary on the starboard side while Bush gave the orders that brought the *Sutherland* up to windward of the convoy again that he calmed down and began to experience internal misgivings once more. He was on the point of retiring below when a sudden cry from Bush recalled him to the quarterdeck.

'*Walmer Castle*'s hauled her wind, sir.'

Hornblower put his glass to his eye. The *Walmer Castle* was the leading ship of the convoy, and the farthest to port. She was about three miles away, and there was no mistaking the fact that she had spun round on her heel and was now clawing frantically up to windward towards them.

'She's signalling, sir,' said Vincent, 'but I can't read it. It might be No. Twenty-nine, but that's "Discontinue the action" and she can't mean that.'

'Masthead!' bellowed Bush. 'What can you see on the port bow?'

'Northin', sir.'

'She's hauled it down now, sir,' went on Vincent. 'There goes another one! No. Eleven, sir. Enemy in sight.'

'Here, Savage,' said Bush. 'Take your glass and up with you.'

The next ship in the straggling line had come up into the wind, too; Savage was half-way up the rigging, when the masthead lookout hailed.

'I can see 'em now, sir. Two luggers, sir, on the port bow.'

Luggers off Ushant could only mean French priva-teers.

Swift, handy, and full of men, with a length of ex-perience at sea only equalled by that of the British navy, they would court any danger to make a prize of a fat East Indiaman. Such a capture would make their captains wealthy men. Bush, Vincent, everyone on the quarterdeck looked at Hornblower. If he were to lose such a ship entrusted to his charge he would forfeit every bit of credit at the Admiralty that he possessed.

'Turn up the hands, Mr Bush,' said Hornblower. In the excitement of instant action he had no thought for the dramatic aspect of affairs, forgot the need to pose, and made no attempt to impress his subordinates with his calm; and the calculations which came flooding up into his mind had so rapidly engrossed him that he betrayed no excitement whatever, as they saw.

The Indiamen all carried guns – the *Lord Mornington* actually had eighteen ports a side – and could beat off any long-range attack by a small privateer. The luggers' tactics would be to swoop alongside and board; no boarding nettings manned by an Indiaman's crew would keep out a hundred Frenchmen mad for gold. They would manoeuvre so as to cut off a ship to windward of him – while he was beating up against the wind they could rush her in three minutes and carry her off under his very eyes. He must not allow such a situation to arise, and yet the Indiamen were slow, his crew was undrilled, and French luggers were as quick as lightning in stays – there were two of them, as well, and he would have to parry two thrusts at once.

They were in sight now from the deck, their dark

sails lifting above the horizon, two-masted and close-hauled. The dark squares of their sails were urgent with menace, and Hornblower's eye could read more than the mere dreams of the silhouettes against the clear horizon. They were small, with not more than twenty guns apiece, and no more than nine pounders at that – the *Sutherland* could sink them with a couple of broadsides if they were ever foolish enough to come within close range. But they were fast; already they were hull-up, and Hornblower could see the white water under their bows. And they were lying at least a point nearer the wind than ever he could induce the *Sutherland* to lie. Each would have at least a hundred and fifty men on board, because French privateers had little thought for the comfort of their crews, nor needed to when they only intended to dash out of port, snap up a prize, and dash back again.

'Shall I clear for action, sir?' asked Bush, greatly daring.

'No,' snapped Hornblower. 'Send the men to quarters and put out the fires.'

There was no need to knock down bulwarks and risk spoiling his property and imperil the livestock on board, because there was no chance of a stand-up fight. But a stray nine-pounder ball into the galley fire might set the whole ship ablaze. The men went to their stations, were pushed there, or led there – some of the men were still confused between port and starboard sides – to the accompaniment of the low-voiced threats and curses of the petty officers.

'I'll have the guns loaded and run out, too, if you please, Mr Bush.'

More than half the men had never seen a cannon fired in their lives. This was the first time they had even heard the strange mad music of the gun trucks rumbling over the planking. Hornblower heard it with a catch in his breath – it called up many memories. The privateers gave no sign of flinching when the *Sutherland* showed her teeth, as Hornblower, watching them closely, saw. They held steadily on their course, heading closehauled to meet the convoy. But their appearance, Hornblower was glad to see, had done more to herd the merchantmen together than his orders had done. They were huddled together in a mass, each ship closer aboard its neighbour than any merchant captain could be induced to steer save under the impulse of fear. He could see boarding nettings being run up on board them, and they were running out their guns. The defence they could offer would only be feeble, but the fact that they could defend themselves at all was important in the present state of affairs.

A puff of smoke and a dull report from the leading privateer showed that she had opened fire; where the shot went Hornblower could not see, but the tricolour flag soared up each of the luggers' mainmasts, and at a word from Hornblower the red ensign rose to the *Sutherland*'s peak in reply to this jaunty challenge. Next moment the luggers neared the *Walmer Castle*, the leading ship to port, with the evident intention of running alongside.

'Set the t'gallants, Mr Bush,' said Hornblower. 'Helm a-starboard. Meet her. Steady.'

The *Walmer Castle* had sheered off in fright, almost running on board her starboard side neighbour, who had been forced to put her helm over as well. Then, in the nick of time, the *Sutherland* came dashing down. The luggers put up their helms and moved away to avoid the menace of her broadside, and their first clumsy rush had been beaten off.

'Main tops'l aback!' roared Hornblower.

It was of supreme importance to preserve his position of advantage to windward of the convoy, whence he could dash forward to the threatened point of danger. The convoy drew slowly ahead, with the luggers leading them. Hornblower watched them steadily, the practice of years enabling him to keep them in the focus of his telescope as he stood on the heaving deck. They spun round suddenly on the starboard tack again, moving like clockwork, leaping to meet the *Lord Mornington* on the starboard wing like hounds at the throat of a stag. The *Lord Mornington* sheered out of her course, the *Sutherland* came tearing down upon her, and the luggers went about, instantly, heading for the *Walmer Castle* again.

'Hard a-starboard,' rasped Hornblower. The *Walmer Castle*, to his vast relief, managed to throw her topsails aback, and the *Sutherland* reached her just in time. She swept across her stern; Hornblower could see her whiskered captain in his formal blue frockcoat beside her wheel, and half-a-dozen Lascar sailors leaping hysterically over her deck. The luggers wore away, just out of gunshot of the *Sutherland*. There was smoke eddying round one of the other Indiamen; apparently she had loosed off her broadside straight into the blue.

'They're wasting powder there, sir,' volunteered Bush, but Hornblower made no reply, being too busy with his mental calculations.

'As long as they have the sense not to scatter –' said Crystal.

That was an important consideration; if the convoy once divided he could not hope to defend every portion of it. There was neither honour nor glory to be won in this contest between a ship of the line and two small privateers – if he beat them off the world would think nothing of it, while if any one of the convoy was lost he could imagine only too well the ensuing public outcry. He had thought of signalling to his charges that they should keep together, but he had rejected the idea. Signalling would only confuse them, and half of them would probably misread the signal. It was better to rely on their natural instinct of self-preservation.

The privateers had come up into the wind again, and were working to windward directly astern of the *Sutherland*. From the very look of them, of their sharp black hulls and far-raked masts, Hornblower could guess that they had concerted some new move. He faced aft, watching them closely. Next moment the plan revealed itself. He saw the bows of the leader swing to starboard, those of the second one to port. They were diverging, and each with the wind on her quarter came racing down, white water foaming at their bows, lying over to the stiff breeze, each of them a picture of malignant efficiency. As soon as they were clear of the *Sutherland* they would converge again attacking opposite wings of the convoy. He would hardly have time to beat off the first one and then return to chase the other away.

He thought wildly for a moment of trying to bring the whole convoy to the wind together, and rejected the plan at once. They would probably spread out in the attempt, if they did not fall foul of each other, and in either case, scattered or crippled, they would fall easy victims to their enemies. All he could do was to attempt to tackle both ships in succession. It might seem hopeless, but there was nothing to be gained in abandoning the only plan possible. He would play it out to the last second.

He dropped his telescope on the deck, and sprang up on to the rail, hanging on by the mizzen rigging. He stared at his enemies, turning his head from side to side, calculating their speeds and, observing their courses, his face set rigid in an intensity of concentration. The lugger to starboard was slightly nearer, and consequently would arrive at the convoy first. He would have a minute or so more in hand to get back to deal with the second if he turned on this one. Another glance confirmed his decision, and he risked his reputation upon it – without a thought now, in the excitement of action, for that reputation of his.

'Starboard two points,' he called.

'Starboard two points,' echoed the quartermaster.

The *Sutherland* swung round, out of the wake of the convoy, and headed to cross the bows of the starboard-side lugger. In turn, to avoid the ponderous broadside which was menacing her, the latter edged away, farther and farther as the *Sutherland* moved down upon her. By virtue of her vastly superior speed she was forereaching both upon the convoy and the escort; and the *Sutherland* in her effort to keep between the privateer and the merchantmen was being lured farther and farther away from her proper position to interfere with the designs of the other lugger. Hornblower was aware of that, but it was a risk he was compelled to take, and he knew, despairingly, that if the Frenchmen played the right game he would be beaten. He could never drive the first lugger so far away and to leeward as to render her innocuous and still have time enough to get back and deal with the other. Already he was dangerously astray, but he held on his course, almost abreast now both of the convoy and of the lugger to starboard. Then he saw the other lugger turn to make its dash in upon the convoy.

'Hands to the braces, Mr Bush!' he called. 'Hard a-starboard!'

The *Sutherland* came round, heeling over with the wind abeam and a trifle more canvas than was safe. She seemed to tear through the water as she raced for the convoy, which was wheeling in confusion away from the attack. As if through a forest of masts and sails Hornblower could see the dark sails of the lugger swooping down upon the helpless *Walmer Castle*, which must have responded slowly to her helm, or been badly commanded, and was being left astern by the others. A dozen simultaneous calculations raced through Hornblower's mind. He was thinking like a highly complex machine, forecasting the course of the lugger, and of the six Indiamen, and making allowances for the possible variations resulting from their captains' personal traits. He had to bear in mind the speed of the *Sutherland*, and the rate at which she was drifting to leeward under her press of canvas. To circumnavigate the scattering convoy would take too much time and would deprive him of any opportunity of surprise. He called his orders quietly down to the helmsman, steering for the narrowing gap between two ships. The *Lord Mornington* saw the two-decker rushing down upon her, and swerved as Hornblower had anticipated.

'Stand to your guns, there!' he bellowed. 'Mr Gerard! Give the lugger a broadside as we pass her!'

The *Lord Mornington* was past and gone in a flash; beyond her was the *Europe* – she had worn round a little and seemed to be heading straight for a collision.

'God blast her!' roared Bush. 'God –' The *Sutherland* had shaved across her bows, her jib boom almost brushing the *Sutherland*'s mizzen rigging. Next moment the *Sutherland* had dashed through the narrowing gap between two more ships. Beyond was the *Walmer Castle*, and alongside her the lugger taken completely by surprise at this unexpected appearance. In the stillness which prevailed on board the *Sutherland* they could hear the pop-popping of small arms – the Frenchmen were scrambling up to the lofty deck of the Indiaman. But as the big two-decker came hurtling down upon him the French captain tried for safety. Hornblower could see the French boarders leaping down again to the lugger and her vast mainsail rose ponderously under the united effort of two hundred frantic arms. She had boomed off from the Indiamen and came round like a top, but she was five seconds too late.

'Back the mizzen tops'l,' snapped Hornblower to Bush. 'Mr Gerard!'

The *Sutherland* steadied herself for a crashing blow.

'Take your aim!' screamed Gerard, mad with excitement. He was by the forward section of guns on the main deck, which would bear first. 'Wait till your guns bear! Fire!'

The rolling broadside which followed, as the ship slowly swung round, seemed to Hornblower's tense mind to last for at least five minutes. The intervals between the shots were ragged, and some of the guns were clearly fired before they bore. Elevation was faulty, too, as the splashes both this side of, and far beyond, the lugger bore witness. Nevertheless, some of the shots told. He saw splinters flying in the lugger, a couple of shrouds part. Two sudden swirls in the crowd on her deck showed where cannon balls had ploughed through it.

The brisk breeze blew the smoke of the straggling broadside clear instantly, so that his view of the lugger a hundred yards away was uninterrupted. She had still a chance of getting away. Her sails were filled, and she was slipping fast through the water. He gave the orders to the helmsman which would cause the *Sutherland* to yaw again and bring her broadside to bear. As he did so nine puffs of smoke from the lugger's side gave warning that she was firing her nine-pounder popguns.

The Frenchmen were game enough. A musical tone like a brief expiring note on an organ sang in his ear as a shot passed close overhead, and a double crash below told him that the *Sutherland* was hit. Her thick timbers ought to keep out nine-pounder shot at that range.

He heard the rumble of the trucks as the *Sutherland*'s guns were run out again, and he leaned over the rail to shout to the men on the maindeck.

'Take your aim well!' he shouted. 'Wait till your sights bear!'

The guns went off in ones or twos down the *Sutherland*'s side as she yawed. There was only one old hand at each of the *Sutherland*'s seventy-four guns, and although the officers in charge of the port-side battery had sent over some of their men to help on the starboard side they would naturally keep the trained layers in case the port-side guns had to be worked suddenly. And there were not seventy-four good gun layers left over from the Lydia's old crew – he remembered the difficulty he had experienced in drawing up the watch bill.

'Stop your vents!' shouted Gerard, and then his voice went up into a scream of excitement. 'There it goes! Well done, men!'

The big main mast of the lugger, with the mainsail and topmast and shrouds and all, was leaning over to one side. It seemed to hang there naturally, for a whole breathing space, before it fell with a sudden swoop. Even then a single shot fired from her aftermost gun proclaimed the Frenchman's defiance. Hornblower turned back to the helmsman to give the orders that would take the Sutherland within pistol shot and complete the little ship's destruction. He was aflame with excitement. Just in time he remembered his duty; he was granting the other lugger time to get in among the convoy, and every second was of value. He noted his excitement as a curious and interesting phenomenon, while his orders brought the Sutherland round on the other tack. As she squared away a long shout of defiance rose from the lugger, lying rolling madly in the heavy sea, her black hull resembling some crippled waterbeetle. Someone was waving a tricolour flag from the deck.

'Goodbye, Mongseer Crapaud,' said Bush. 'You've a long day's work ahead of you before you see Brest again.'

The Sutherland threshed away on her new course; the convoy had all turned and were beating up towards her, the lugger on their heels like a dog after a flock of sheep. At the sight of the *Sutherland* rushing down upon her she sheered off again. Obstinately, she worked round to make a dash at the *Walmer Castle* – steering wide as usual – but Hornblower swung the *Sutherland* round and the *Walmer Castle* scuttled towards her for protection. It was easy enough, even in a clumsy ship like the *Sutherland*, to fend off the attacks of a single enemy. The Frenchman realized this after a few minutes more, and bore away to the help of her crippled consort.

Hornblower watched the big lugsail come round and fill, and the lugger lying over as she thrashed her way to windward; already the dismasted Frenchman was out of sight from the *Sutherland*'s quarterdeck. It was a relief to see the Frenchman go. If he had been in command of her he would have left the other to look after herself and hung on to the convoy until nightfall; it would have been strange if he had not been able to snap up a straggler in the darkness.

'You can secure the guns, Mr Bush,' he said, at length.

Someone on the main deck started to cheer, and the cheering was taken up by the rest of the crew. They were waving their hands or their hats as if a Trafalgar had just been won.

'Stop that noise,' shouted Hornblower, hot with rage. 'Mr Bush, send the hands aft here to me.'

They came, all of them, grinning with excitement, pushing and playing like schoolboys; even the rawest of them had forgotten his seasickness in the excitement of the battle. Hornblower's blood boiled as he looked down at them, the silly fools.

'No more of that!' he rasped. 'What have you done?

Frightened off a couple of luggers not much bigger than our long boat! Two broadsides from a seventy-four, and you're pleased with yourselves for knocking away a single spar! God, you ought to have blown the Frenchie out of the water! Two broadsides, you pitiful baby school! You must lay your guns better than that when it comes to real fighting, and I'll see you learn how – me and the cat between us. And how d'you make sail? I've seen it done better by Portuguese niggers!'

There was no denying the fact that words spoken from a full heart carry more weight than all the artifices of rhetoric. Hornblower's genuine rage and sincerity had made a deep impression, so stirred up had he been at the sight of botched and bungling work. The men were hanging their heads now, and shifting uneasily from one foot to the other, as they realized that what they had done had not been so marvellous after all. And to do them justice, half their exhilaration arose from the mad excitement of the *Sutherland*'s rush through the convoy, with ships close on either hand. In later years, when they were spinning yarns of past commissions, the story would be embroidered until they began to affirm that Hornblower had steered a two-decker in a howling storm through a fleet of two-hundred sail all on opposing courses.

'You can pipe down now, Mr Bush,' said Hornblower. 'And when the hands have had their breakfasts you can exercise them aloft.'

In the reaction following his excitement he was yearning to get away to the solitude of the stern gallery again. But here came Walsh the surgeon, trotting up the quarterdeck and touching his hat.

'Surgeon's report, sir,' he said. 'One warrant officer killed. No officers and no seamen wounded.'

'Killed?' said Hornblower, his jaw dropping. 'Who's killed?'

'John Hart, midshipman,' answered Walsh.

Hart had been a promising seaman in the *Lydia*, and it was Hornblower himself who had promoted him to the quarterdeck and obtained his warrant for him.

'Killed?' said Hornblower again.

'I can mark him "mortally wounded", sir, if you prefer it,' said Walsh. 'He lost a leg when a nine-pounder ball came in through No. Eleven gun port on the lower deck. He was alive when they got him down to the cockpit, but he died the next minute. Popliteal artery.'

Walsh was a new appointment, who had not served under Hornblower before. Otherwise he might have known better than to indulge in details of this sort with so much professional relish.

'Get out of my road, blast you,' snarled Hornblower.

His prospect of solitude was spoiled now. There would have to be a burial later in the day, with flag half-mast and yards a-cockbill. That in itself was irksome. And it was Hart who was dead – a big gangling young man with a wide, pleasant smile. The thought of it robbed him of all pleasure in his achievements this morning. Bush was there on the quarterdeck, smiling happily both at the thought of what had been done today and at the thought of four solid hours' exercise aloft for the hands. He would have liked to talk, and Gerard was there, eager to discuss the working of his beloved guns. Hornblower glared at them, daring them to address one single word to him; but they had served with him for years, and knew better.

He turned and went below; the ships of the convoy were sending up flags – the sort of silly signals of congratulations one might expect of Indiamen, probably half of them misspelled. He could rely on Bush to hoist 'Not understood' until the silly fools got it right, and then to make a mere acknowledgement. He wanted nothing to do with them, or with anybody else. The one shred of comfort in a world which he hated was that, with a following wind and the convoy to leeward, he would be private in his stern gallery, concealed even from inquisitive telescopes in the other ships.

Hornblower took a last pull at his cigar when he heard the drum beating to divisions. He exhaled a lungful of smoke, his head thrown back, looking out from under the cover of the stern gallery up at the blissful blue sky, and then down at the blue water beneath, with the dazzling white foam surging from under the *Sutherland's* counter into her wake. Overhead he heard the measured tramp of the marines as they formed up across the poop deck, and then a brief shuffle of heavy boots as they dressed their line in obedience to the captain's order. The patter of hundreds of pairs of feet acted as a subdued accompaniment as the crew formed up round the decks. When everything had fallen still again Hornblower pitched his cigar overboard, hitched his full dress coat into position, settled his cocked hat on his head, and walked with dignity, his left hand on his sword-hilt, forward to the half-deck and up the companion ladder to the quarterdeck. Bush was there, and Crystal, and the midshipmen of the watch. They saluted him, and from farther aft came the snick-snack-snick of the marines presenting arms.

Hornblower stood and looked round him in leisurely fashion; on this Sunday morning it was his duty to inspect the ship, and he could take advantage of the fact to drink in all the beauty and the artistry of the scene. Overhead the pyramids of white canvas described slow cones against the blue sky with the gentle roll of the ship. The decks were snowy white – Bush had succeeded in that in ten days' labour – and the intense orderliness of a ship of war was still more intense on this morning of Sunday inspection. Hornblower shot a searching glance from under lowered eyelids at the crew ranged in long single lines along the gangways and on the maindeck. They were standing still, smart enough in their duck frocks and trousers. It was their bearing that he wished to study, and that could be done more effectively in a sweeping glance from the quarterdeck than at the close range of the inspection. There could be a certain hint of insolence in the way a restive crew stood to attention, and one could perceive lassitude in a dispirited crew. He could see neither now, for which he was thankful.

Ten days of hard work, of constant drill, of unsleeping supervision, of justice tempered by good humour, had done much to settle the hands to their duty. He had had to order five floggings three days ago, forcing himself to stand apparently unmoved while the whistle and crack of the cat-o'-nine-tails sickened his stomach. One of those floggings might do a little good to the recipient – an old hand who had apparently forgotten what he had learned and needed a sharp reminder of it. The other four would do none to the men whose backs had been lacerated; they would never make good sailors and were mere brutes whom brutal treatment could at least make no worse. He had sacrificed them to show the wilder spirits what might happen as a result of inattention to orders – it was only by an actual demonstration that one could work on the minds of uneducated men. The dose had to be prescribed with the utmost accuracy, neither too great nor too small. He seemed, so his sweeping glance told him, to have hit it off exactly.

Once more he looked round to enjoy the beauty of it all – the orderly ship, the white sails, the blue sky; the scarlet and pipeclay of the marines, the blue and gold of the officers; and there was consummate artistry in the subtle indications that despite the inspection the real pulsating life of the ship was going on beneath it. Where four hundred and more men stood at attention awaiting his lightest word the quartermaster at the wheel kept his mind on the binnacle and the leach of the main course, the lookouts at the masthead and the officer of the watch with his telescope were living demonstrations of the fact that the ship must still be sailed and the King's service carried on.

Hornblower turned aside to begin his inspection. He walked up and down the quadruple ranks of the marines, but although he ran his eye mechanically over the men he took notice of nothing. Captain Morris and his sergeants could be relied upon to attend to details like the pipeclaying of belts and the polishing of buttons. Marines could be drilled and disciplined into machines in a way sailors could not be; he could take the marines for granted and he was not interested in them. Even now, after ten days, he hardly knew the faces and names of six out of the ninety marines on board.

He passed on to the lines of seamen, the officers of each division standing rigidly in front. This was more interesting. The men were trim and smart in their whites

– Hornblower wondered how many of them ever realized that the cost of their clothing was deducted from the meagre pay they received when they were paid off. Some of the new hands were horribly sunburned, as a result of unwise exposure to the sudden blazing sun of yesterday. A blond burly figure here had lost the skin from his forearms as well as from his neck and forehead. Hornblower recognized him as Waites, condemned for sheep-stealing at Exeter assizes – that explained the sunburn, for Waites had been blanched by months of imprisonment awaiting trial. The raw areas looked abominably painful.

'See that this man Waites,' said Hornblower to the petty officer of the division, 'attends the surgeon this afternoon. He is to have goose grease for those burns, and whatever lotions the surgeon prescribes.'

'Aye aye, sir,' said the petty officer.

Hornblower passed on down the line, scanning each man closely. Faces well remembered, faces it was still an effort to put a name to. Faces that he had studied two years back in the far Pacific on board the *Lydia*, faces he had first seen when Gerard brought back his boatload of bewildered captures from St Ives. Swarthy faces and pale, boys and elderly men, blue eyes, brown eyes, grey eyes. A host of tiny impressions were collecting in Hornblower's mind; they would be digested together later during his solitary walks in the stern gallery, to form the raw material for the plans he would make to further the efficiency of his crew.

'That man Simms ought to be rated captain of the mizzentop. He's old enough now. What's this man's name? Dawson? No, Dawkins. He's looking sulky. One of Goddard's gang – it looks as if he's still resenting Goddard's flogging. I must remember that.'

The sun blazed down upon them, while the ship lifted and swooped over the gentle sea. From the crew he turned his attention to the ship – the breechings of the guns, the way the falls were flemished down, the cleanliness of the decks, the galley, and the forecastle. At all this he need only pretend to look – the skies would fall before Bush neglected his duty. But he had to go through with it, with a show of solemnity. Men were oddly influenced – the poor fools would work better for Bush if they thought Hornblower was keeping an eye on him, and they would work better for Hornblower if they thought he inspected the ship thoroughly. This wretched business of capturing men's devotion set Hornblower smiling cynically when he was unobserved.

'A good inspection, Mr Bush,' said Hornblower, returning to the quarterdeck. 'The ship is in better order than I hoped for. I shall expect the improvement to continue. You may rig the church now.'

It was a Godfearing Admiralty who ordered church service every Sunday morning, otherwise Hornblower would have dispensed with it, as befitted a profound student of Gibbon. As it was, he had managed to evade having a chaplain on board – Hornblower hated parsons. He watched the men dragging up mess stools for themselves, and chairs for the officers. They were working diligently and cheerfully, although not with quite that disciplined purposefulness which characterized a fully trained crew. His coxswain Brown covered the compass-box on the quarterdeck with a cloth, and laid on it, with due solemnity, Hornblower's Bible and prayer book. Hornblower disliked these services; there was always the chance that some devout member of his compulsory congregation might raise objections to having to attend – Catholic or Nonconformist. Religion was the only power which could ever pit itself against the bonds of discipline; Hornblower remembered a theologically minded master's mate who had once protested against his reading the Benediction, as though he, the King's representative at sea – God's representative, when all was said and done – could not read a Benediction if he chose!

He glowered at the men as they settled down, and began to read. As the thing had to be done, it might as well be done well, and, as ever, while he read he was struck once more by the beauty of Cranmer's prose and the deftness of his adaptation. Cranmer had been burned alive two hundred and fifty years before – did it benefit him at all to have his prayer book read now?

Bush read the lessons in a tuneless bellow as if he were hailing the foretop. Then Hornblower read the opening lines of the hymn, and Sullivan the fiddler played the first bars of the tune. Bush gave the signal for the singing to start – Hornblower could never bring himself to do that; he told himself he was neither a mountebank nor an Italian opera conductor – and the crew opened their throats and roared it out.

But even hymn singing had its advantages. A captain could often discover a good deal about the spirits of his crew by the way they sang their hymns. This morning either the hymn chosen was specially popular or the crew were happy in the new sunshine, for they were singing lustily, with Sullivan sawing away at an ecstatic obbligato on his fiddle. The Cornishmen among the crew apparently knew the hymn well, and fell upon it with a will, singing in parts to add a leavening of harmony to the tuneless bellowings of the others. It all meant nothing to Hornblower – one tune was the same as another to his tone-deaf ear, and the most beautiful music was to him no more than comparable with the noise of a cart along a gravel road. As he listened to the unmeaning din, and gazed at the hundreds of gaping mouths, he found himself wondering as usual whether or not there was any basis of fact in this legend of music – whether other people actually heard something more than mere noise, or whether he was the only person on board not guilty of wilful self-deception.

Then he saw a ship's boy in the front row. The hymn meant something to him, at least. He was weeping broken-heartedly, even while he tried to keep his back straight and to conceal his emotions, with the big tears running down his cheeks and his nose all beslobbered. The poor little devil had been touched in one way or another – some chord of memory had been struck. Perhaps the last time he had heard that hymn was in the little church at home, beside his mother and brothers. He was homesick and heartbroken now. Hornblower was glad for his sake as well as for his own when the hymn came to an end; the next ceremony would steady the boy again.

He took up the Articles of War and began to read them as the Lords Commissioners of the Admiralty had ordained should be done each Sunday in every one of His Britannic Majesty's Ships. He knew the solemn sentences by heart at this, his five hundredth reading, every cadence, every turn of phrase, and he read them well. This was better than any vague religious service or Thirty Nine Articles. Here was a code in black and white, a stern, unemotional call to duty pure and simple. Some Admiralty clerk or pettifogging lawyer had had a gift of phrasing just as felicitous as Cranmer's. There was no trumpet-call about it, no clap-trap appeal to sentiment; there was merely the cold logic of the code which kept the British Navy at sea, and which had guarded England during seventeen years of a struggle for life. He could tell by the deathlike stillness of his audience as he read that their attention had been caught and held, and when he folded the paper away and looked up he could see solemn, set faces. The ship's boy in the front row had forgotten his tears. There was a faraway look in his eyes; obviously he was making good resolutions to attend more strictly to his duty in future. Or perhaps he was dreaming wild dreams of the time to come when he would be a captain in a gold-laced coat commanding a seventy-four, or of brave deeds which he would do.

In a sudden revulsion of feeling Hornblower wondered if lofty sentiment would armour the boy against cannon shot – he remembered another ship's boy who had been smashed into a red jam before his eyes by a shot from the *Natividad*.

8

In the afternoon Hornblower was walking his quarter-deck; the problem before him was so difficult that he had quitted his stern gallery – he could not walk fast enough there, owing to his having to bend his head, to set his thoughts going. The people on the quarterdeck saw his mood, and kept warily over to the lee side, leaving the whole weather side, nearly thirty yards of quarterdeck and gangway, to him. Up and down, he walked, up and down, trying to nerve himself to make the decision he hankered after. The *Sutherland* was slipping slowly through the water with a westerly breeze abeam; the convoy was clustered together only a few cables' lengths to leeward.

Gerard shut his telescope with a snap.

'Boat pulling toward us from *Lord Mornington*, sir,' he said. He wanted to warn his captain of the approach of visitors, so that if he thought fit he could make himself unapproachable in his cabin; but he knew, as well as Hornblower did, that it might be unwise for a captain to act in too cavalier a fashion towards the notabilities on board the East India convoy.

Hornblower looked across at the boat creeping beetle-like towards him. Ten days of a strong north-easterly wind had not merely hurried the convoy to the latitude of North Africa where he was to leave them to their own devices, but had prevented all intercourse and visiting between ships, until yesterday. Yesterday there had been a good deal of coming and going between the ships of the convoy; it was only natural that today he should receive formal calls, which he could not well refuse. In another two hours they would be parting company – it could not be a prolonged ordeal.

The boat ran alongside, and Hornblower walked forward to receive his two guests – Captain Osborn of the *Lord Mornington*, in his formal frock coat, and someone else, tall and bony, resplendent in civilian full dress with ribbon and star.

'Good afternoon, Captain,' said Osborn. 'I wish to present you to Lord Eastlake, Governor-designate of Bombay.'

Hornblower bowed; so did Lord Eastlake.

'I have come,' said Lord Eastlake, clearing his throat, 'to beg of you, Captain Hornblower, to receive on behalf of your ship's company this purse of four hundred guineas. It has been subscribed by the passengers of the East India convoy in recognition of the skill and courage displayed by the *Sutherland* in the action with the two French privateers off Ushant.'

'In the name of my ship's company I thank your Lordship,' said Hornblower.

It was a very handsome gesture, and as he took the purse he felt like Judas, knowing what designs he was cherishing against the East India convoy.

'And I,' said Osborn, 'am the bearer of a most cordial invitation to you and to your first lieutenant to join us at dinner in the *Lord Mornington*.'

At that Hornblower shook his head with apparent regret.

'We part company in two hours,' he said. 'I was about to hang out a signal to that effect. I am deeply hurt by the necessity of having to refuse.'

'We shall all be sorry on board the *Lord Mornington*,' said Lord Eastlake. 'Ten days of bad weather have deprived us of the pleasure of the company of any of the officers of the Navy. Cannot you be persuaded to alter your decision?'

'This has been the quickest passage I have made to these latitudes,' said Osborn. 'I begin to regret it now that it appears to have prevented our seeing anything of you.'

'I am on the King's service, my lord, and under the most explicit orders from the Admiral.'

That was an excuse against which the Governor-designate of Bombay could not argue.

'I understand,' said Lord Eastlake. 'At least can I have the pleasure of making the acquaintance of your officers?'

Once more that was a handsome gesture; Hornblower called them up and presented them one by one; horny-handed Bush, and Gerard handsome and elegant, Captain Morris of the marines and his two gawky subalterns, the other lieutenants and the master, down to the junior midshipman, all of them delighted and embarrassed at this encounter with a lord.

At last Lord Eastlake turned to go.

'Goodbye, Captain,' he said, proffering his hand. 'A prosperous voyage in the Mediterranean to you.'

'Thank you, my lord. And a good passage to Bombay to you. And a successful and historic term of office.'

Hornblower stood weighing the purse – an embroidered canvas bag at which someone had laboured hard recently – in his hand. He felt the weight of the gold, and under his fingers he felt the crackle of the banknotes. He would have liked to treat it as prize money, and take his share under prize money rules, but he knew he could not accept that sort of reward from civilians. Still, his crew must show full appreciation.

'Mr Bush,' he said, as the boat shoved off. 'Man the yards. Have the men give three cheers.'

Lord Eastlake and Captain Osborn acknowledged the compliment as they pulled away; Hornblower watched the boat creep back to the *Lord Mornington*. Four hundred guineas. It was a lot of money, but he was not going to be bought off with four hundred guineas. In that very moment he came to his decision after twenty-four hours of vacillation. He would display to the East India convoy the independence of Captain Hornblower.

'Mr Rayner,' he said. 'Clear away the launch and the longboat. Have the helm put up and run down to leeward of the convoy. I want those boats in the water by the time we reach them. Mr Bush. Mr Gerard. Your attention please.'

Amid the bustle and hurry of wearing the ship, and tailing on at the stay tackles, Hornblower gave his orders briefly. For once in his life Bush ventured to demur when he realized what Hornblower had in mind.

'They're John Company's ships, sir,' he said.

'I had myself fancied that such was the case,' said Hornblower with elaborate irony. He knew perfectly well the risk he was running in taking men from ships of the East India Company – he would be both offending the most powerful corporation in England and contravening

Admiralty orders. But he needed the men, needed them desperately, and the ships from whom he was taking them would sight no land until they reached St Helena. It would be three or four months before any protest could reach England, and six months before any censure could reach him in the Mediterranean. A crime six months old might not be prosecuted with extreme severity, and perhaps in six months' time he would be dead.

'Give the boats' crews pistols and cutlasses,' he said, 'just to show that I'll stand no nonsense. I want twenty men from each of those ships.'

'Twenty!' said Bush, gaping with admiration. This was flouting the law on the grand scale.

'Twenty from each. And mark you, I'll have only white men. No Lascars. And able seamen every one of them, men who can hand, reef, and steer. And find out who their quarter gunners are and bring them. You can use some trained gunners, Gerard?'

'By God I can, sir.'

'Very good.'

Hornblower turned away. He had reached his decision unaided, and he did not want to discuss it further. The *Sutherland* had run down to the convoy. First the launch and then the cutter dropped into the water and pulled over to the clustered ships while the *Sutherland* dropped farther down to leeward to await their return, hove to with main topsail to the mast. Through his glass Hornblower saw the flash of steel as Gerard with his boarding party ran up on to the deck of the *Lord Mornington* – he was displaying his armed force early so as to overawe any thought of resistance. Hornblower was in a fever of anxiety which he had to struggle hard to conceal. He shut his glass with a snap and began to pace the deck.

'Boat pulling towards us from *Lord Mornington*, sir,' said Rayner, who was as excited as his captain, and far more obviously.

'Very good,' said Hornblower with careful unconcern.

That was a comfort. If Osborn had given Gerard a pointblank refusal, had called his men to arms and defied him, it might give rise to a nasty situation. A court of law might call it murder if someone got killed in a scuffle while illegal demands were being enforced. But he had counted on Osborn being taken completely by surprise when the boarding party ran on to his deck. He would be able to offer no real resistance. Now Hornblower's calculations were proving correct; Osborn was sending a protest, and he was prepared to deal with any number of protests – especially as the rest of the convoy would wait on their commodore's example and could be relieved of their men while the protesting was going on.

It was Osborn himself who came in through the entry port, scarlet with rage and offended dignity.

'Captain Hornblower!' he said, as he set foot on the deck. 'This is an outrage! I must protest against it, sir. At this very moment your lieutenant is parading my crew with a view to impressment.'

'He is acting by my orders, sir,' said Hornblower.

'I could hardly believe it when he told me so. Are you aware, sir, that what you propose to do is contrary to the law? It is a flagrant violation of Admiralty regulations. A perfect outrage, sir. The ships of the Honourable East India Company are exempt from impressment, and

I, as Commodore, must protest to the last breath of my body against any contravention of the law.'

'I shall be glad to receive your protest when you make it, sir.'

'But – but –' spluttered Osborn. 'I have delivered it. I have *made* my protest, sir.'

'Oh, I understand,' said Hornblower. 'I thought these were only remarks preliminary to a protest.'

'Nothing of the sort,' raved Osborn, his portly form almost dancing on the deck. 'I have protested, sir, and I shall continue to protest. I shall call the attention of the highest in the land to this outrage. I shall come from the ends of the earth, gladly, sir, to bear witness at your court martial. I shall not rest – I shall leave no stone unturned – I shall exert all my influence to have this crime punished as it deserves. I'll have you cast in damages, sir, as well as broke.'

'But, Captain Osborn –' began Hornblower, changing his tune just in time to delay the dramatic departure which Osborn was about to make. From the tail of his eye Hornblower had seen the *Sutherland*'s boats pulling towards two more victims, having presumably stripped the first two of all possible recruits. As Hornblower began to hint at a possible change of mind on his part, Osborn rapidly lost his ill temper.

'If you restore the men, sir, I will gladly retract all I have said,' said Osborn. 'Nothing more will be heard of the incident, I assure you.'

'But will you not allow me to ask for volunteers from among your crews, Captain?' pleaded Hornblower. 'There may be a few men who would like to join the King's service.'

'Well – yes, I will even agree to that. As you say, sir, you may find a few restless spirits.'

That was the height of magnanimity on Osborn's part, although he was safe in assuming that there would be few men in his fleet foolish enough to exchange the comparative comfort of the East India Company's service for the rigours of life in the royal navy.

'Your seamanship in that affair with the privateers, sir, was so admirable that I find it hard to refuse you anything,' said Osborn, pacifically. The *Sutherland*'s boats were alongside the last of the convoy now.

'That is very good of you, sir,' said Hornblower, bowing. 'Allow me, then, to escort you into your gig. I will recall my boats. Since they will have taken volunteers first, we can rely upon it that they will have all the willing ones on board, and I shall return the unwilling ones. Thank you, Captain Osborn. Thank you.'

He saw Captain Osborn over the side and walked back to the quarterdeck. Rayner was eyeing him with amazement on account of his sudden volte-face, which gave him pleasure, for Rayner would be still more amazed soon. The cutter and launch, both of them as full of men as they could be, were running down now to rejoin, passing Osborn's gig as it was making its slow course to windward. Through his glass Hornblower could see Osborn wave his arm as he sat in his gig; presumably he was shouting something to the boats as they went by. Bush and Gerard very properly paid him no attention. In two minutes they were alongside, and the men came pouring on deck, a hundred and twenty men laden with their small possessions, escorted by thirty of the *Sutherland*'s hands. They were made welcome by the rest of the crew all with broad grins. It was a peculiarity of the British pressed sailor that he was always glad to see other men pressed – in the same way, thought Hornblower, as the fox who lost his brush wanted all the other foxes to lose theirs.

Bush and Gerard had certainly secured a fine body of men; Hornblower looked them over as they stood in apathy, or bewilderment, or sullen rage, upon the *Sutherland*'s main deck. At no warning they had been snatched from the comfort of an Indiaman, with regular pay, ample food, and easy discipline, into the hardships of the King's service, where the pay was problematic, the food bad, and where their backs were liable to be flogged to the bones at a simple order from their new captain. Even a sailor before the mast could look forward with pleasure to his visit to India, with all its possibilities; but these men were destined instead now to two years of monotony only varied by danger, where disease and the cannon balls of the enemy lay in wait for them.

'I'll have those boats hoisted in, Mr Rayner,' said Hornblower.

Rayner's eyelids flickered for a second – he had heard Hornblower's promise to Captain Osborn, and he knew that more than a hundred of the new arrivals would refuse to volunteer. The boats would only have to be hoisted out again to take them back. But if Hornblower's wooden expression indicated anything at all, it was that he meant what he said.

'Aye aye, sir,' said Rayner.

Bush was approaching now, paper in hand, having agreed his figures regarding the recruits with Gerard.

'A hundred and twenty, total, sir, as you ordered,' said

Bush. 'One cooper's mate – he was a volunteer, one hundred and nine able seamen – two of 'em volunteered; six quarter gunners; four landsmen, all volunteers.'

'Excellent, Mr Bush. Read 'em in. Mr Rayner, square away as soon as those boats are inboard. Mr Vincent! Signal to the convoy: "All-men-have-volunteered. Thank you. Goodbye." You'll have to spell out "volunteered" but it's worth it.'

Hornblower's high spirits had lured him into saying an unnecessary sentence. But when he took himself to task for it he could readily excuse himself. He had a hundred and twenty new hands, nearly all of them able seamen – the *Sutherland* had nearly her full complement now. More than that, he had guarded himself against the wrath to come. When the inevitable chiding letter arrived from the Admiralty he would be able to write back and say that he had taken the men with the East India Company's Commodore's permission; with any good fortune he could keep the ball rolling for another six months. That would give him a year altogether in which to convince the new hands that they had volunteered – by that time some of them at least might be sufficiently enamoured of their new life to swear to that; enough of them to befog the issue, and to afford to an Admiralty, prepared of necessity to look with indulgence on breaches of the pressing regulations, a loophole of excuse not to prosecute him too hard.

'*Lord Mornington* replying, sir,' said Vincent. '"Do not understand the signal. Await boat"!'

'Signal "Goodbye" again,' said Hornblower.

Down on the maindeck Bush had hardly finished reading through the Articles of War to the new hands – the necessary formality to make them servants of the King, submissive to the hangman and the cat.

9

The *Sutherland* had reached her rendezvous off Palamos Point, apparently the first of the squadron, for there was no sign as yet of the flagship or of the *Caligula*. As she beat slowly up under easy sail against the gentle south-easterly wind Gerard was taking advantage of this period of idleness to exercise the crew at the guns. Bush had too long had his way in drilling the crew aloft; it was time for practice with the big guns, as Hornblower had agreed. Under the scorching sun of a Mediterranean midsummer the men, naked to the waist, had sweated rivers running the guns out and in again, training round with handspikes, each man of the crew learning the knack of the flexible rammer – all the mechanical drill which every man at the guns had to learn until he could be trusted to run up, fire, clean, and reload, and to go on doing so for hour after hour, in thick powder smoke and with death all around him. Drill first, marksmanship a long way second, but all the same it was policy to allow the men to fire off the guns a few times – they found compensation in that for the arduous toil at the guns.

A thousand yards to port the quarter boat was bobbing over the glittering sea. There was a splash, and then they could see the black dot of the cask she had thrown overboard before pulling hastily out of the line of fire.

'No. One gun!' bellowed Gerard. 'Take your aim! Cock your locks! Fire – stop your vents!'

The foremost eighteen-pounder roared out briefly while a dozen glasses looked for the splash.

'Over and to the right!' announced Gerard. 'No. Two gun!'

The maindeck eighteen-pounders, the lower deck twenty-four-pounders, spoke each in turn. Even with experienced gun layers it would have been too much to expect to hit a cask at such a long range in thirty-seven shots; the cask still bobbed unharmed. Every gun of the port battery tried again, and still the cask survived.

'We'll shorten the range. Mr Bush, have the helm put up and run the ship past the cask at a cable's length away. Now, Mr Gerard.'

Two hundred yards was a short enough range even for carronades; the forecastle and quarterdeck carronades' crews stood to their weapons as the *Sutherland* ran down to the cask. The guns went off nearly simultaneously as they bore, the ship trembling to the concussions, while the thick smoke eddied upwards round the naked men. The water boiled all round the cask, as half a ton of iron tore it up in fountains, and in the midst of the splashes the cask suddenly leaped clear of the water, dissolving into its constituent staves as it did so. All the guns' crews cheered while Hornblower's silver whistle split the din as a signal to cease fire, and the men clapped each other on the shoulder exultantly. They were heartily pleased with themselves. As Hornblower knew, the fun of knocking a cask to pieces was full compensation for two hours' hard work at gun drill.

The quarter boat dropped another cask; the starboard-side battery prepared to bombard it, while Hornblower stood blinking gratefully in the sunshine on the quarterdeck, feeling glad to be alive. He had as full a crew as any captain could hope for, and more trained topmen than he could ever have dared to expect. So far everyone was healthy; his landsmen were fast becoming seamen, and he would train them into gunners even quicker than that. This blessed midsummer sunshine, hot and dry, suited his health admirably. He had left off fretting over Lady Barbara, thanks to the intense pleasure which it gave him to see his crew settling down into a single efficient unit. He was glad to be alive, with high spirits bubbling up within him.

'Good shot, there!' said Hornblower. An extraordinarily lucky shot from one of the lower deck guns had smashed the second cask to fragments. 'Mr Bush, see that every man of that gun's crew gets a tot of rum tonight.'

'Aye aye, sir.'

'Sail ho!' came from the masthead. 'Deck, there. Sail right to wind'ard, an' coming down fast.'

'Mr Bush, have the quarter boat recalled. Heave the ship to on the starboard tack, if you please.'

'Aye aye, sir.'

Even now, no more than fifty miles from France, and not more than twenty from a corner of Spain under French domination, there was very small chance of any sail being French, especially on the course this one was steering – any French vessel crept along the coast without venturing a mile to sea.

'Masthead! What do you make of the sail?'

'She's a ship, sir, wi' all sail set. I can see her royals an' t'garn stuns'ls.'

'Belay!' roared the boatswain's mate to the hands hoisting in the quarter boat.

The fact that the approaching vessel was a full-rigged ship made it more unlikely still that she was French – French commerce was confined to small craft, luggers and brigs and tartanes, now. Probably she was one of the ships the *Sutherland* had come to meet. A moment later the suspicion was confirmed from the masthead.

'Deck, there! Sail looks like *Caligula* to me, sir. I can see her torps'ls now, sir.'

So she was; Captain Bolton must have completed his task of escorting the storeships into Port Mahon. Within an hour the *Caligula* was within gunshot.

'*Caligula* signalling, sir,' said Vincent. 'Captain to Captain. Delighted to see you. Will you dine with me now?'

'Hoist the assent,' replied Hornblower.

The pipes of the boatswain's mates twittered into one last weird wail as Hornblower went up the side of the *Caligula*; the sideboys stood at attention; the marines presented arms; and Captain Bolton came forward, his hand held out and his craggy face wreathed in smiles.

'First at the rendezvous!' said Bolton. 'Come this way, sir. It does my heart good to see you again. I've twelve dozen sherry here I'll be glad to hear your opinion of. Where are those glasses, steward? Your very good health, sir!'

Captain Bolton's after cabin was furnished with a luxury which contrasted oddly with Hornblower's. There were satin cushions on the lockers; the swinging lamps were of silver, and so were the table appointments on the white linen cloth on the table. Bolton had been lucky in the matter of prize money when in command of a frigate – a single cruise had won him five thousand pounds – and Bolton had started life before the mast. The momentary jealousy which Hornblower experienced evaporated as he noted the poor taste of the cabin fittings, and remembered how dowdy Mrs Bolton had looked when he saw her last. More than anything else, Bolton's obvious pleasure at seeing him, and the genuine respect he evinced in his attitude towards him, combined to give Hornblower a better opinion of himself.

'From the rapidity with which you reached the rendezvous, it appears that your passage was even quicker than ours,' said Bolton, and the conversation lapsed into technicalities, which endured even after dinner was served.

And clearly Bolton had little idea of what kind of dinner to offer in this scorching heat. There was pea soup, excellent, but heavy. Red mullet – a last minute purchase in Port Mahon at the moment of sailing. A saddle of mutton. Boiled cabbage. A Stilton cheese, now a little past its best. A syrupy port which was not to Hornblower's taste. No salad, no fruit, not one of the more desirable products of the Minorca Bolton had just left.

'Minorquin mutton, I fear,' said Bolton, carvers in hand. 'My last English sheep died mysteriously at Gibraltar and provided dinner for the gunroom. But you will take a little more, sir?'

'Thank you, no,' said Hornblower. He had eaten manfully through a vast helping, and, gorged with mutton fat, was sitting sweating now in the sweltering cabin. Bolton pushed the wine back to him, and Hornblower poured a few drops into his half-empty glass. A lifetime of practice had made him adept at appearing to drink level with his host while actually drinking one glass to three. Bolton emptied his own glass and refilled it.

'And now,' said Bolton, 'we must await in idleness the arrival of Sir Mucho Pomposo, Rear Admiral of the Red.'

Hornblower looked at Bolton quite startled. He himself would never have risked speaking of his superior officer as Mucho Pomposo to anyone. Moreover, it had not occurred to him to think of Sir Percy Leighton in that fashion. Criticism of a superior who had yet to demonstrate to him his capacity one way or the other was not Hornblower's habit; and possibly he was specially slow to criticize a superior who was Lady Barbara's husband.

'Mucho Pomposo, I said,' repeated Bolton. He had drunk one glass more of port than was quite wise, and was pouring himself out another one. 'We can sit and polish our backsides while he works that old tub of a *Pluto* round from Lisbon. Wind's sou'easterly. So it was yesterday, too. If he didn't pass the Straits two days back it'll be a week or more before he appears. And if he doesn't leave all the navigation to Elliott he'll never arrive at all.'

Hornblower looked up anxiously at the skylight. If any report of his conversation were to reach higher quarters it would do Bolton no good. The latter interpreted the gesture correctly.

'Oh, never fear,' he said. 'I can trust my officers. They don't respect an admiral who's no seaman any more than I do. Well, what have you to say?'

Hornblower proffered the suggestion that one of the two ships might push to the northward and begin the task of harassing the French and Spanish coast while the other stayed on the rendezvous awaiting the admiral.

'That's a worthy suggestion,' said Bolton.

Hornblower shook off the lassitude occasioned by the heat and the vast meal inside him. He wanted the *Sutherland* to be dispatched on this duty. The prospect of immediate action was stimulating. He could feel his pulse quickening at the thought, and the more he considered it the more anxious he was that the choice should fall on him. Days of dreary beating about on and off the rendezvous made no appeal to him at all. He could bear it if necessary – twenty years in the navy would harden anyone to waiting – but he did not want to have to. He did not want to.

'Who shall it be?' said Bolton. 'You or me?'

Hornblower took a grip of his eagerness.

'You are the senior officer on the station, sir,' he said. 'It is for you to say.'

'Yes,' said Bolton, meditatively. 'Yes.'

He looked at Hornblower with a considering eye.

'You'd give three fingers to go,' he said suddenly, 'and you know it. You're the same restless devil that you were in the *Indefatigable*. I remember beating you for it, in 93, or was it 94?'

Hornblower flushed hotly at the reminder. The bitter humiliation of being bent over a gun and beaten by the lieutenant of the midshipman's berth rankled to this day when it was recalled to him. But he swallowed his resentment; he had no wish to quarrel with Bolton, especially at this juncture, and he knew he was exceptional in regarding a beating as an outrage.

''93, sir,' he said. 'I'd just joined.'

'And now you're a post captain, and the most note-worthy one in the bottom half of the list,' said Bolton. 'God, how time flies. I'd let you go, Hornblower, for old times' sake, if I didn't want to go myself.'

'Oh,' said Hornblower. His evident disappointment made his expression ludicrous. Bolton laughed.

'Fair's fair,' he said. 'I'll spin a coin for it. Agreed?'

'Yes, sir,' said Hornblower, eagerly. Better an even chance than no chance at all.

'You'll bear me no malice if I win?'

'No, sir. None.'

With maddening slowness Bolton reached into his fob and brought out his purse. He took out a guinea and laid it on the table, and then, with the same delib-eration, while Hornblower wrestled with his eagerness, he replaced the purse. Then he took up the guinea, and poised it on his gnarled thumb and forefinger.

'King or spade?' he asked, looking across at Hornblower.

'Spade,' said Hornblower, swallowing hard.

The coin rang as Bolton spun it in the air; he caught it, and crashed it on to the table.

'Spade it is,' he said, lifting his hand.

Bolton went through all the motions once more of taking out his purse, putting the guinea back, and thrusting the purse into his fob, while Hornblower forced himself to sit still and watch him. He was cool again now, with the immediate prospect of action.

'Damn it, Hornblower,' he said. 'I'm glad you won. You can speak the Dago lingo, which is more than I can. You've had experience with 'em in the South Sea. It's the sort of duty just made for you. Don't be gone more than three days. I ought to put that in writing, in case his High Mightiness comes back. But I won't trouble. Good luck to you, Hornblower, and fill your glass.'

Hornblower filled it two-thirds full – if he left a little in the bottom he would only have drunk half a glass more than he wanted then. He sipped, and leaned back in his chair, restraining his eagerness as long as possible. But it overcame him at last, and he rose.

'God damn it, man, you're not going?' said Bolton. Hornblower's attitude was unmistakable, but he could not believe the evidence of his eyes.

'If you would permit me, sir,' said Hornblower. 'There's a fair wind –'

Hornblower was actually stammering as he tried to make all his explanations at once. The wind might change; if it was worth while separating it was better to go now than later; if the *Sutherland* were to stand in towards the coast during the dark hours there was a chance that she might snap up a prize at dawn – every sort of explanation except the true one that he could not bear to sit still any longer with immediate action awaiting him just over the horizon.

'Have it your own way, then,' grumbled Bolton. 'If you must, you must. You're leaving me with a half-empty bottle. Does that mean you don't like my port?'

'No, sir,' said Hornblower, hastily.

'Another glass, then, while your boat's crew is making ready. Pass the word for Captain Hornblower's gig.'

The last sentence was bellowed towards the closed door of the cabin, and was immediately repeated by the sentry outside.

Boatswain's pipes twittered as Hornblower went down the *Caligula*'s side, officers stood to attention, side boys held the lines. The gig rowed rapidly over the silver water in the fading evening; Coxswain Brown looked sidelong, anxiously, at his captain, trying to guess what this hurried and early departure meant. In the *Sutherland* there was similar anxiety; Bush and Gerard and Crystal and Rayner were all on the quarterdeck awaiting him – Bush had obviously turned out of bed at the news that the captain was returning.

Hornblower paid no attention to their expectant glances. He had made it a rule to offer no explanation – and there was a pleasurable selfish thrill in keeping his subordinates in ignorance of their future. Even as the gig came leaping up to the tackles he gave the orders which squared the ship away before the wind, heading back to the Spanish coast where adventure awaited them.

'*Caligula*'s signalling, sir,' said Vincent. 'Good luck.'

'Acknowledge,' said Hornblower.

The officers on the quarterdeck looked at each other, wondering what the future held in store for them for the commodore to wish them good luck. Hornblower noted the interchange of glances without appearing to see them.

'Ha-h'm,' he said, and walked with dignity below, to

pore over his charts and plan his campaign. The timbers creaked faintly as the gentle wind urged the ship over the almost placid sea.

IO

'Two bells, sir,' said Polwheal, waking Hornblower from an ecstatic dream. 'Wind East by South, course Nor' by East, an' all sail set to the royal, sir. An' Mr Gerard says to say land in sight on the larboard beam.'

This last sentence jerked Hornblower from his cot without a moment's more meditation. He slipped off his nightshirt and put on the clothes Polwheal held ready for him. Unshaved and uncombed he hurried up to the quarterdeck. It was full daylight now, with the sun half clear of the horizon and looking over the starboard quarter, and just abaft the port beam a grey mountain shape reflecting its light. That was Cape Creux, where a spur of the Pyrenees came jutting down to the Mediterranean, carrying the Spanish coastline out of its farthest easterly point.

'Sail ho!' yelled the lookout at the masthead. 'Nearly right ahead. A brig, sir, standing out from the land on the starboard tack.'

It was what Hornblower had been hoping for; it was for this reason that he had laid his course so as to be on this spot at this moment. All the seaboard of Catalonia, as far south as Barcelona and beyond, was in the hands of the French, and a tumultuous French army – the 'Account of the Present War in Spain' estimated it at nearly eighty thousand men – was endeavouring to extend its conquests southwards and inland.

But they had Spanish roads to contend against as well as Spanish armies. To supply an army eighty thousand strong, and a large civilian population as well, was impossible by land over the Pyrenean passes, even though Gerona had surrendered last December after a heroic defence. Food and siege materials and ammunition had to be sent by sea, in small craft which crept along the coast, from shore battery to shore battery, through the lagoons and the shallows of the coast of the Gulf of Lions, past the rocky capes of Spain, as far as Barcelona.

Since Cochrane's recall, this traffic had met with hardly any interference from the British in the Mediterranean. When Hornblower first reached his rendezvous off Palamos Point he had been careful to disappear again over the horizon immediately, so as to give no warning of the approach of a British squadron. He had hoped that the French might grow careless. With the wind nearly in the east, and Cape Creux running out almost directly eastwards, there was a chance that some supply ship or other, compelled to stand far out from the land to weather the point, might be caught at dawn out of range of the shore batteries, having neglected to make this dangerous passage at night. And so it had proved.

'Hoist the colours, Mr Gerard,' said Hornblower. 'And call all hands.'

'The brig has wore, sir,' hailed the lookout. 'She's running before the wind.'

'Head so as to cut her off, Mr Gerard. Set stu'ns'ls both sides.'

Before the wind, and with only the lightest of breezes

blowing, was the *Sutherland*'s best point of sailing, as might be expected of her shallow build and clumsy beam. In these ideal conditions she might easily have the heels of a deep-laden coasting brig.

'Deck, there!' hailed the lookout. 'The brig's come to the wind again, sir. She's on her old course.'

That was something very strange. If the chase had been a ship of the line, she might have been challenging battle. But a mere brig, even a brig of war, would be expected to fly to the shelter of the shore batteries. Possibly she might be an English brig.

'Here, Savage. Take your glass and tell me what you can see.'

Savage dashed up the main rigging at the word.

'Quite right, sir. She's closehauled again on the starboard tack. We'll pass her to leeward on this course. She's wearing French national colours, sir. And she's signalling now, sir. Can't read the flags yet, sir, and she's nearly dead to leeward, now.'

What the devil was the brig up to? She had settled her own fate by standing to windward again; if she had dashed for the land the moment she had sighted the *Sutherland* she might possibly have escaped. Now she was a certain capture – but why was the French brig signalling to a British ship of the line? Hornblower sprang up on to the rail; from there he could see the brig's topsails over the horizon, as she held her windward course.

'I can read the signal now, sir. MV.'

'What the devil does MV mean?' snapped Hornblower to Vincent, and then regretted that he had said it. A look would have done as well.

'I don't know, sir,' said Vincent, turning the pages of the signal book. 'It's not in the code.'

'We'll know soon enough,' said Bush. 'We're coming up to her fast. Hullo! She's wearing round again. She's come before the wind. But it's no use now. Mongseer. You're ours. A handsome bit of prize money there for us, my lads.'

The excited chatter of the quarterdeck reached Hornblower's ears to be unheard. This last attempt at flight on the Frenchman's part had explained his previous movements. Bush, Gerard, Vincent, Crystal, were all too careless to have thought about it, too excited at the prospect of prize money. Hornblower could guess now what had happened. At first sight of the *Sutherland*, the brig had turned to fly. Then she had seen the red ensign which the *Sutherland* had hoisted, and misread it as the French colours – both sides had made the same mistake before this, the red fly both of tricolour and of red ensign led easily to confusion.

It was fortunate this time that Leighton had been Rear-Admiral of the Red, so that the *Sutherland* had worn his colours. What was more, the *Sutherland* had the round bow given her by her Dutch builders, the same as nearly every French ship of the line, and unlike every English ship save three or four. So the brig had taken the *Sutherland* to be French, and as soon as she was sure of this had held to the wind again, anxious to make her offing so as to weather Cape Creux. Then the MV signal which she had flown had been the private French recognition signal – that was something well-worth knowing. It was only when the *Sutherland* did not make the expected conventional reply that the French captain had realized his mistake, and made one last dash for liberty.

A quite unavailing dash, for the *Sutherland* had cut her off from all chance of escape to leeward. The ships were only two miles apart now, and converging. Once more the brig came round, this time with the very faint hope of clawing away out of range to windward. But the *Sutherland* was hurtling close upon her.

'Fire a shot near him,' snapped Hornblower.

At that threat the French captain yielded. The brig hove to, and the tricolour came down from her peak. A cheer went up from the *Sutherland*'s main deck.

'Silence, there!' roared Hornblower. 'Mr Bush, take a boat and board her. Mr Clarke, you're prize-master. Take six hands with you and navigate her to Port Mahon.'

Bush was all smiles on his return.

'Brig *Amélie*, sir. Six days out from Marseille for Barcelona. General cargo of military stores. Twenty-five tons powder. One hundred and twenty-five tons of biscuit. Beef and pork in casks. Brandy. Admiralty agent at Port Mahon'll buy her, sure as a gun, ship, stores, and all.' Bush rubbed his hands. 'And we the only ship in sight!'

If any other British ship had been in sight she would have shared the prize money. As it was, the only shares to be given away were those of the admiral commanding in the Mediterranean and of Admiral Leighton commanding the squadron. Between them they would have one-third of the value, so that Hornblower's share would be about two-ninths – several hundred pounds at least.

'Bring the ship before the wind,' said Hornblower. Not for worlds would he give any sign of his delight at being several hundred pounds richer. 'We've no time to lose.'

He went below to shave, and as he scraped the lather from his cheeks and contemplated the melancholy face in the glass he meditated once more on the superiority of sea over land. The *Amélie* was a small vessel, almost inconsiderable in size. But she carried between two and three hundred tons of stores; and if the French had tried to send that amount overland to Barcelona it would have called for a first-class military convoy – a hundred or more wagons, hundreds of horses, taking up a mile or more of road and needing a guard of thousands of troops to protect it from the attacks of the Spanish partisans. Troops and horses would have needed food, too, and that would call for more wagons still, all crawling along at fifteen miles a day at most over the Spanish roads. Small wonder, then, that the French preferred to run the risk of sending their stores by sea. And what a blow it would be for the harassed French army to find a British squadron on their flank, and their best route of communication broken.

Walking forward to take his bath with Polwheal in attendance, a new idea struck him.

'Pass the word for the sailmaker,' he said.

Potter the sailmaker came aft and stood at attention while Hornblower rotated himself under the jet of the washdeck pump.

'I want a French ensign, Potter,' said Hornblower. 'There's not one on board?'

'French ensign, sir? No, sir.'

'Then make one. I'll give you twenty minutes, Potter.'

Hornblower continued to rotate under the jet of the pump, rejoicing in its refreshing impact on this hot morning. The chances were that no Frenchman had observed the capture of the *Amélie* from Cape Creux, and that was the only land in sight at the time. Even if someone had done so, it would take many hours to warn all the coastline of the presence of a British ship of the line. Having taken the French by surprise, the right game to play was to go on exploiting that surprise to the utmost, making use of every device that would make the blow effective. He went back to his cabin and put on refreshing clean linen, still turning over in his mind the details of his plans which were now losing their nebulousness of the night before and growing more and more clear cut.

'Breakfast, sir?' asked Polwheal, tentatively.

'Bring me some coffee on the quarterdeck,' said Hornblower. He could not bear the thought of food – perhaps because of his present excitement, perhaps because of his vast dinner of the night before.

From the quarterdeck could be seen shadowy blue masses on the horizon right ahead – the peaks of the Pyrenees; between them and the sea crawled the road from France to Spain. The sailmaker's mate came running aft with his arms full of a vast bundle.

'Mr Vincent,' said Hornblower. 'I'll have this flag hoisted instead of our own.'

The officers of the quarterdeck eyed the strange tricolour as it rose to the peak, and they looked from the flag to their captain, whispering among themselves.

Grouped on the lee side, not one of them dared to try to open a conversation with Hornblower on the weather side. Hornblower exulted both in their excitement and their silence.

'Send the hands to quarters as soon as they have breakfasted, Mr Bush,' said Hornblower. 'Clear for action, but keep the ports shut, I want the longboat and launch ready to be hoisted out at a moment's notice.'

The hands came tumbling up from breakfast in a perfect babble of sound – the order to clear for action, the tricolour at the peak, the mountains of Spain ahead, the morning's capture, all combining to work them up into wild excitement.

'Keep those men silent on the maindeck, there!' bellowed Hornblower. 'It sounds like Bedlam turned loose.'

The noise dwindled abruptly, the men creeping about like children in a house with an irascible father. The bulkheads came down, the galley fire was tipped overside. The boys were running up with powder for the guns; the shot garlands between the guns were filled with the black iron spheres ready for instant use.

'Cleared for action, sir,' said Bush.

'H-h'm,' said Hornblower. 'Captain Morris, if I send away the longboat and launch, I want twenty marines in each. Have your men told off ready.'

Hornblower took his glass and studied once more the rapidly nearing coastline. There were cliffs here, and the coast road wound at the foot of them, at the water's edge, and the shore was steep-to, according to his charts. But it would be a sensible precaution to start the lead going soon. He was taking a risk in approaching a lee shore guarded by heavy batteries – the *Sutherland* might be badly knocked about before she could beat to windward out of range again. Hornblower was counting not merely on the disguise he had adopted, but on the very fact that the French would not believe that an English ship could take that risk.

To the French in the batteries the presence of a French ship of the line off that coast was susceptible of explanation – she might have ventured forth from Toulon, or have come in from the Atlantic, or she might be a refugee from some Ionian island attacked by the British, seeking refuge after long wanderings. He could not believe that they would open fire without allowing time for explanation.

At a word from Hornblower the *Sutherland* turned on a course parallel with the shore, heading northward with the wind abeam. She was creeping along now, in the light breeze, only just out of gunshot of the shore. The sun was blazing down upon them, the crew standing silently at their stations, the officers grouped on the quarterdeck, Hornblower with the sweat running down his face, sweeping the coast with his glass in search of an objective. The little wind was calling forth only the faintest piping from the rigging; the rattle of the blocks to the gentle roll of the ship sounded unnaturally loud in the silence as did the monotonous calling of the man at the lead. Suddenly Savage hailed from the foretop.

'There's a lot of small craft, sir, at anchor round the point, there. I can just see 'em from here, sir.'

A dark speck danced in the object glass of Hornblower's telescope. He lowered the instrument to rest his aching eye, and then he raised it again. The speck was still there; it was a tricolour flag waving lazily in the wind from a flagstaff on the point. That was what Hornblower had been seeking. A French battery perched on the top of the cliff. Forty-two pounders, probably, sited with a good command, probably with furnaces for heating the shot – no ship that floated could fight them. Clustered underneath, a little coasting fleet, huddling there for shelter at the sight of a strange sail.

'Tell your men to lie down,' said Hornblower to Morris. He did not want the red coats of the marines drawn up on the quarterdeck to reveal his ship prematurely for what she was.

The *Sutherland* crept along, the grey cliffs growing more clearly defined as at Hornblower's order she was edged closer in shore. Beyond the cliffs mountain peaks were revealing themselves with startling suddenness whenever Hornblower's rigid concentration on the battery relaxed. He could see the parapets now in his glass, and he almost thought he could see the big guns peeping over them. At any moment now the battery might burst into thunder and flame and smoke, and in that case he would have to turn and fly, baffled. They were well within gunshot now. Perhaps the French had guessed the *Sutherland*'s identity, and were merely waiting to have her well within range. Every minute that the *Sutherland* approached meant another minute under fire when she tried to escape. The loss of a mast might mean in the end the loss of the ship.

'Mr Vincent,' said Hornblower, without shifting his gaze from the battery. 'Hoist MV.'

The words sent a stir through the group of officers.

They could be certain now of what plan Hornblower had in mind. The trick increased the risk of detection at the same time as, if it were successful, it gave them more opportunity of approaching the battery. If MV were the French recognition signal, and was being correctly employed, well and good. If not – the battery would soon tell them so. Hornblower, his heart thumping in his breast, judged that at any rate it might confuse the issue for the officer in the battery and induce him to delay a little longer. The signal rose up the halliards, and the battery still stayed silent. Now a signal hoist soared up the battery's flagstaff.

'I can't read that, sir,' said Vincent. 'One of 'em's a swallowtail we don't use.'

But the mere fact of the battery's signalling in reply meant that they were at least doubtful of the *Sutherland*'s identity – unless it were part of the plan to lure her closer in. Yet if the battery delayed much longer it would be too late.

'Mr Bush, do you see the battery?'

'Yes, sir.'

'You will take the longboat. Mr Rayner will take the launch, and you will land and storm the battery.'

'Aye aye, sir.'

'I will give you the word when to hoist out.'

'Aye aye, sir.'

'Quarter less eight,' droned the leadsman – Hornblower had listened to each cast subconsciously; now that the water was shoaling he was compelled to give half his attention up to the leadsman's cries while still scrutinizing the battery. A bare quarter of a mile from it now; it was time to strike.

'Very good, Mr Bush. You can go now.'

'Aye aye, sir.'

'Back the maintops'l, Mr Gerard.'

At Bush's orders the dormant ship sprang to life. The shrilling of the pipes brought the boats' crews to the falls at the run. This was the time when the painful drill would reveal its worth; the more quickly those boats were swung out, manned, and away, the less would be the danger and the greater the chance of success. Longboat and launch dropped to the water, the hands swarming down the falls.

'Throw the guns down the cliff, Mr Bush. Wreck the battery if you can. But don't stay a moment longer than necessary.'

'Aye aye, sir.'

They were off, the men tugging like maniacs at the oars.

'Helm a-lee! Mr Gerard, put the ship about. And down with that flag, and send up our own. Ah!'

The air was torn with the passage of cannon shot overhead. The whole ship shook as something struck her a tremendous blow forward. Hornblower saw the smoke billow up round the battery – it had opened fire at last. And thank God it was firing at the ship; if one of those shots hit a boat he would be in a pretty scrape. So pleased was he at the thought that it never occurred to him to wonder about his own personal safety.

'Mr Gerard, see if the guns can reach the battery. See that every shot is properly aimed. It is no use unless the embrasures can be swept.'

Another salvo from the battery, and too high again, the shots howling overhead. Little Longley, strutting the quarterdeck with his dirk at his hip, checked in his stride to duck, instinctively, and then, with a side glance at his captain, walked on with his neck as stiff as a ramrod. Hornblower grinned.

'Mr Longley, have that maintopgallant halliard spliced at once.'

It was a kindness to keep the boy busy so that he would have no time to be afraid. Now the *Sutherland*'s starboard broadside began to open fire, irregularly, as the gun captains fancied their weapons bore. Flying jets of dust from the face of the cliff showed that most of the shots were hitting thirty feet too low. But if even one or two shots got in through the embrasures and killed someone working the guns it would be a valuable help in unsettling the artillery men. Another salvo. This time they had fired at the boats. The launch almost vanished under the jets of water flung up by the plunging fire, and Hornblower gulped with anxiety. But the next moment the launch reappeared, limping along crabwise – a shot must have smashed some of the oars on one side. But the boats were safe now; close up to the cliffs as they were the guns up above could surely not be depressed sufficiently to hit them. The longboat was in the very surf now, with the launch at her heels. Now the men were tumbling out and splashing up to the beach.

For a moment Hornblower wished that, contrary to etiquette, he had taken command of the landing party, fearing lest a disorderly and piecemeal attack should waste all the advantages gained. No, Bush was safe enough. He could see him through his glass, leaping up on to the road and then turning to face the landing party. Hornblower could see Bush's arms wave as he gave his orders. Someone led off a party of seamen to the right – that was Rayner, for Hornblower's straining eyes could perceive his bald head and unmistakable round-shouldered gait. Morris was taking the marines – a solid block of scarlet – off to the left. Bush was forming up the remainder in the centre – Bush was clear-headed enough. There were three gullies in the face of the cliff, marked with straggling greenery, and indicating the easiest points of ascent. As the flanking parties reached the bottom of their paths, Hornblower saw Bush's sword flash as he called his men on. They were breasting the cliffs now, all three parties simultaneously. A tiny faint cheer crept out over the water to the ship.

One or two of the maindeck guns were making better practice now. Twice Hornblower thought he saw earth flying from the embrasures as shots struck them; so much the better, but the firing must stop now that the men were mounting the cliff. He pealed on his whistle and bellowed the order. In dead silence the ship slid on through the water while every eye watched the landing party. They were pouring over the top now. Sudden gusts of smoke showed that the guns were firing again – canister or grape, probably. Any of those parties caught in a whirlpool of canister from a forty-two pounder might well be wiped out. Weapons were sparkling on the parapet; little pinpricks of smoke indicated small-arms fire. Now out on the left the red coats of the marines were on the very top of the parapet, a white-clad sailor was waving from the centre. They were pouring over, although red dots and white dots littered the face of the parapet to mark where men had fallen.

One anxious minute with nothing to see seemed to last for hours. And then the tricolour flag came slowly down its staff, and the hands on the maindeck burst into a storm of cheering. Hornblower shut his glass with a snap.

'Mr Gerard, put the ship about. Send in the quarter boats to take possession of the craft in the bay.'

There were four tartanes, a felucca, and two cutter-rigged boats clustered at anchor in the tiny bay below the battery – a fine haul especially if they were fully laden. Hornblower saw the dinghies pulling madly from them for the shore on the side away from the battery, as the crews fled to escape captivity. Hornblower was glad to see them go; he did not want to be burdened with prisoners, and he had been a prisoner himself for two weary years in Ferrol. Something fell in an avalanche down the cliff, crashing on to the road at its foot in a cloud of dust and debris. It was a forty-two pounder heaved up by brute force over the parapet; Bush had got to work quickly enough at dismantling the battery – if Bush were still alive. Another gun followed at an interval, and another after that.

The small craft, two of them towing the quarter boats, were beating out towards the *Sutherland* where she lay hove-to awaiting them, and the landing party was coming down the cliff face again and forming up on the beach. Lingering groups indicated that the wounded were being brought down. All these necessary delays seemed to stretch the anticlimax into an eternity. A bellowing roar from the battery and a fountain of earth and smoke – momentarily like those volcanoes at whose foot the *Lydia* had anchored last commission – told that the magazine had been fired. Now at last the launch and the longboat were pulling back to the ship, and Hornblower's telescope, trained on the sternsheets of the longboat, revealed Bush sitting there, alive and apparently well. Even then, it was a relief to see him come rolling aft, his big craggy face wreathed in smiles, to make his report.

'The Frogs bolted out of the back door as we came in at the front,' he said. 'They hardly lost a man. We lost –'

Hornblower had to nerve himself to listen to a pitiful list. Now that the excitement was over he felt weak and ill, and it was only by an effort that he was able to keep his hands from trembling. And it was only by an effort that he could make himself smile and mouth out words of commendation first to the men whom Bush singled out for special mention and then to the whole crew drawn up on the maindeck. For hours he had been walking the quarterdeck pretending to be imperturbable, and now he was in the throes of the reaction. He left it to Bush to deal with the prizes, to allot them skeleton crews and send them off to Port Mahon, while without a word of excuse he escaped below to his cabin. He had even forgotten that the ship had been cleared for action, so that in his search for privacy he had to sit in his hammock chair at the end of the stern gallery, just out of sight from the stern windows, while the men were replacing the bulkheads and securing the guns. He lay back, his arms hanging and his eyes closed, with the water bubbling under the counter below him and the rudder pintles groaning at his side. Each time the ship went about as Bush worked her out to make an offing his head sagged over to the opposite shoulder.

What affected him most was the memory of the risks he had run; at the thought of them little cold waves ran down his back and legs. He had been horribly reckless in his handling of the ship – only by the greatest good fortune was she not now a dismasted wreck, with half her crew killed and wounded, drifting on to a lee shore, with an exultant enemy awaiting her. It was Hornblower's nature to discount his achievements to himself, to make no allowance for the careful precautions he had taken to ensure success, for his ingenuity in making the best of circumstances. He cursed himself for a reckless fool, and for his habit of plunging into danger and only counting the risk afterwards.

A rattle of cutlery and crockery in the cabin recalled him to himself, and he sat up and resumed his unmoved countenance just in time as Polwheal came out into the stern gallery.

'I've got you a mouthful to eat, sir,' he said. 'You've had nought since yesterday.'

Hornblower suddenly knew that he was horribly hungry, and at the same time he realized that he had forgotten the coffee Polwheal had brought him, hours ago, to the quarterdeck. Presumably that had stayed there to grow cold until Polwheal fetched it away. With real pleasure he got up and walked into the cabin; so tempting was the prospect of food and drink that he felt hardly a twinge of irritation at having Polwheal thus fussing over him and trying to mother him and probably getting ready to take overmuch advantage of his position. The cold tongue was delicious, and Polwheal with uncanny intuition had put out a half-bottle of claret

– not one day a month did Hornblower drink anything stronger than water when by himself, yet today he drank three glasses of claret, knowing that he wanted them, and enjoying every drop.

And as the food and the wine strengthened him, and his fatigue dropped away, his mind began to busy itself with new plans, devising, without his conscious volition, fresh methods of harassing the enemy. As he drank his coffee the ideas began to stir within him, and yet he was not conscious of them. All he knew was the cabin was suddenly stuffy and cramped, and that he was yearning again for the fresh air and fierce sunshine outside. Polwheal, returning to clear the table, saw his captain through the stern windows pacing the gallery, and years of service under Hornblower had taught him to make the correct deductions from Hornblower's bent, thoughtful head, and the hands which, although clasped behind him, yet twisted and turned one within the other as he worked out each prospective development.

In consequence of what Polwheal had to tell, the lower deck all knew that another move was imminent, fully two hours before Hornblower appeared on the quarterdeck and gave the orders which precipitated it.

II

'They're shooting well, sir,' said Bush, as a fountain of water leaped suddenly and mysteriously into brief life a hundred yards from the port beam.

'Who couldn't shoot well with their advantages?' answered Gerard. 'Forty-two pounders, on permanent mounts fifty feet above the water, and soldiers to serve 'em ten years in the ranks?'

'I've seen 'em shoot worse, all the same,' said Crystal.

'It's a mile an' a half if it's a yard,' said Bush.

'More than that,' said Crystal.

'A scant mile,' said Gerard.

'Nonsense,' said Bush.

Hornblower broke into their wrangling.

'Your attention, please, gentlemen. And I shall want Rayner and Hooker – pass the word, there, for Mr Rayner and Mr Hooker. Now, study the place with care.'

A dozen telescopes trained on Port Vendres, with the sunset reddening behind. In the background Mount Canigou stood out with a startling illusion of towering height; to the left the spurs of the Pyrenees ran clean down into the sea at Cape Cerbera, marking where Spain had ended and France began. In the centre the white houses of Port Vendres showed pink under the sunset, clustering round the head of the little bay. In front of them a vessel swung at anchor, under the protection of the batteries on either side of the bay which were marked by occasional puffs of smoke as the guns there tried repeatedly, at extremely long range, to hit the insolent ship which was flaunting British colours within sight of the Empire's coasts.

'Mark that battery to the left, Mr Gerard,' said Hornblower. 'Mr Rayner, you see the battery to the right – there goes a gun. Mark it well. I want no mistake made. Mr Hooker, you see how the bay curves? You must be able to take a boat straight up to the ship there tonight.'

'Aye aye, sir,' said Hooker, while the other officers exchanged glances.

'Put the ship upon the port tack, Mr Bush. We must stand out to sea. These are your orders, gentlemen.'

Turning from one officer to another, Hornblower ran briefly through their instructions. The ship sheltering in Port Vendres was to be cut and taken that night as a climax to the twenty-four hours which had begun with the capture of the *Amélie* and continued with the storming of the battery at Llanza.

'The moon rises at one o'clock. I shall take care to be back in our present position here at midnight,' said Hornblower.

With good fortune, the garrison of Port Vendres might be lured into tranquillity by the sight of the *Sutherland* sailing away now, and she could return un-observed after nightfall. An hour of darkness would suffice to effect a surprise, and the rising moon would give sufficient light for the captured ship to be brought out if successful, and for the attackers to rally and escape if unsuccessful.

'Mr Bush will remain in command of the ship,' said Hornblower.

143

'Sir!' protested Bush. 'Please sir –'

'You've won sufficient distinction today, Bush,' said Hornblower.

Hornblower was going in with the attack. He knew that he would not be able to bear the anxiety of waiting outside with the firing and the fighting going on inside – he was in a fever already, now that he was allowing his mind to dwell on the prospective action, although he was taking care not to show it.

'Every man in the boarding party must be a seaman,' said Hornblower. 'Mr Gerard and Mr Rayner can divide the marines between them.'

His listeners nodded, understanding. To set sail in a strange ship and get her under way in darkness would call for seamanship.

'You all understand what is expected of you?' asked Hornblower, and they nodded again. 'Mr Hooker, repeat your orders.'

Hooker repeated them accurately. He was a good officer as Hornblower had known when he had recommended him for promotion to lieutenant on the *Lydia's* return.

'Good,' said Hornblower. 'Then, gentlemen, you will please set your watches with mine. There will be enough light from the stars to read them. What, no watch, Mr Hooker? Perhaps Mr Bush will be good enough to lend you his.'

Hornblower could see, from his officers' expressions, that this synchronization of the watches had impressed upon them the necessity for accurately conforming to the timetable which he had laid down, in a fashion nothing else could have done. Otherwise they would have paid only casual attention to the intervals of 'five minutes' and 'ten minutes' which he had given, and he could appreciate in a manner they could not, the necessity for exact adherence to schedule in a complex operation carried out in the darkness.

'You are all agreed now? Then perhaps all you gentlemen with the exception of the officer of the watch will give me the pleasure of your company at dinner.'

Again the officers interchanged glances; those dinners in Hornblower's cabin on the eve of action were famous. Savage could remember one on board the *Lydia* before the duel with the *Natividad*. The other two present then had been Galbraith, the lieutenant of his division, and Clay, his best friend. And Galbraith had died of gangrene in the far Pacific, and Clay's head had been smashed by a cannon ball.

'There'll be no whist tonight,' smiled Hornblower, reading his thoughts. 'There will be too much to do before midnight.'

Often before, Hornblower had insisted on whist before action, and had concealed his own nervousness by criticism of the play of his preoccupied fellow players. Now he was forcing himself to be smiling, genial, and hospitable as he led the way into the cabin. His nervous tension inclined to make him talkative, and this evening, when his guests were more tongue-tied even than usual, he could for once give rein to his inclinations, and chat freely in an attempt to keep conversation going. The others eyed him, wondering as he smiled and gossiped. They never saw him in this mood except on the eve of action, and they had forgotten how human and fascinating he could be when he employed all his wiles to

145

captivate them. For him it was a convenient way to keep his mind off the approaching action, thus to exercise himself in fascination while still drawing the rigid line which divided the captain from his subordinates.

'I am afraid,' said Hornblower in the end, crumpling his napkin and tossing it on to the table, 'it is time for us to go on deck again, gentlemen. What a mortal pity to break up this gathering!'

They left the lamplit brilliance of the cabin for the darkness of the deck. The stars were glowing in the dark sky, and the *Sutherland* was stealing ghostlike over the sea which reflected them; her pyramids of canvas soared up to invisibility, and the only sounds to be heard were the rattle of the rigging and the periodic music of the water under her forefoot as she rode over the tiny invisible waves. The crew was resting on the gangways and the maindeck, conversing in whispers, and when the subdued voices of their officers called them to duty they mustered silently, each division assembling for its particular duty. Hornblower checked the position of the ship with Bush, and strained his eye through his night-glass towards the invisible shore.

'Longboat crew here!' called Gerard softly.

'Launch crew here!' echoed Rayner, and their allotted parties formed up quietly abreast the mainmast.

The cutters' crews were assembling on the quarter-deck; Hornblower was taking two hundred and fifty men altogether – if the expedition were a complete disaster Bush would hardly have sufficient men to navigate the *Sutherland* back to the rendezvous.

'You can heave-to, Mr Bush,' he said.

One by one the boats were hoisted out, and lay on

their oars a few yards off. Last of all, Hornblower went down the side and seated himself beside Brown and Longley in the stern of the barge; the men at the oars pushed off at a growl from Brown, and the flotilla, with muffled oars, began to pull steadily away from the ship. The darkness was intense, and, by the usual optical illusion, seemed still more intense close to the surface of the sea than up on the deck of the *Sutherland*. Slowly the barge drew ahead, and as the longboat and launch diverged out on each quarter they were rapidly lost to sight. The oars seemed to touch the velvety blackness of the sea without a sound.

Hornblower made himself sit still, his hand resting on the hilt of his fifty-guinea sword. He wanted to crane his neck round and look at the other boats; with every minute's inaction he grew more nervous. Some fool of a marine might fiddle with the lock of his musket, or someone's pistol, carelessly left at full cock, might go off as its owner tugged at his oar. The slightest warning given on shore would ruin the whole attack; might mean the loss of hundreds of lives, and call down upon his head – if he survived – a withering rebuke from his admiral. Grimly he made himself sit still for five more minutes before taking up his nightglass.

Then at last he caught the faintest possible glimpse of grey cliff. With his hand on the tiller he altered course until they were almost in the mouth of the inlet.

'Easy!' he breathed, and the boat glided silently forward under the stars. Close astern two tiny nuclei of greater darkness indicated where the two cutters rested on their oars. Holding his watch under his nose he could just see the time – he must wait three full minutes.

A distant sound reached his ears; there were oars pulling in the harbour. He heard them splashing two hundred yards ahead; he fancied he could see the splashes. The French were, as he expected, rowing a guard round their precious ship. Yet her captain had not realized that a guard boat rowing with muffled oars, creeping very slowly along, would be a far more dangerous obstacle to a cutting-out expedition than any boat merely busily rowing up and down across the entrance. He looked at his watch again.

'Oars,' he whispered, and the men braced themselves ready to pull. 'There's the guard boat ahead. Remember, men, cold steel. If any man fires before I do I'll shoot him with my own hand. Give way!'

The barge crept forward again, stealing into the harbour. In a few more seconds she would be at the point where the batteries' fire crossed, the point which sentries would have under constant observation, upon which the guns would be laid at nightfall so that a salvo would blow any approaching boat out of the water. For a horrible second Hornblower wondered whether launch and longboat had gone astray. Then he heard it. A loud challenge on his right, heard clearly across the water, followed by another on his left, and both instantly drowned in a wild rattle of musketry fire. Rayner and Gerard were leading their parties against the batteries, and both of them as their orders had dictated, were making an infernal noise about it so as to distract the gunners at the vital moment.

His eye caught the splashes of the guard boat's oars, more noticeable than ever with the crew pulling wildly as they paid attention to the din on shore instead of to their own business. The barge shot silently and un-noticeable towards it. She was only fifty yards from the guard boat when someone at last caught sight of her.

'*Qui va là?*' cried someone, sharply, but before any answer could be expected the barge came crashing up against the guard boat's side, as Hornblower dragged the tiller round.

His quick order had got the oars in a second before the collision, while the impact of the barge swept the oars of the guard boat away, tumbling half her crew in a tangle into the bottom of the boat. Hornblower's sword was out, and at the instant of contact he leaped madly from the barge to the guard boat, choking with excitement and nervousness as he did so. He landed with both feet on someone in the stern, trod him down, and miraculously kept his own footing. There was a white face visible down by his knee, and he kicked at it, wildly, felt a jar up his leg as the kick went home, and at the same moment he cut with all his strength at another head before him. He felt the sword bite into bone; the boat rolled frightfully under him as more of the barge's crew came tumbling into the guard boat. Someone was heaving himself upright before him – someone with a black gash of a mous-tache across his face in the starlight, and therefore no Englishman. Hornblower lunged fiercely as he reeled in the rocking boat, and he and his opponent came down together upon the men under their feet. When he scrambled up the struggle was over, without a shot being fired. The guard boat's crew was dead, or over-board, or knocked unconscious. Hornblower felt his neck and his wrist wet and sticky – with blood, presumably, but he did not have time to think about that.

'Into the barge, men,' he said. 'Give way.'

The whole fight had hardly taken more than a few seconds. At the batteries the racket of the attack was still continuing, and even as the barge pushed away from the derelict guard boat there came a sudden splutter of musketry fire from higher up the bay. The two cutters had reached the anchored ship without impediment, rowing, as Hornblower's orders had dictated, past the two locked boats straight for her. With his hands on the tiller he set a course for the musket flashes. Apparently the cutters' crews had not succeeded in carrying the ship at the first rush, for the sparkle of the firing stayed steady along the ship's bulwark – she must have had her boarding nettings rigged and her crew fairly wide awake.

The child Longley at his side was leaping about in his seat with excitement.

'Sit still, boy,' growled Hornblower.

He put the tiller over and the barge swept under the ship's stern towards the disengaged side of the ship.

'Oars!' hissed Hornblower. 'Take hold, there, bowman. Now, all together, men, and give a cheer.'

It was a hard scramble up the side of the ship, and her boarding nettings were rigged, sure enough. Hornblower found foot-hold on the bulwark through the netting, swaying perilously, leaning far out over the water, for the nettings were rigged from the yardarms and sloped sharply outwards. He struggled in them like a fly in a web. Beside him he saw Longley, writhing similarly. The boy had his dirk between his teeth in the fashion he had heard about in sailors' yarns. He looked so foolish hanging in the netting with that great clumsy weapon in his mouth that Hornblower giggled insanely on his insecure foothold. He snatched his sword from its sheath, clutching with the other hand, and slashed at the tarry cordage. The whole net was heaving and tossing as the barge's crew wrenched at it; he was almost jerked from his hold.

But everyone around him was cheering madly. This surprise attack on the unguarded side must be shaking the nerve of the defenders trying to beat off the cutters' crews. The fifty-guinea sword was of the finest steel and had a razor edge; it was cutting through strand after strand of the netting. Suddenly something parted with a rush. For one horrible second Hornblower lost his footing and nearly fell outwards, but with a convulsive effort he recovered and swung himself forward, falling through the net on his hands and knees, the sword clattering on the deck before him. A Frenchman was rushing at him; his eye caught a glimpse of the steel head of a levelled pike. He snatched hold of the shaft, twisting on to his back, guiding the weapon clear. The Frenchman's knee crashed into the back of his head, and his neck was badly wrenched as the Frenchman tumbled over on top of him. He kicked himself clear, found his sword, miraculously, and stood to face the other dark shapes rushing at him.

A pistol banged off at his ear, half deafening him, and it seemed as if the whole mass of those attacking him melted away into nothing at the finish. Those others crossing the deck now were English; they were cheering.

'Mr Crystal!'

'Sir!'

'Cut the cable. Is Mr Hooker there?'

'Aye aye, sir.'

'Get aloft with your boat's crew and set sail.'

There was no time for self-congratulation yet. Boats might come dashing out from the shore with reinforcements for the ship's crew; and Rayner and Gerard might be repulsed by the garrisons of the batteries so that he would have to run the gauntlet of the guns.

'Brown!'

'Sir!'

'Send up that rocket.'

'Aye aye, sir.'

The rocket which Brown had brought with him at Hornblower's orders was to be the signal to the landing parties that the ship was taken. And there was a decided breath of air coming off the land which would carry the ship out of the bay; Hornblower had counted on that – after the scorching heat of the day a land breeze was only to be expected.

'Cable's parted, sir!' hailed Crystal from forward.

Hooker had loosed the maintopsail, and the ship was already gathering sternway.

'Hands to the braces, there, barge's crew, first cutter's crew. Benskin! Ledly! Take the wheel. Hard a-starboard.'

Brown's flint and steel were clicking and flashing as he crouched on the deck. The rocket rose in an upward torrent of sparks and burst high above into stars. As the forestaysail was set the ship's head came round, and as she steadied on her course down the bay with the wind abaft, the moon cleared the horizon right ahead – a gibbous, waning moon, giving just enough light for Hornblower to be able to con the ship easily out of the bay between the batteries. Hornblower could hear whistles blowing, piercing the sound of the musketry which was still popping round the batteries. Rayner and Gerard were calling off their men now.

Two splashes overside indicated that a couple of the ship's crew were swimming for the shore rather than face captivity. It had been a well-timed and successful operation.

12

This Gulf of the Lion was not likely to be a very profitable cruising ground, so Hornblower decided as he scanned the French coast through his telescope. It was so deeply embayed that any wind from north to west through south would find his ship with land under her lee; it was shallow, treacherous, and liable to be whipped by storms into a tremendous sea. Navigational risks were worth taking if a suitable prize offered, but, thought Hornblower looking at the coast, there was small chance of any prize. From Port Vendres as far round as Marseille – the limit of the Inshore Squadron's sector – the flat shore was bordered by vast dreary lagoons which were separated from the sea by long spits of sand and even by peninsulas of cultivated land. There were batteries here and there upon the sand spits, and regular forts to support them, and the little towns, Cette, Aigues-Mortes, and so on were encompassed by medieval fortifications which could defy any effort he could make against them.

But the main factor was that chain of lagoons, linked together since Roman times by a series of canals. Vessels up to two hundred tons could creep along inside the coastline – he could actually see through his glass, at this very moment, brown sails apparently sailing over the green vineyards. The entrances to the chain were all defended by solid works, and if he were to try to surprise one of these it would involve running all the risk of taking his ship in through the tortuous channels between the sandbanks, under gunfire. Even if he should succeed he could still hardly attack the shipping in the lagoons.

The blue Mediterranean under the glaring blue sky shaded to green and even to yellow as it shoaled here and there in patches, a constant reminder to Hornblower as he walked his deck of the treacherous water he was navigating. Forward the ship was a hive of industry. Bush, watch in hand, had fifty men whom he was drilling aloft – they had set and furled the fore-topgallant sail a dozen times in the last hour and a half, which must be puzzling the numerous telescopes trained on the ship from the shore. Harrison the boatswain down on the maindeck was squatting on a stool with two of his mates and twenty landsmen cross-legged in a ring round him – he was teaching the advanced class some of the refinements of knotting and splicing. From the lower gun deck the squeal and rumble of gun trucks told how Gerard was exercising embryo gun layers at the six forward twenty-four pounders – Gerard's ambition was to have six trained gun captains at every gun, and he was a long way yet from achieving it. On the poop Crystal with his sextant was patiently trying to instruct the midshipmen in the elements of navigation – the young devils were fidgety and restless as Crystal droned on. Hornblower was sorry for them. He had delighted in mathematics since his boyhood; logarithms had been playthings to him at little Longley's age, and a problem in spherical trigonometry was to him but a source of pleasure, analogous, he realized, to the pleasure some of those lads found in the music which was so incomprehensible to him.

A monotonous hammering below indicated that the carpenter and his mates were putting the finishing touches to their repair of the big hole which had been made yesterday morning – incredible that it was hardly more than twenty-four hours ago – by the forty-two pounder at Llanza, while the clanking of the pumps showed that the petty criminals of the ship were pumping her out. The *Sutherland*, thanks to her recent docking, leaked extraordinarily little, less than an inch a day in calm weather, and Hornblower was able to deal with this small amount by an hour's pumping every morning, allotting to it the miscreants who had found themselves in Bush's or Harrison's black books by being last up the hatchway, or lashing up their hammocks by fore and aft turns, or by committing any of the numerous crimes of omission or commission which annoy boatswains and first lieutenants. A turn at pumping – the most monotonous and uninviting work in the ship – was a far more economical punishment than the cat, and Hornblower believed it to be more deterrent, rather to Bush's amusement.

Smoke was pouring from the galley chimney, and even on the quarterdeck Hornblower could smell the cooking that was going on. The men were going to have a good dinner today, with duff; yesterday they had eaten and drunk nothing save biscuit and cold water, thanks to the ship having been engaged three times in twenty-four hours. They did not mind that as long as they were successful – it was amazing how beneficial a little success was to discipline. Today, with eleven dead and sixteen wounded, with thirty-four men away in prizes – less two prisoners who had elected to serve the King of England rather than face one of his prisons – the *Sutherland* was more effective as a fighting unit than the day before yesterday with practically a full complement. Hornblower could see, from the quarterdeck, the cheerfulness and high spirits of everyone in sight.

He was cheerful and in high spirits himself. For once his self-depreciation was in abeyance. He had forgotten his fears of yesterday, and three successful actions in a day had re-established his self-confidence. He was at least a thousand pounds the richer by his captures, and that was good to think about. He had never before in his life had a thousand pounds. He remembered how Lady Barbara had tactfully looked away after a single glance at the pinchbeck buckles on his shoes. Next time he dined with Lady Barbara he would be wearing solid gold buckles, with diamonds set in them if he chose, and by some inconspicuous gesture he would call her attention to them. Maria would have bracelets and rings to flaunt his success before the eyes of the world.

Hornblower remembered with pride that he had not known a moment's fear last night in Port Vendres, not when he leaped on board the guard boat, not even when he had found himself in the nightmare embrace of the boarding netting. Just as he now had the wealth for which he had longed, so he had proved to himself to his own surprise that he possessed the brute physical courage which he had envied in his subordinates. Even though, characteristically, he attached no importance to the moral courage and organizing ability and ingenuity he had displayed he was on the crest of a wave of optimism and self-confidence. With high spirits bubbling inside him he turned once more to scan the flat repulsive coast on his left hand, applying himself to the problem of how to stir up confusion there. Down below there were the captured French charts with which the Admiralty had supplied him – as they had the *Pluto* and *Caligula* as well, presumably. Hornblower spent the earliest hours of daylight in poring over them. He called up their details before his mind's eye as he looked across the shallows at the green bar of coast, and the brown sails beyond. He was as close in as he dared, and yet that sail was half a mile beyond cannon shot.

Over to the left was Cette, perched up on the top of a little hill prominent above the surrounding flat land. Hornblower was reminded of Rye overlooking Romney Marsh, but Cette was a gloomy little town of a prevailing black colour, unlike Rye's cheerful grey and reds. And Cette, he knew, was a walled town, with a garrison, against which he could attempt nothing. Behind Cette was the big lagoon called the Étang de Thau, which constituted a major link in the chain of inland waterways which offered shelter and protection to French shipping all the way from Marseille and the Rhône Valley to the foot of the Pyrenees. Cette was invulnerable as far as he was concerned, and vessels on the Étang de Thau were safe from him.

Of all the whole inland route he was opposite the most vulnerable part, this short section where the navigable channel from Aigues-Mortes to the Étang de Thau was only divided from the sea by a narrow spit of land. If a blow were to be struck, it was here that he must strike it; moreover, at this very moment he could see something at which to strike – that brown sail no more than two miles away. That must be one of the French coasters, plying between Port Vendres and Marseille with wine and oil. It would be madness to attempt anything against her, and yet – and yet – he felt mad today.

'Pass the word for the captain's coxswain,' he said to the midshipman of the watch. He heard the cry echo down the maindeck, and in two minutes Brown was scurrying towards him along the gangway, halting breathless for orders.

'Can you swim, Brown?'

'Swim, sir? Yes, sir.'

Hornblower looked at Brown's burly shoulders and thick neck. There was a mat of black hair visible through the opening of his shirt.

'How many of the barge's crew can swim?'

Brown looked first one way and then the other before he made the confession which he knew would excite contempt. Yet he dared not lie, not to Hornblower.

'I dunno, sir.'

Hornblower refraining from the obvious rejoinder was more scathing than Hornblower saying, 'You ought to know.'

'I want a crew for the barge,' said Hornblower. 'Everyone a good swimmer, and everyone a volunteer. It's for a dangerous service, and, mark you, Brown, they must be true volunteers – none of your pressgang ways.'

'Aye aye, sir,' said Brown, and after a moment's hesitation, 'Everyone'll volunteer, sir. It'll be hard to pick 'em. Are you going, sir?'

'Yes. A cutlass for every man. And a packet of combustibles for every man.'

'Com – combustibles, sir?'

'Yes. Flint and steel. A couple of port-fires, oily rags, and a bit of slowmatch, in a watertight packet for each man. Go to the sailmaker and get oilskin for them. And a lanyard each to carry it if we swim.'

'Aye aye, sir.'

'And give Mr Bush my compliments. Ask him to step this way, and then get your crew ready.'

Bush came rolling aft, his face alight with excitement; and before he had reached the quarterdeck the ship was abuzz with rumours – the wildest tales about what the captain had decided to do next were circulating among the crew, who had spent the morning with one eye on their duties and the other on the coast of France.

'Mr Bush,' said Hornblower. 'I am going ashore to burn that coaster over there.'

'Aye aye, sir. Are you going in person, sir?'

'Yes,' snapped Hornblower. He could not explain to Bush that he was constitutionally unable to send men away on a task for which volunteers were necessary and not go himself. He eyed Bush defiantly, and Bush eyed him back, opened his mouth to protest, thought better of it, and changed what he was going to say.

'Longboat and launch, sir?'

'No. They'd take the ground half a mile from the shore.'

That was obvious; four successive lines of foam showed where the feeble waves were breaking, far out from the water's edge.

'I'm taking my barge and a volunteer crew.'

Still Hornblower, by his expression, dared Bush to

make any protest at all, but this time Bush actually ventured to make one.

'Yes, sir. Can't I go, sir?'

'No.'

There was no chance of further dispute in the face of that blank negative. Bush had the queer feeling – he had known it before – as he looked at Hornblower's haughty expression that he was a father dealing with a high-spirited son; he loved his captain as he would have loved a son if ever he had had one.

'And mark this, too, Bush. No rescue parties. If we're lost, we're lost. You understand? Shall I give you that in writing?'

'No need, sir. I understand.'

Bush said the words sadly. When it came to the supreme test of practice, Hornblower, however much he respected Bush's qualities and abilities, had no opinion whatever of his first lieutenant's capacity to make original plans. The thought of Bush blundering about on the mainland of France throwing away valuable lives in a hopeless attempt to rescue his captain frightened him.

'Right. Heave the ship to, Mr Bush. We'll be back in half an hour if all goes well. Stand off and wait for us.'

The barge pulled eight oars; as Hornblower gave the word he had high hopes that her launching had passed unobserved from the shore. Bush's morning sail drill must have accustomed the French to seemingly purposeless manoeuvres by the *Sutherland*; her brief backing of her topsails might be unnoticed. He sat at Brown's side while the men went to their oars. The boat danced quickly and lightly over the sea; he set a course so as to reach the shore a little ahead of the brown sail which was showing just over the green strip of coast. Then he looked back at the *Sutherland*, stately under her pyramids of sails, and dwindling with extraordinary rapidity as the barge shot away from her. Even at that moment Hornblower's busy mind set to work scanning her lines and the rake of her masts, debating how he could improve her sailing qualities.

They had passed the first line of breakers without taking ground – breakers they could hardly be called, so sluggish was the sea – and darted in towards the golden beach. A moment later the boat baulked as she slid over the sand, moved on a few yards, and grounded once more.

'Over with you, men,' said Hornblower.

He threw his legs over the side and dropped thigh deep into the water. The crew were as quick as he, and seizing the gunwales, they ran the lightened boat up until the water was no higher than their ankles. Hornblower's first instinct was to allow excitement to carry him away and head a wild rush inland, but he checked himself.

'Cutlasses?' he asked, sternly. 'Fire packets?'

Running his eye over his nine men he saw that everyone was armed and equipped, and then he started his little expedition steadily up the beach. The distance was too great to expect them to run all the way and swim afterwards. The sandy beach was topped by a low shingle bank where samphire grew. They leaped over this and found themselves among green vines; not twenty yards away an old, bent man and two old women were hoeing along the rows. They looked up in blank surprise at this sudden apparition, standing and staring voiceless at the chattering group of seamen. A quarter of a mile away, across the level vineyard, was the brown spritsail. A small mizzen was visible now behind it. Hornblower picked out a narrow path leading roughly in that direction.

'Come along men,' he said, and broke into a dog trot. The old man shouted something as the seamen tramped the vines; they laughed like children at hearing French spoken for the first time in their lives. To most of them this was their first sight of a vineyard, too – Hornblower could hear them chattering behind him in amazement at the orderly rows of seemingly worthless stumps, and the tiny bunches of immature grapes.

They crossed the vineyard; a sharp drop on the further side brought them on to a rough towpath along the canal. Here the lagoon was no more than two hundred yards wide, and the navigable channel was evidently close up to the towpath, for a sparse line of beacons a hundred yards out presumably marked the shallows. Two hundred yards away the coaster was creeping slowly towards them, still unconscious of her danger. The men uttered a wild cheer and began tearing off their jackets.

'Quiet, you fools,' growled Hornblower. He unbuckled his sword belt and stripped off his coat.

At the sound of the men's shouting the crew of the coaster came tumbling forward. There were three men, and a moment later they were joined by two sturdy women, looking at them under their hands. It was one of the women, quicker witted, who guessed what the group of men stripping on the bank implied. Hornblower, tearing off his breeches, heard one of them give a shriek and saw her running aft again. The coaster still crept over the water towards them, but when it was nearly opposite the big spritsail came down with a run and she swung away from the towpath as her helm was put over. It was too late to save her, though. She passed through the line of beacons and grounded with a jerk in the shallows beyond. Hornblower saw the man at the wheel quit his charge and turn and stare at them, with the other men and the women grouped round him. He buckled his sword about his naked body. Brown was naked, too, and was fastening his belt round his waist, and against his bare skin lay a naked cutlass.

'Come along, then,' said Hornblower; the quicker the better. He put his hands together and dropped into the lagoon in an ungainly dive; the men followed him, shouting and splashing. The water was as warm as milk, but Hornblower swam as slowly and as steadily as he could. He was a poor swimmer, and the coaster a hundred and fifty yards away seemed very distant. The sword dangling from his waist already seemed heavy. Brown came surging past him, swimming a lusty overarm stroke, with the lanyard of his packet of combustibles between his white teeth, and his thick black hair sleek with water. The other men followed; by the time they neared the coaster Hornblower was a long way last. They all scrambled up before him into the low waist of the vessel, but then discipline reasserted itself and they turned and stooped to haul him on board. He pressed aft, with sword drawn. Women and men were there in a sullen group, and for a moment he was puzzled to know what to do with them. French and English faced each other in the dazzling sunlight, the water streaming from the naked men, but in the tenseness of that meeting no one thought of their nakedness. Hornblower remembered with relief the dinghy towing behind; he pointed to it and tried to remember his French.

'Au bateau,' he said. 'Dans le bateau.'

The French hesitated. There were four middle-aged men and one old one; one old woman and one middle-aged. The English seamen closed up behind their captain, drawing their cutlasses from their belts.

'Entrez dans le bateau,' said Hornblower. 'Hobson, pull that dinghy up alongside.'

The middle-aged woman broke into a storm of invective, screeching, high pitched, her hands gesticulating wildly and her wooden shoes clattering on the deck.

'I'll do it, sir,' interposed Brown. ''Ere, you, 'op in there.'

He took one of the men by the collar, flourished his cutlass and dragged him across the deck to the side. The man yielded, and lowered himself over the side, and once the example was set, the others followed it. Brown cast off the painter and the crowded dinghy drifted away, the woman still shrieking curses in her Catalan French.

'Set the ship on fire,' said Hornblower. 'Brown, take three men below and see what you can do there.'

The late crew had got out a couple of oars and were paddling cautiously over to the towpath, the dinghy laden down to within an inch of the water's edge. Hornblower watched them as they crawled across, and climbed the bank to the path.

His picked crew did their work quickly and neatly. A mighty crashing from below showed that Brown's party was bursting into the cargo to make a nest for a fire. Smoke emerged almost at once from the cabin skylight; one of the men had piled the furniture there together, soused it in oil from the lamps, and got the whole thing into a blaze at once.

'Cargo is oil in barr'ls and grain in sacks, sir,' reported Brown. 'We stove in some barr'ls an' ripped some sacks open, sir. That'll burn. Look, sir.'

From the main hatchway a thin ghost of black smoke was already rising, and the heat pouring up from the hatch made all the forward part of the ship appear to dance and shimmer in the sunshine. There was a fire in the dry timberwork of the deck just forward of the hatch, too. It was crackling and banging explosively, although this fire was hardly visible thanks to the strong sunlight and the absence of smoke, and there was fire in the forecastle – smoke was billowing out of the bulk-head door and rolling towards them in a sullen wave.

'Get some of the deck planks up,' said Hornblower hoarsely.

The splintering crash of the work was followed by a contrasting silence – and yet no silence, for Hornblower's ear caught a muffled, continuous roaring. It was the noise of the flames devouring the cargo, as the increased draught caused by the piercing of the decks set the flames racing through the inflammable stuff.

'God! There's a sight!' exclaimed Brown.

The whole waist of the ship seemed to open as the fire poured up through the deck. The heat was suddenly unbearable.

'We can go back now,' said Hornblower. 'Come along, men.'

He set the example by diving once more into the lagoon, and the little naked band began to swim slowly back to the towpath. Slowly, this time; the high spirits of the attack had evaporated. The awful sight of the red fire glowing under the deck had sobered every man. They swam slowly, clustered round their captain, while he set a pace limited by his fatigue and unscientific breaststroke. He was glad when he was able at last to stretch out a hand and grasp the weeds growing on the towpath bank. The others scrambled out before him; Brown offered him a wet hand and helped him up to the top.

'Holy Mary!' said one of the men. 'Will ye look at th' old bitch?'

They were thirty yards from where they had left their clothes, and at that spot the coaster's crew had landed. At the moment when the Irishman called their attention to them the old woman who had reviled them cast one last garment into the lagoon. There was nothing left lying on the bank. One or two derelict shirts still floated in the lagoon, buoyed up by the air they contained, but practically all their clothes were at the bottom.

'What did you do that for, damn you?' raved Brown – all the seamen had rushed up to the coaster's crew and were dancing and gesticulating naked round them. The old woman pointed across at the coaster. It was ablaze from end to end, with heavy black smoke pouring from her sides. They saw the rigging of the mainmast whisk away in smouldering fragments, and the mast suddenly sag to one side, barely visible flames licking along it.

'I'll get your shirt back for you, sir,' said one of the men to Hornblower, tearing himself free from the fascination of the sight.

'No. Come along,' snapped Hornblower.

'Would you like the old man's trousers, sir?' asked Brown. 'I'll take 'em off him and be damned to him, sir. 'Tisn't fit –'

'No!' said Hornblower again.

Naked, they climbed up to the vineyard. One last glance down showed that the two women were weeping, heartbroken, now. Hornblower saw one of the men patting one of the women on the shoulder; the others watched with despairing apathy the burning of their ship – their all. Hornblower led the way over the vines. A horseman was galloping towards them; his blue uniform and cocked hat showed that he was one of Bonaparte's gendarmes. He reined up in front of them, reaching for his sabre, but at the same time, not too sure of himself, he looked to right and to left for the help which was not in sight.

'Ah, would you!' said Brown, dashing to the front waving his cutlass.

The other seamen closed up beside him, their weapons ready, and the gendarme hastily wheeled his horse out of harm's way; a gleam of white teeth showed under his black moustache. They hurried past him; he had dismounted when Hornblower looked back, and was trying, as well as his restless horse would allow, to take his carbine out of the boot beside his saddle. At the top of the beach stood the old man and the two women who had been hoeing; the old man brandished his hoe and threatened them, but the two women stood smiling shamefaced, looking up under lowered eyelids at their nakedness. There lay the barge, just in the water, and far out there was the *Sutherland* – the men cheered at the sight of her.

Lustily they ran the boat out over the sand, paused while Hornblower climbed in, pushed her out farther, and then came tumbling in over the side and took the oars. One man yelped with pain as a splinter in a thwart pricked his bare posterior. Hornblower grinned automatically, but the man was instantly reduced to silence by a shocked Brown.

''Ere 'e comes, sir,' said stroke oar, pointing aft over Hornblower's shoulder.

The gendarme was leaping clumsily down the beach in his long boots, his carbine in his hand. Hornblower, craning round, saw him kneel and take aim; for a second Hornblower wondered, sickly, whether his career was going to be ended by the bullet of a French gendarme, but the puff of smoke from the carbine brought not even the sound of the bullet – a man who had ridden far, and run fast in heavy boots, could hardly be expected to hit a ship's boat at two hundred yards with a single shot.

Over the spit of land between sea and lagoon they could see a vast cloud of smoke. The coaster was destroyed beyond any chance of repair. It had been a wicked waste to destroy a fine ship like that, but war and waste were synonymous terms. It meant misery and poverty for the owners; but at the same time it would mean that the length of England's arm had been demonstrated now to the people of this enemy land whom the war had not affected during these eighteen years save through Bonaparte's conscription. More than that; it meant that the authorities responsible for coast defence would be alarmed about this section of the route from Marseille to Spain, the very section which they had thought safest. That would mean detaching troops and guns to defend it against future raids, stretching the available forces thinner still along the two hundred miles of coast. A thin screen of that sort could easily be pierced at a selected spot by a heavy blow struck without warning – the sort of blow a squadron of ships of the line, appearing and disappearing at will over the horizon, could easily strike. If the game were played properly, the whole coast from Barcelona to Marseille could be kept in a constant state of alarm. That was the way to wear down the strength of the Corsican colossus; and a ship favoured by the weather could travel ten, fifteen times as fast as troops could march, as fast even as a well-mounted messenger could carry a warning. He had struck at the French centre, he had struck at the French left wing. Now he must hasten and strike at the French right wing on his way back to the rendezvous. He uncrossed and recrossed his knees as he sat in the sternsheets of the barge, his desire for instant action filling him with restlessness while the boat drew closer to the *Sutherland*.

He heard Gerard's voice saying 'What the devil –?' come clearly over the water to him; apparently Gerard had just detected the nakedness of everyone in the approaching boat. The pipes twittered to call the watch's attention to the arrival of the ship's captain. He would have to come in naked through the entry port, receiving the salutes of the officers and marines, but keyed up as he was he gave no thought to his dignity. He ran up to the deck with his sword hanging from his naked waist – it was an ordeal which could not be avoided, and he had learned in twenty years in the Navy to accept the inevitable without lamentation. The faces of the side boys and of the marines were wooden in their effort not to smile, but Hornblower did not care. The black pall of smoke over the land marked an achievement any man might be proud of. He stayed naked on the deck until he had given Bush the order to put the ship about which would take the *Sutherland* southward again in search of fresh adventure. The wind would just serve for a south-westerly course, and he was not going to waste a minute of a favourable wind.

13

The *Sutherland* had seen nothing of the *Caligula* during her long sweep south-westward. Hornblower had not wanted to, and, more, had been anxious not to. For it was just possible that the *Pluto* had reached the rendezvous, and in that case the admiral's orders would override Captain Bolton's, and he would be deprived of this further opportunity before his time limit had elapsed. It was during the hours of darkness that the *Sutherland* had crossed the latitude of Cape Bugar – the Palamos Point of the rendezvous – and morning found the *Sutherland* far to the south-westward, with the mountains of Catalonia a blue streak on the horizon over the starboard bow.

Hornblower had been on deck since dawn, a full hour before the land was sighted; at his orders the ship wore round and stood close-hauled to the north-eastward again, edging in to the shore as she did so until the details of the hilly country were plainly visible. Bush was on deck, standing with a group of other officers; Hornblower, pacing up and down, was conscious of the glances they were darting at him, but he did his best not to notice them, as he kept his telescope steadily directed at the land. He knew that Bush and all the others thought he had come hither with a set purpose in mind, and that they were awaiting the orders which would plunge the ship again into the same kind of adventures which had punctuated the last two days. They credited him with diabolical foresight and ingenuity; he was not going to admit to them how great a part good fortune had played, nor was he going to admit that he had brought the *Sutherland* down here, close in to Barcelona, merely on general principles and in the hope that something might turn up.

It was stiflingly hot already; the blue sky glared with a brassy tint to the eastward, and the easterly breeze seemed not to have been cooled at all by its passage across four hundred miles of the Mediterranean from Italy. It was like breathing the air of a brick kiln; Hornblower found himself running with sweat within a quarter of an hour of cooling himself off under the washdeck pump. The land slipping by along their larboard beam seemed to be devoid of all life. There were lofty grey-green hills, many of them capped with a flat table-top of stone with precipitous rocky slopes; there were grey cliffs and brown cliffs, and occasional dazzling beaches of golden sand. Between the sea and those hills ran the most important high road in Catalonia, that connecting Barcelona with France. Surely, thought Hornblower, something ought to show up somewhere along here. He knew there was a bad mountain road running parallel ten miles inland, but the French would hardly use it of their own free will. One of the reasons why he had come here was to force them to abandon the high road in favour of the by-road where the Spanish partisans would have a better chance of cutting up their convoys; he might achieve that merely by flaunting the British flag here within gunshot of the beach, but he would rather bring it about by administering a sharp lesson. He did not want this blow of his against the French right flank to be merely a blow in the air.

The hands were skylarking and laughing as they washed the decks; it was comforting to see their high spirits, and peculiarly comforting to allow oneself to think that those high spirits were due to the recent successes. Hornblower felt a glow of achievement as he looked forward, and then, as was typical of him, began to feel doubts as to whether he could continue to keep his men in such good order. A long, dreary cruise on blockade service might soon wear down their spirits. Then he spurned away his doubts with determined optimism. Everything had gone so well at present; it would continue to go well. This very day, even though the chances were a hundred to one against, something was certain to happen. He told himself defiantly that the vein of good fortune was not yet exhausted. A hundred to one against or a thousand to one, something was going to happen again today, some further chance of distinction.

On the shore over there was a little cluster of white cottages above a golden beach. And drawn up on the beach were a few boats – Spanish fishing boats, presumably. There would be no sense in risking a landing party, for there was always the chance that the village would have a French garrison. Those fishing boats would be used to supply fish to the French army, too, but he could do nothing against them, despite that. The poor devils of fishermen had to live; if he were to capture or burn those boats he would set the people against the alliance with England – and it was only in the Peninsula, out of the whole world, that England had any allies.

There were black dots running on the beach now. One of the fishing boats was being run out into the sea. Perhaps this was the beginning of today's adventure; he felt hope, even certainty, springing up within him. He put his glass under his arm and turned away, walking the deck apparently deep in thought, his head bent and his hands clasped behind him.

'Boat putting off from the shore, sir,' said Bush, touching his hat.

'Yes,' said Hornblower carelessly.

He was endeavouring to show no excitement at all. He hoped that his officers believed that he had not yet seen the boat and was so strong-minded as not to step out of his way to look at her.

'She's pulling for us, sir,' added Bush.

'Yes,' said Hornblower, still apparently unconcerned. It would be at least ten minutes before the boat could near the ship – and the boat must be intending to approach the *Sutherland*, or else why should she put off so hurriedly as soon as the *Sutherland* came in sight? The other officers could train their glasses on the boat, could chatter in loud speculation as to why she was approaching. Captain Hornblower could walk his deck in lofty indifference, awaiting the inevitable hail. No one save himself knew that his heart was beating faster. Now the hail came, high pitched, across the glittering water.

'Heave to, Mr Bush,' said Hornblower, and stepped with elaborate calm to the other side to hail back.

It was Catalan which was being shouted to him; his wide and exact knowledge of Spanish – during his two years as a prisoner on parole when a young man he had learned the language thoroughly to keep himself from fretting into insanity – and his rough and ready French enabled him to understand what was being spoken, but he could not speak Catalan. He hailed back in Spanish.

'Yes,' he said. 'This is a British ship.'

At the sound of his voice someone else stood up in the boat. The men at the oars were Catalans in ragged civilian dress; this man wore a brilliant yellow uniform and a lofty hat with a plume.

'May I be permitted to come on board?' he shouted in Spanish. 'I have important news.'

'You will be very welcome,' said Hornblower, and then, turning to Bush, 'A Spanish officer is coming on board, Mr Bush. See that he is received with honours.'

The man who stepped on to the deck and looked curiously about him, as the marines saluted and the pipes twittered, was obviously a hussar. He wore a yellow tunic elaborately frogged in black, and yellow breeches with broad stripes of gold braid. Up to his knees he wore shiny riding boots with dangling gold tassels in front and jingling spurs on the heels; a silver-grey coat trimmed with black astrakhan, its sleeves empty, was slung across his shoulders. On his head was a hussar busby, of black astrakhan with a silver-grey bag hanging out of the top behind an ostrich plume, and gold cords from the back of it round his neck, and he trailed a broad curved sabre along the deck as he advanced to where Hornblower awaited him.

'Good day, sir,' he said, smiling. 'I am Colonel José Gonzales de Villena y Danvila, of His Most Catholic Majesty's Olivenza Hussars.'

'I am delighted to meet you,' said Hornblower. 'And

I am Captain Horatio Hornblower, of His Britannic Majesty's ship *Sutherland*.'

'How fluently your Excellency speaks Spanish!'

'Your Excellency is too kind. I am fortunate in my ability to speak Spanish, since it enables me to make you welcome on board my ship.'

'Thank you. It was only with difficulty that I was able to reach you. I had to exert all my authority to make those fishermen row me out. They were afraid lest the French should discover that they had been communicating with an English ship. Look! They are rowing home already for dear life.'

'There is no French garrison in that village at present, then?'

'No, sir, none.'

A peculiar expression played over Villena's face as he said this. He was a youngish man of fair complexion, though much sunburned, with a Hapsburg lip (which seemed to indicate that he might owe his high position in the Spanish army to some indiscretion on the part of one of his female ancestors) and hazel eyes with drooping lids. Those eyes met Hornblower's without a hint of shiftiness. They merely seemed to be pleading with him not to continue his questioning, but Hornblower ignored the appeal – he was far too anxious for data.

'There are Spanish troops there?' he asked.

'No, sir.'

'But your regiment, Colonel?'

'It is not there, Captain,' said Villena, and continued hastily. 'The news I have to give you is that a French army – Italian, I should say – is marching along the coast road there, three leagues to the north of us.'

'Ha!' said Hornblower. That was the news he wanted.

'They were at Malgret last night, on their way to Barcelona. Ten thousand of them – Pino's and Lecchi's divisions of the Italian army.'

'How do you know this?'

'It is my duty to know it, as an officer of light cavalry,' said Villena with dignity.

Hornblower looked at Villena and pondered. For three years now, he knew, Bonaparte's armies had been marching up and down the length and breadth of Catalonia. They had beaten the Spaniards in innumerable battles, had captured their fortresses after desperate sieges, and yet were no nearer subjecting the country than when they had first treacherously invaded the province. The Catalans had not been able to overcome in the field even the motley hordes Bonaparte had used on this side of Spain – Italians, Germans, Swiss, Poles, all the sweepings of his army – but at the same time they had fought on nobly, raising fresh forces in every unoccupied scrap of territory, and wearing out their opponents by the incessant marches and counter-marches they imposed on them. Yet that did not explain how a Spanish colonel of hussars found himself quite alone near the heart of the Barcelona district where the French were supposed to be in full control.

'How did you come to be there?' he demanded, sharply.

'In accordance with my duty, sir,' said Villena, with lofty dignity.

'I regret very much that I still do not understand, Don José. Where is your regiment?'

'Captain –'

'Where is it?'

'I do not know, sir.'

All the jauntiness was gone from the young hussar now. He looked at Hornblower with big pleading eyes as he was made to confess his shame.

'Where did you see it last?'

'At Tordera. We – we fought Pino there.'

'And you were beaten?'

'Yes. Yesterday. They were on the march back from Gerona and we came down from the mountains to cut them off. Their cuirassiers broke us, and we were scattered. My – my horse died at Arens de Mar there.'

The pitiful words enabled Hornblower to understand the whole story in a wave of intuition. Hornblower could visualize it all – the undisciplined hordes drawn up on some hillside, the mad charges which dashed them into fragments, and the helter-skelter flight. In every village for miles round there would be lurking fugitives today. Everyone had fled in panic. Villena had ridden his horse until it dropped, and being the best mounted, had come farther than anyone else – if his horse had not died he might have been riding now. The concentration of the French forces to put ten thousand men in the field had led to their evacuation of the smaller villages, so that Villena had been able to avoid capture, even though he was between the French field army and its base at Barcelona.

Now that he knew what had happened there was no advantage to be gained from dwelling on Villena's misfortunes; indeed it was better to hearten him up, as he would be more useful that way.

'Defeat,' said Hornblower, 'is a misfortune which

179

every fighting man encounters sooner or later. Let us hope we shall gain our revenge for yesterday today.'

'There is more than yesterday to be revenged,' said Villena.

He put his hand in the breast of his tunic and brought out a folded wad of paper; unfolded it was a printed poster, which he handed over to Hornblower who glanced at it and took in as much of the sense as a brief perusal of the Catalan in which it was printed permitted. It began, 'We, Luciano Gaetano Pino, Knight of the Legion of Honour, Knight of the Order of the Iron Crown of Lombardy, General of Division, commanding the forces of His Imperial and Royal Majesty Napoleon, Emperor of the French and King of Italy in the district of Gerona hereby decree –' There were numbered paragraphs after that, dealing with all the offences anyone could imagine against His Imperial and Royal Majesty. And each paragraph ended – Hornblower ran his eye down them – 'will be shot'; 'penalty of death'; 'will be hanged'; 'will be burned' – it was a momentary relief to discover that this last referred to villages sheltering rebels.

'They have burned every village in the uplands,' said Villena. 'The road from Figueras to Gerona – ten leagues long, sir – is lined with gallows, and upon every gallows is a corpse.'

'Horrible!' said Hornblower, but he did not encourage the conversation. He fancied that if any Spaniard began to talk about the woes of Spain he would never stop. 'And this Pino is marching back along the coast road, you say?'

'Yes.'

'Is there deep water close into the shore at any spot?'

The Spaniard raised his eyebrows in protest at that question, and Hornblower realized that it was hardly fair to ask a colonel of hussars about soundings.

'Are there batteries protecting the road from the sea?' he asked, instead.

'Oh yes,' said Villena. 'Yes, I have heard so.'

'Where?'

'I do not know exactly, sir.'

Hornblower realized that Villena was probably incapable of giving exact topographical information about anywhere, which was what he would expect of a Spanish colonel of light cavalry.

'Well, we shall go and see,' he said.

14

Hornblower had shaken himself free from the company of Colonel Villena, who showed, now that he had told of his defeat, a hysterical loquacity and a pathetic unwillingness to allow him out of sight. He had established him in a chair by the taffrail out of the way, and escaped below to the security of his cabin, to pore once more over the charts. There were batteries marked there – most of them apparently dated from the time, not so long ago, when Spain had been at war with England, and they had been erected to protect coasting vessels which crept along the shore from battery to battery. In consequence they were established at points where there was not merely deep water close in, but also a bit of shelter given by projecting points of land in which the fugitives could anchor. There had never been any thought in men's minds then that marching columns might in the future be attacked from the sea, and exposed sections of the coast – like this twenty miles between Malgret and Arens de Mar – which offered no anchorage might surely be neglected. Since Cochrane was here a year ago in the *Impérieuse* no British ship had been spared to harass the French in this quarter.

The French since then had had too many troubles on their hands to have time to think of mere possibilities. The chances were that they had neglected to take precautions – and in any case they could not have enough heavy guns and trained gunners to guard the whole coast. The *Sutherland* was seeking a spot a mile and a half at least from any battery, where the water was deep enough close in for her to sweep the road with her guns. She had already hauled out of range of one battery, and that was marked on his chart and, moreover, was the only one marked along the stretch. It was most unlikely that the French had constructed others since the chart was last brought up to date. If Pino's column had left Malgret at dawn the *Sutherland* must be nearly level with it now. Hornblower marked the spot which his instinct told him would be the most suitable, and ran up on deck to give the orders which would head the *Sutherland* in towards it.

Villena climbed hastily out of his chair at sight of him, and clinked loudly across the deck towards him, but Hornblower contrived to ignore him politely by acting as if his whole attention was taken up by giving instructions to Bush.

'I'll have the guns loaded and run out, too, if you please, Mr Bush,' he concluded.

'Aye aye, sir,' said Bush.

Bush looked at him pleadingly. This last order, with its hint of immediate action, set the pinnacle on his curiosity. All he knew was that a Dago colonel had come on board. What they were here for, what Hornblower had in mind, he had no means of guessing. Hornblower always kept his projected plans to himself, because then if he should fail his subordinates would not be able to guess the extent of the failure. But Bush felt sometimes that his life was being shortened by his captain's reticence. He was pleasantly surprised this time when

Hornblower condescended to make explanations, and he was never to know that Hornblower's unusual loquaciousness was the result of a desire to be saved from having to make polite conversation with Villena.

'There's a French column expected along the road over there,' he said. 'I want to see if we can get in a few shots at them.'

'Aye aye, sir.'

'Put a good man in the chains with the lead.'

'Aye aye, sir.'

Now that Hornblower actually wanted to be conversational he found it impossible – for nearly three years he had checked every impulse to say an unnecessary word to his second in command; and Bush's stolid 'Aye aye, sirs' were not much help. Hornblower took refuge from Villena by gluing his eye to his telescope and scanning the nearing shore with the utmost diligence. Here there were bold grey-green hills running almost to the water's edge, and looping along the foot of them, now ten feet up, and now a hundred feet, ran the road.

As Hornblower looked at it his glass revealed a dark tiny speck on the road far ahead. He looked away, rested his eye, and looked again. It was a horseman, riding towards them. A moment later he saw a moving smudge behind, which fixed his attention by an occasional sparkle and flash from the midst of it. That was a body of horsemen; presumably the advanced guard of Pino's army. It would not be long before the *Sutherland* was up opposite to them. Hornblower gauged the distance of the ship from the road. Half a mile, or a little more – easy cannon shot, though not as easy as he would like.

'By the deep nine!' chanted the man at the lead. He

could edge in a good deal closer at this point, if, when he turned the ship about and followed Pino along the shore, they came as far as here. It was worth remembering. As the *Sutherland* proceeded to meet the advancing army, Hornblower's brain was busy noting landmarks on the shore and the corresponding soundings opposite them. The leading squadron of cavalry could be seen distinctly now – men riding cautiously, their sabres drawn, looking searchingly on all sides as they rode; in a war where every rock and hedge might conceal a musketeer determined on killing one enemy at least their caution was understandable.

Some distance behind the leading squadron Hornblower could make out a longer column of cavalry, and beyond that again a long, long line of white dots, which puzzled him for a moment with its odd resemblance to the legs of a caterpillar all moving together. Then he smiled. They were the white breeches of a column of infantry marching in unison; by some trick of optics their blue coats as yet showed up not at all against their grey background.

'And a half ten!' called the leadsman.

He could take the *Sutherland* much closer in here when he wanted to. But at present it was better to stay out at half gunshot. His ship would not appear nearly as menacing to the enemy at that distance. Hornblower's mind was hard at work analysing the reactions of the enemy to the appearance of the *Sutherland* – friendly hat-waving by the cavalry of the advanced guard, now opposite him, gave him valuable additional data. Pino and his men had never yet been cannonaded from the sea, and had had no experience so far of the destructive effect of a ship's heavy broadside against a suitable target. The graceful two-decker, with her pyramids of white sails, would be something outside their experience. Put an army in the field against them, and they could estimate its potentialities instantly, but they had never encountered ships before. His reading told him that Bonaparte's generals tended to be careless of the lives of their men; and any steps taken to avoid the *Sutherland*'s fire would involve grave inconvenience – marching back to Malgret to take the inland road, or crossing the pathless hills to it direct. Hornblower guessed that Pino, somewhere back in that long column and studying the *Sutherland* through his glass, would make up his mind to chance the *Sutherland*'s fire and would march on hoping to get through without serious loss. Pino would be disappointed, thought Hornblower.

The cavalry at the head of the main column were opposite them. The second regiment twinkled and sparkled in the flaming sunshine like a river of fire.

'Those are the cuirassiers!' said Villena, gesticulating wildly at Hornblower's elbow. 'Why do you not fire, Captain?'

Hornblower realized that Villena had probably been gabbling Spanish to him for the last quarter of an hour, and he had not heard a word he had said. He was not going to waste his surprise attack on cavalry who could gallop away out of range. This opening broadside must be reserved for slow-moving infantry.

'Send the men to the guns, Mr Bush,' he said, forgetting all about Villena again in a flash, and to the man at the wheel, 'Starboard a point.'

'And a half nine,' called the leadsman.

The *Sutherland* headed closer into shore.

'Mr Gerard!' hailed Hornblower. 'Train the guns on the road, and only fire when I give you the signal.'

A horse artillery battery had followed the cavalry – popgun six-pounders whose jolting and lurching showed well how bad was the surface of the road, one of the great highways of Spain. The men perched on the limbers waved their hands in friendly fashion to the beautiful ship close in upon them.

'By the mark six!' from the leadsman.

He dared not stand closer in.

'Port a point. Steady!'

The ship crept on through the water; not a sound from the crew, standing tense at their guns – only the faint sweet music of the breeze in the rigging, and the lapping of the water over side. Now they were level with the infantry column, a long dense mass of blue-coated and white-breeched soldiers, stepping out manfully, a little unreal in the haze of dust. Above the blue coats could be seen the white lines of their faces – every face was turned towards the pretty white-sailed ship creeping over the blue-enamel water. It was a welcome diversion in a weary march, during a war when every day demanded its march. Gerard was giving no orders for change of elevation at the moment – here the road ran level for half a mile, fifty feet above the sea. Hornblower put his silver whistle to his lips. Gerard had seen the gesture. Before Hornblower could blow, the centre maindeck gun had exploded, and a moment later the whole broadside followed with a hideous crash. The *Sutherland* heeled to the recoil, and the white, bitter-tasting smoke came billowing up.

'God, look at that!' exclaimed Bush.

The forty-one balls from the *Sutherland's* broadside and carronades had swept the road from side to side. Fifty yards of the column had been cut to fragments. Whole files had been swept away; the survivors stood dazed and stupid. The guntrucks roared as the guns were run out again, and the *Sutherland* lurched once more at the second broadside. There was another gap in the column now, just behind the first.

'Give it 'em again, boys!' yelled Gerard.

The whole column was standing stock still and silly to receive the third broadside; the smoke from the firing had drifted to the shore now, and was scattering over the rocks in thin wreaths.

'Quarter less nine!' called the leadsman.

In the deepening water Hornblower could close nearer in. The next section of the column, seeing the terrible ship moving down upon them implacably, about to blast them into death, was seized with panic and bolted wildly down the road.

'Grape, Mr Gerard!' shouted Hornblower. 'Starboard a point!'

Farther down the road the column had not fled. Those who stood firm and those who ran jammed the road with a struggling mass of men, and the *Sutherland*, under the orders of her captain, closed in upon them pitilessly, like a machine, steadied again, brought her guns to bear upon the crowd, and then swept the road clear with her tempest of grapeshot as though with a broom.

'God blast me!' raved Bush. 'That'll show 'em.'

Villena was snapping his fingers and dancing about

the deck like a clown, dolman flying, plume nodding, spurs jangling.

'By the deep seven!' chanted the leadsman. But Hornblower's eye had caught sight of the little point jutting out from the shore close ahead, and its hint of jagged rock at its foot.

'Stand by to go about!' he rasped.

His mind was working at a feverish pace – there was water enough here, but that point indicated a reef – a ridge of harder rock which had not been ground away like the rest of the shore, and remained as a trap below the surface on which the *Sutherland* might run without warning between two casts of the lead. The *Sutherland* came up to the wind, and stood out from the shore. Looking aft, they could see the stretch of road which she had swept with her fire. There were dead and wounded in heaps along it. One or two men stood among the wreck; a few were bending over the wounded, but most of the survivors were on the hillside above the road, scattered on the steep slopes, their white breeches silhouetted against the grey background.

Hornblower scanned the shore. Beyond the little point there would be deep water close in again, as there had been on the other side of it.

'We will wear ship again, Mr Bush,' he said.

At the sight of the *Sutherland* heading for them the infantry on the road scattered wildly upon the hillside, but the battery of artillery beyond had no such means of escape open to it. Hornblower saw drivers and gunners sitting helplessly for an instant; then saw the officer in command, his plume tossing, gallop along the line, calling the men to action with urgent gesticulations. The drivers wheeled their horses on the road, swinging their guns across it, the gunners leaning down from the limbers, unhooking the gun trails, and bending over their guns as they worked frantically to bring them into action. Could a battery of nine-pounder field pieces effect anything against the *Sutherland*'s broadside?

'Reserve your fire for the battery, Mr Gerard,' shouted Hornblower.

Gerard waved his hat in acknowledgement. The *Sutherland* swung slowly and ponderously round. One gun went off prematurely – Hornblower was glad to see Gerard noting the fact so as to punish the gun's crew later – and then the whole broadside was delivered with a crash, at the moment when the Italian artillerymen were still at work with the rammers loading the guns. The rush of smoke obscured the view from the quarterdeck; it did not clear until already one or two well-served guns were rumbling up into firing position again. By that time the wind had rolled it away in a solid bank, and they could see the hard-hit battery. One gun had had a wheel smashed, and was leaning drunkenly over to one side; another, apparently hit full on the muzzle, had been flung back from its carriage and was pointing up to the sky. There were dead men lying around the guns, and the living were standing dazed by the torrent of shot which had delayed them. The mounted officer had just flung himself from his saddle and let his horse go free while he ran to the nearest gun. Hornblower could see him calling the men about him, determined on firing one shot at least in defiance of the thundering tormentor.

'Give 'em another, men!' shouted Gerard, and the *Sutherland* heeled once more to the broadside.

By the time the smoke cleared away the *Sutherland* had passed on, leaving the battery behind. Hornblower could see it wrecked and ruined, another of its guns dismounted, and not a soul visible on his feet near the guns. Now the *Sutherland* was opposite more infantry – the second division of the column, presumably – which shredded away in a panic up the hillside section by section as the *Sutherland* neared them. Hornblower saw them scattering. He knew that it was as damaging to an army to be scattered and broken up like this as for it to be decimated by fire; he would as soon not kill the poor devils, except that his own men would be more delighted at casualties among the enemy than at a mere demoralization whose importance they could not appreciate.

There was a group of horsemen on the hillside above the road. Through his telescope he could see that they were all splendidly mounted, and dressed in a variety of uniforms flashing with gold and diversified with plumes. Hornblower guessed them to be the staff of the army; they would serve well as a target in the absence of larger bodies of formed troops. He attracted Gerard's notice and pointed. Gerard waved back. His two midshipmen-messengers went running below to point out the new target to the officers on the lower gun-deck; Gerard himself bent over the nearest gun and squinted along it, while the gun captains set the tangent sights in accordance with the orders he bellowed through his speaking trumpet. Gerard stood aside and jerked the lanyard, and the whole broadside followed the shot he fired.

The blast of shot reached the group of horsemen. Men and horses went down together; there was hardly a rider left in his saddle. So universal was the destruction that Hornblower guessed that close under the surface soil must be rock, flying chips of which had scattered like grapeshot. He wondered if Pino were among those hit, and found himself to his surprise hoping that Pino had had both legs shot off. He told himself that until that morning he had not even heard Pino's name, and he felt a momentary scorn for himself, for feeling a blind animosity towards a man merely because he was his opponent.

Some officer a little farther down the road had kept his men together, drawn up stubbornly in a mass along the road, refusing to allow them to scatter. It was small advantage that his stern discipline brought his men. Hornblower brought his ship steadily round until the guns bore, and then tore the steady regiment to fragments with a fresh broadside. As the smoke eddied around him a sharp rap on the rail at his side made him look down. There was a musket ball stuck there – someone had fired at long range, two hundred yards or more, and succeeded in hitting the ship. The ball must have been nearly spent when it arrived, for it was embedded to half its depth and had retained its shape. It was just too hot to touch; he picked it out with his handkerchief over his fingers, and juggled with it idly, as he had done, he told himself, with hot chestnuts when he was a boy.

The clearing smoke revealed the new destruction he had wrought, the slaughtered files and heaped-up dead; he fancied that he could hear even the screaming of the wounded. He was glad that the troops were scattering up the hillside and presented no target, for he was sick of slaughter although Bush was still blaspheming with excitement and Villena still capering at his side. Surely he must reach the rear of the column soon – from advanced guard to rearguard the army could not occupy more than eight or nine miles of road. As the thought came into his head he saw the road here was full of stationary wagons – the baggage train of the army. Those squat vehicles with four horses apiece must be ammunition caissons; beyond was a string of country carts, each with its half-dozen patient oxen, dun-coloured, with sheepskins hanging over their foreheads. Filling the rest of the road beside the carts were pack-mules, hundreds of them, looking grotesquely malformed with their ungainly burdens on their backs. There was no sign of a human being – the drivers were mere dots, climbing the hillside having abandoned their charges.

The *Account of the Present War in the Peninsula* which Hornblower had so attentively studied had laid great stress on the difficulties of transport in Spain. A mule or horse was as valuable – several times as valuable, for that matter – as any soldier. Hornblower set his expression hard.

'Mr Gerard!' he shouted. 'Load with grape. I want those baggage animals killed.'

A little wail went up from the men at the guns who heard the words. It was just like those sentimental fools to cheer when they killed men and yet to object to killing animals. Half of them would deliberately miss if they had the chance.

'Target practice. Single guns only,' bellowed Hornblower to Gerard.

The patient brutes would stand to be shot at, unlike their masters, and the gun layers would have no opportunity to waste ammunition. As the *Sutherland* drifted slowly along the shore her guns spoke out one by one, each one in turn hurling a hatful of grape, at extreme grapeshot range, on to the road. Hornblower watched horses and mules go down, kicking and plunging. One or two of the packmules, maddened with fear, managed to leap the bank out of the road and scrambled up the hill, scattering their burdens as they did so. Six oxen attached to a cart all went down together, dead simultaneously. Held together by their yokes they stayed, two by two, on their knees and bellies, their heads stretched forward, as if in prayer. The maindeck murmured again in pity as the men saw the result of the good shot.

'Silence there!' roared Gerard, who could guess at the importance of the work in hand.

Bush plucked at his captain's sleeve, daring greatly in thus breaking in on his preoccupation with a suggestion.

'If you please, sir. If I took a boat's crew ashore I could burn all those wagons, destroy everything there.'

Hornblower shook his head. It was like Bush not to see the objections to such a plan. The enemy might fly before guns to which they had no chance of replying, but if a landing party were put within their reach they would fall upon it fiercely enough – more fiercely than ever as a result of their recent losses. It was one thing to land a small party to attack fifty artillery men in a battery taken completely by surprise, but it was quite another to land in the face of a disciplined army ten thousand strong. The words with which Hornblower tried to soften his refusal were blown into inaudibility by the explosion of the quarterdeck carronade beside them, and when Hornblower again opened his mouth to speak there was a fresh distraction on the shore to interrupt him.

Someone was standing up in the next cart destined to receive fire, waving a white handkerchief frantically. Hornblower looked through his glass; the man appeared to be an officer of some sort, in his blue uniform with red epaulettes. But if he were trying to surrender he must know that his surrender could not be accepted in that it could not be put into effect. He must take his chance of the next shot. The officer suddenly seemed to realize it. He stooped down in the cart and rose again still waving his handkerchief and supporting someone who had been lying at his feet. Hornblower could see that the man hung limp in his arms; there was a white bandage round his head and another round his arm, and Hornblower suddenly realized that these carts were the ambulance vehicles of the army, full of the sick and of the wounded from yesterday's skirmish. The officer with the handkerchief must be a surgeon.

'Cease fire!' bellowed Hornblower, shrilling on his whistle. He was too late to prevent the next shot being fired, but luckily it was badly sighted and merely raised a cloud of dust from the cliff face below the road. It was illogical to spare draught animals which might be invaluable to the French for fear of hitting wounded men who might recover and again be active enemies, but it was the convention of war, deriving its absurdity from war itself.

Beyond the wagon train was the rearguard, but that was scattered over the hillside sparsely enough not to be worth powder and shot. It was time to go back and harass the main body once more.

'Put the ship about, Mr Bush,' said Hornblower. 'I want to retrace our course.'

It was not so easy on a course diametrically opposite to the previous one. The wind had been on the *Sutherland*'s quarter before; now it was on her bow and she could only keep parallel to the shore by lying as close-hauled as she would sail. To make any offing at all when they reached the little capes which ran out from the shore the ship would have to go about, and the leeway she made might drift her into danger unless the situation were carefully watched. But the utmost must be done to harass the Italians and to demonstrate to them that they could never use the coast road again; Bush was delighted – as Hornblower could see from the fierce light in his eyes – that his captain was going to stick to his task and not sail tamely off after defiling once along the column, and the men at the starboard-side guns rubbed their hands with pleasure at the prospect of action as they bent over the weapons that had stood unused so far.

It took time for the *Sutherland* to go about and work into position again for her guns to command the road; Hornblower was pleased to see the regiments which had re-formed break up again as their tormentor neared them and take to the hillside once more. But close-hauled the *Sutherland* could hardly make three knots past the land, allowing for the vagaries of the coast line and the wind; troops stepping out as hard as they could go along the road could keep their distance from her if necessary, and perhaps the Italian officers might realize this soon enough. He must do what damage he could now.

'Mr Gerard!' he called, and Gerard came running to his beckoning, standing with face uplifted to hear his orders from the quarterdeck. 'You may fire single shots at any group large enough to be worth it. See that every shot is well aimed.'

'Aye aye, sir.'

There was a body of a hundred men or so massed on the hillside opposite them now. Gerard himself laid the gun and estimated the range, squatting on his heels to look along the dispart sights with the gun at full elevation. The ball struck the rock in front of them and ricocheted into the group; Hornblower saw a sudden swirl in the crowd, which scattered abruptly leaving two or three white-breeched figures stretched on the ground behind them. The crew cheered at the sight of it. Marsh the gunner had been hurriedly sent for by Gerard to take part in this accurate shooting; the gun he was training killed more men in another group, over which flashed something on a pole which Hornblower, straining his eye through his telescope, decided must be one of the imperial eagles which Bonaparte's bulletins so often mentioned, and at which British cartoonists so often jeered.

Shot after shot crashed out from the *Sutherland*'s starboard battery as she made her slow way along the coast. Sometimes the crew cheered when some of the scrambling midgets on the hillside were knocked over; sometimes the shot was received in chill silence when no effect could be noted. It was a valuable demonstration to the gunners on the importance of being able to lay their guns truly, to estimate range and deflexion, even though it was traditional in a ship of the line that all the gunners had to do was to serve their guns as fast as possible with no necessity for taking aim with their ship laid close alongside the enemy.

Now that the ear was not deafened by the thunder of a full broadside, it could detect after each shot the flattened echo thrown back by the hills, returning from the land with its quality oddly altered in the heated air. For it was frightfully hot; Hornblower, watching the men drinking eagerly at the scuttle butt as their petty officers released them in turns for the purpose, wondered if those poor devils scrambling over the rocky hillsides in the glaring sun were suffering from thirst. He feared they were. He had no inclination to drink himself – he was too preoccupied listening to the chant of the man at the lead, with watching the effect of the firing, and with seeing that the *Sutherland* was running into no danger.

Whoever was in command of the shattered field-artillery battery farther along the road was a man who knew his duty. Midshipman Savage in the foretop attracted Hornblower's attention to it with a hail. The three serviceable guns had been slewed round to point diagonally across the road straight at the ship, and they fired the moment Hornblower trained his glass on them. Wirra-wirra-wirra; one of the balls passed high over Hornblower's head, and a hole appeared in the

Sutherland's main topsail. At the same time a crash forward told where another shot had struck home. It would be ten minutes before the *Sutherland*'s broadside could bear on the battery.

'Mr Marsh,' said Hornblower. 'Turn the starboard bow-chasers on that battery.'

'Aye aye, sir.'

'Carry on with your target practice, Mr Gerard.'

'Aye aye, sir.'

As part of the programme for training his men into fighting machines it would be invaluable to give them firing practice while actually under fire from the enemy – no one knew better than Hornblower the difference between being fired at and not being fired at. He found himself in the act of thinking that one or two unimportant casualties might be worth receiving in these circumstances as part of the crew's necessary experience, and then he drew back in horror from the thought that he was casually condemning some of his own men to mutilation or death – and he might himself be one of those casualties. It was intolerably easy to separate mentally the academic theories of war from the human side of it, even when one was engaged in it oneself. To his men down below, the little uniformed figures scrambling over the hillside were not human beings suffering agonies from heat and thirst and fatigue; and the still figures which littered the road here were not disembowelled corpses, lately fathers or lovers. They might as well be tin soldiers for all his men thought about them. It was mad that at that moment, irrelevantly in the heat and the din of firing, he should start thinking about Lady Barbara and her pendant of sapphires, and

Maria, who must now be growing ungainly with her child within her. He shook himself free from such thoughts – while they had filled his mind the battery had fired another salvo whose effect he actually had not noticed.

The bow-chasers were banging away at the battery; their fire might unsteady the men at the field guns. Meanwhile the broadside guns were finding few targets offered them, for the Italian division opposite them had scattered widely all over the hillside in groups of no more than half a dozen at the most – some of them were right up on the skyline. Their officers would have a difficult time reassembling them, and any who wished to desert – the *Account of the Present War in the Peninsula* had laid stress on the tendency of the Italians to desert – would have ample opportunity today.

A crash and a cry below told that a shot from the battery had caused one at least of the casualties Hornblower had been thinking about – from the high-pitched scream of agony it must have been one of the ship's boys who had been hit; he set his lips firm as he measured the distance the ship still had to sail before bringing her broadside to bear. He would have to receive two more salvoes; it was the tiniest bit difficult to wait for them. Here came one – it passed close overhead with a sound like an infinity of bees on an urgent mission; apparently the gunners had made inadequate allowance for the rapidly decreasing range. The main topgallant backstay parted with a crack, and a gesture from Bush sent a party to splice it. The *Sutherland* would have to swing out now in readiness to weather the point and reef ahead.

'Mr Gerard! I am going to put the ship about. Be ready to open fire on the battery when the guns bear.'

'Aye aye, sir.'

Bush sent the hands to the braces. Hooker was forward in charge of the headsail sheets. The *Sutherland* came beautifully up into the wind as her helm was put down, and Hornblower watched the field guns, now less than a quarter of a mile away, through his glass. The gunners saw the *Sutherland* swinging round – they had seen that before, and knew the tempest of shot that would follow. Hornblower saw one man run from the guns, and saw others follow him, clawing their way desperately up the bank on to the hillside. Others flung themselves flat on their faces – only one man was left standing, raving and gesticulating beside the guns. Then the *Sutherland* heaved to the recoil of her guns once more, the acrid smoke came billowing up, and the battery was blotted out of sight. Even when the smoke cleared the battery could not be seen. There were only fragments – shattered wheels, an axle tree pointing upwards, the guns themselves lying tumbled on the ground. That had been a well-aimed broadside; the men must have behaved as steadily as veterans.

Hornblower took his ship out round the reef and stood in again for the shore. On the road just ahead was the rear of an infantry column; the leading division must have been formed up again on the road while the *Sutherland* was dealing with the second one. Now it was marching off down the road at a great pace, embanked in a low, heavy cloud of dust.

'Mr Bush! We must try and catch that column.'

'Aye aye, sir.'

But the *Sutherland* was a poor sailor close-hauled, and time and again when she was on the point of overtaking the rear of the column she had to go out and head out from the shore in order to weather a projecting point of land. Sometimes she was so close to the hurrying infantry that Hornblower could see through his glass the white faces above the blue tunics of the men looking back over their shoulders. And here and there along the road in the track of the division he saw men who had fallen out – men sitting by the roadside with their heads in their hands, men leaning exhausted on their muskets staring at the ship gliding by, sometimes men lying motionless and unconscious on their faces where they had fallen, overwhelmed by fatigue and heat.

Bush was fretting and fuming as he hastened about the ship trying to coax a little more speed out of her, setting every spare man to work carrying hammocks laden with shot from the lee side to the weather side, trimming the sails to the nicest possible degree of accuracy, blaspheming wildly whenever the gap between the ship and men showed signs of lengthening.

But Hornblower was well content. An infantry division which had been knocked about as badly as this one, and then sent flying helter skelter in panic for miles, dropping stragglers by the score, and pursued by a relentless enemy, would have such a blow to its self-respect as to be vastly weakened as a fighting force for weeks. Before he came into range of the big coastal battery on the farther side of Arens de Mar he gave over the pursuit – he did not want the flying enemy to recover any of its lost spirit by seeing the *Sutherland* driven off by the fire of the heavy guns there, and to circle round out of range would consume so much time that night would be upon them before they could be back on the coast again.

'Very good, Mr Bush. You can put the ship on the starboard tack and secure the guns.'

The *Sutherland* steadied to an even keel, and then heeled over again as she paid off on the other tack.

'Three cheers for the cap'n,' yelled someone on the maindeck – Hornblower could not be sure who it was, or he would have punished him. The storm of cheering that instantly followed drowned his voice and prevented him from checking the men, who shouted until they were tired, all grinning with enthusiasm for the captain who had led them to victory five times in three days. Bush was grinning, too, and Gerard, beside him on the quarterdeck. Little Longley was dancing and yelling with an utter disregard for an officer's dignity, while Hornblower stood sullenly glowering down at the men below. Later he might be delighted at the recollection of this spontaneous proof of the men's affection and devotion, but at present it merely irritated and embarrassed him.

As the cheering died away the voice of the leadsman made itself heard again.

'No bottom! No bottom with this line!'

He was still doing the duty to which he had been assigned, and would continue to do it until he received orders to rest – a most vivid example of the discipline of the Navy.

'Have that man taken out of the chains at once, Mr Bush!' snapped Hornblower, annoyed at the omission to relieve the man.

'Aye aye, sir,' said Bush, chagrined at having been for once remiss in his work.

The sun was dipping in purple and red into the mountains of Spain, in a wild debauch of colour that made Hornblower catch his breath as he looked at the extravagant beauty of it. He was mazed and stupid now, in reaction from his exalted quickness of thought of the preceding hours; too stupid as yet even to be conscious of any fatigue. Yet he must still wait to receive the surgeon's report. Someone had been killed or wounded today – he remembered vividly the crash and the cry when the shot from the field guns hit the ship.

The gunroom steward had come up on the quarterdeck and touched his forehead to Gerard.

'Begging your pardon, sir,' he said. 'But Tom Cribb's been killed.'

'What?'

'Yes indeed, sir. Knocked 'is 'ead clean off. Dretful, 'e looks, laying there, sir.'

'What's this you say?' interrupted Hornblower. He could remember no man on board of the name of Tom Cribb – which was the name of the heavyweight champion of England – nor any reason why the gunroom steward should report a casualty to a lieutenant.

'Tom Cribb's been killed, sir,' explained the steward. 'And Mrs Siddons, she's got a splinter in 'er – in 'er backside, begging your pardon, sir. You could 'ave 'eard 'er squeak from 'ere, sir.'

'I did,' said Hornblower.

Tom Cribb and Mrs Siddons must be a pig and a sow belonging to the gunroom mess. It was a comfort to realize that.

'She's all right now, sir. The butcher clapped a 'andful o'tar on the place.'

Here came Walsh the surgeon with his report that there had been no casualties in the action.

'Excepting among the pigs in the manger, sir,' added Walsh, with the deprecating deference of one who proffers a joke to his superior officer.

'I've just heard about them,' said Hornblower.

Gerard was addressing the gunroom steward.

'Right!' he was saying. 'We'll have his chitterlings fried. And you can roast the loin. See that you get the crackling crisp. If it's leathery like the last time we killed a pig, I'll have your grog stopped. There's onions and there's sage – yes, and there's a few apples left. Sage and onions and apple sauce – and mark you this, Loughton, don't put any cloves in that sauce. No matter what the other officers say, I won't have 'em. In an apple pie, yes, but not with roast pork. Get started on that at once. You can take a leg to the bos'n's mess with my compliments, and roast the other one – it'll serve cold for breakfast.'

Gerard was striking the fingers of one hand into the palm of the other to accentuate his points; the light of appetite was in his face – Hornblower fancied that when there were no women available Gerard gave all the thought he could spare from his guns to his belly. A man whose eyes could go moist with appetite at the thought of fried chitterlings and roast pork for dinner on a scorching July afternoon in the Mediterranean, and who could look forward with pleasure to cold leg of pork for breakfast next day, should by rights have been fat like a pig himself. But Gerard was lean and handsome and elegant. Hornblower thought of the developing paunch within his own waistband with momentary jealousy.

But Colonel Villena was wandering about the quarterdeck like a lost soul. Clearly he was simply living for the moment when he would be able to start talking again – and Hornblower was the only soul on board with enough Spanish to maintain a conversation. Moreover, as a colonel he ranked with a post captain, and could expect to share the hospitality of the captain's cabin. Hornblower decided that he would rather be overfed with hot roast pork than have to endure Villena's conversation.

'You seem to have planned a feast for tonight, Mr Gerard,' he said.

'Yes, sir.'

'Would my presence be unwelcome in the gunroom to share it?'

'Oh no, sir. Of course not, sir. We would be delighted if you would honour us, sir.'

Gerard's face lit with genuine pleasure at the prospect of acting as host to his captain. It was such a sincere tribute that Hornblower's heart was warmed, even while his conscience pricked him at the memory of why he had invited himself.

'Thank you, Mr Gerard. Then Colonel Villena and myself will be guests of the gunroom tonight.'

With any luck, Villena would be seated far enough from him to save him from the necessity for Spanish conversation.

The marine sergeant drummer had brought out all that the ship could boast of a band – the four marine fifers and the four drummers. They were marching up

and down the gangway to the thunder and the rumble
of the drums while the fifes squealed away bravely at
the illimitable horizon.

'Heart of oak are our ships
Jolly tars are our men –'

The bald words and the trite sentiments seemed to
please the crew, although every man-jack of it would
have been infuriated if he had been called a 'jolly tar'.

Up and down went the smart red coats, and the
jaunty beat of the drums thrilled so that the crushing
heat was forgotten. In the west the marvellous sky still
flamed in glory, even while in the east the night was
creeping up over the purple sea.

15

'Eight bells, sir,' said Polwheal.

Hornblower woke with a start. It seemed to him as if he could not have been asleep more than five minutes, while actually it had been well over an hour. He lay on his cot in his nightshirt, for he had thrown off his coverings during the sweltering heat of the night; his head ached, and his mouth had a foul taste. He had retired to bed at midnight, but – thanks to roast pork for supper – he had tossed and turned in the frightful heat for two or three hours before going to sleep, and now here he was awakened at four o'clock in the morning, simply because he had to prepare his report to Captain Bolton or to the admiral (if the latter had arrived) for delivery that morning at the rendezvous. He groaned miserably with fatigue, and his joints ached as he put his feet to the deck and sat up. His eyes were gummy and hard to open, and they felt sore when he rubbed them.

He would have groaned again except for the need to appear in Polwheal's eyes superior to human weaknesses – at the thought of that he stood up abruptly and posed as somebody feeling perfectly wide awake. A bath under the washdeck pump, and a shave, made the pose almost a reality, and then, with dawn creeping up over the misty horizon, he sat down at his desk and cut himself a new pen, licked its point meditatively before dipping it into the ink, and began to write.

'I have the honour to report that in accordance with the orders of Captain Bolton, on the 20th inst., I proceeded –'

Polwheal came in with his breakfast, and Hornblower turned to the steaming hot coffee for a spur to his already flagging energies. He flipped the pages of the ship's log to refresh his memory – so much had happened latterly that he was actually vague already about the details of the capture of the *Amélie*. The report had to be written badly, avoiding Gibbonesque antitheses or high-flying sentiment, yet at the same time Hornblower disliked the use of the kind of phrasing which was customary in captains' reports. When listing the prizes taken from beside the battery at Llanza he was careful to write 'as named in the margin' instead of the irritating phrase 'as per margin' which had become stereotyped in the Navy since its classic use by an unlettered captain nearly a hundred years before in the War of Jenkins' Ear. He was compelled to use the word 'proceed' even though he hated it – in official reports the Navy never set sail, nor went, nor put to sea, nor journeyed, but always proceeded, just as in the same way captains never suggested or advised or recommended, but always respectfully submitted. Hornblower had respectfully to submit that until the French battery was re-established at Llanza the coastal route from France to Spain was now most vulnerable between Port Vendres and Rosas Bay.

While he struggled with the wording of his description of the raid on the Étang de Thau near Cette he was interrupted by a knock on his door. Longley entered in response to his call.

'Mr Gerard sent me, sir. The squadron's in sight on the starboard bow.'

'The flagship's there, is she?'

'Yes, sir.'

'Right. My compliments to Mr Gerard, and will he please alter course to close her.'

'Aye aye, sir.'

His report would have to be addressed to the admiral, then, and not to Captain Bolton, and it would have to be finished within the next half hour. He dashed his pen into the ink and began to scribble feverishly, describing the harassing of the divisions of Pino and Lecchi on the coast road between Malgret and Arens de Mar. It came as a shock to him when he computed the casualties inflicted on the Italians – they must have numbered five or six hundred, exclusive of stragglers. He had to word that carefully, otherwise he would probably be suspected of gross exaggeration, a serious crime in the eyes of authority. Yesterday five or six hundred men were killed or mutilated who today would have been alive and well if he had not been an active and enterprising officer. The mental eyes with which Hornblower viewed his exploit saw a double image – on the one hand he saw corpses, widows and orphans, misery and pain, while on the other he saw white-breeched figurines motionless on a hillside, tin soldiers knocked over, arithmetical digits recorded on paper. He cursed his analytical mind at the same time as he cursed the heat and the need for writing the report. He was even vaguely conscious of his own cross-grainedness, which always plunged him into depression after a success.

He dashed off his signature to the document, and shouted for Polwheal to bring a candle to melt the sealing wax while he peppered sand over the wet ink. Thanks to the heat his hands stuck clammily to the limp paper. When he came to address the report – 'Rear Admiral Sir P. G. Leighton, K.B.' – the ink spread and ran on the smeared surface as though on blotting paper. But at any rate the thing was done; he went on deck, where already the sunshine was oppressive. The brassiness of the sky, noticeable yesterday, was far more marked today, and Hornblower had noticed that the barometer in his cabin indicated a steady fall which had begun three days ago. There was a storm coming, without a doubt; and moreover a storm which had so long been foretold would be all the more violent when it did come. He turned to Gerard with orders to keep a sharp eye on the weather and to be ready to shorten sail at the first hint of trouble.

'Aye aye, sir,' said Gerard.

Over there rolled the two other ships of the squadron, the *Pluto* with her three tiers of ports, and the red ensign at the mizzen masthead indicating the presence on board of a rear admiral of the red, and the *Caligula* astern of her.

'Pass the word to Mr Marsh to salute the admiral's flag,' said Hornblower.

While the salute was being returned a hoist of flags ran up the *Pluto*'s rigging.

'*Sutherland*'s pendant,' read off Vincent. 'Take station astern.'

'Acknowledge.'

The hoist was succeeded by another.

'*Sutherland*'s pendant,' said Vincent again. 'Flag to captain. Come on board and report.'

'Acknowledge. Mr Gerard, clear away my barge. Where's Colonel Villena?'

'Not seen him yet this morning, sir.'

'Here, Mr Savage, Mr Longley. Run down and get Colonel Villena out of bed. I want him ready as soon as my barge is cleared away.'

'Aye aye, sir.'

It took two and a half minutes before the captain's barge was in the water with Hornblower seated in the stern, and at the very last second Villena made his appearance at the ship's side. He looked as disagreeable as might be expected, at having been routed out of bed by two brusque midshipmen who could speak no word of his language, and dressed with their clumsy and hurried aid. His busby was awry and his coat incorrectly hooked, and his sabre and pelisse still hung over his arm. He was hauled down into the boat by the impatient boat's crew, who did not want to imperil their ship's reputation for smartness by waiting for him after the admiral had signalled for them.

Villena lurched miserably to his thwart beside Hornblower. He was unshaven and bedraggled, and his eyes were as gummy as Hornblower's had been on his awakening. He sat down, muttering and grumbling, still half asleep, trying in dazed fashion to complete his dressing, while the men bent to their oars and sent the barge skimming over the water. It was only as they neared the flagship that Villena was able to open his eyes fully and begin to talk, and for the short remaining period Hornblower felt no need for elaborate politeness.

He was full of hope that the admiral would invite Villena to be his guest for the sake of any information he could give regarding conditions ashore.

Captain Elliott was at the ship's side to greet him as they came on board.

'Glad to see you, Hornblower,' he said, and then in response to Hornblower's introduction he mumbled incoherently to Villena, eyeing the latter's gaudy uniform and unshaven chin in blank astonishment. He was obviously relieved when the formality was over and he could address himself to Hornblower again. 'The admiral's in his cabin. This way, gentlemen, please.'

The flag lieutenant in the admiral's cabin along with the admiral was young Sylvester, whom Hornblower had heard of as a capable young officer even though he was – as might have been expected – a sprig of the nobility. Leighton himself was ponderous and slow of speech this morning; in the stifling heat the sweat was visible in little rivers running down the sides of his heavy chin. He and Sylvester made a brave attempt to welcome Villena. They both of them spoke French fairly well and Italian badly, and by amalgamating what they knew of those two languages with what remained of their schoolboy Latin they were able to make themselves understood, but it was heavy going. Obviously with relief Leighton turned to Hornblower.

'I want to hear your report, Hornblower,' he said.

'I have it here in writing, sir.'

'Thank you. But let us hear a little about your doings verbally. Captain Bolton tells me he spoke a prize you had taken. Where did you go?'

Hornblower began his account – he was glad that

events had moved so fast that he was able to omit all reference to the circumstances in which he had parted company from the East India convoy. He told of his capture of the *Amélie* and of the little fleet of small vessels at Llanza. The admiral's heavy face showed a gleam of extra animation when he heard that he was a thousand pounds the richer as a result of Hornblower's activity, and he nodded sympathetically when Hornblower explained the necessity of burning the last prize he had taken – the coaster near Cette. Cautiously Hornblower put forward the suggestion that the squadron might be most profitably employed in watching between Port Vendres and Rosas, on which stretch, thanks to the destruction of the battery at Llanza, there was now no refuge for French shipping. A hint of a groove appeared between the admiral's eyebrows at that, and Hornblower swerved away from the subject. Clearly Leighton was not the sort of admiral to welcome suggestions from his inferiors.

Hornblower hurriedly began to deal with the next day's action to the south-westward.

'One moment, Captain,' said Leighton. 'You mean you went southward the night before last?'

'Yes, sir.'

'You must have passed close to this rendezvous during the darkness?'

'Yes, sir.'

'You made no attempt to ascertain whether the flagship had arrived?'

'I gave orders for a specially good lookout to be kept, sir.'

The groove between Leighton's eyebrows was very

noticeable now. Admirals were always plagued by the tendency of their captains, when on blockade service, to make excuses to get away and act independently – if only because it increased their share of prize money – and obviously Leighton was not merely determined to deal drastically with any such tendency but also he guessed that Hornblower had been careful to arrange his cruise so as to pass the rendezvous at night.

'I am extremely annoyed, Captain Hornblower, that you should have acted in such a fashion. I have already admonished Captain Bolton for allowing you to go, and now that I find you were within ten miles of here two nights ago I find it difficult to express my displeasure. I reached the rendezvous that very morning, as it happened, and as a result of your behaviour two of His Majesty's ships of the line have been kept idle here for nearly forty-eight hours until you should see fit to rejoin. Please understand, Captain Hornblower, that I am very annoyed indeed, and I shall have to report my annoyance to the admiral commanding in the Mediterranean, for him to take any action he thinks necessary.'

'Yes, sir,' said Hornblower. He tried to look as contrite as he could, but his judgement told him that it was not a court martial matter – he was covered by Bolton's orders – and it was doubtful if Leighton would really carry out his threat of reporting to higher authority.

'Please continue,' said Leighton.

Hornblower began to describe the action against the Italian divisions. He could see by Leighton's expression that he attached little importance to the moral effect achieved, and that his imagination was not powerful enough to allow him to gauge the effect on the Italians of an ignominious retreat before an invulnerable enemy. At Hornblower's suggestion that they had lost five hundred men at least Leighton moved restlessly and exchanged glances with Sylvester – he clearly did not believe him. Hornblower decided discreetly not to put forward his estimate that the Italians had lost at least another five hundred men through straggling and desertion.

'Very interesting,' said Leighton, a trifle insincerely.

A knock at the cabin door and the entrance of Elliott eased the situation.

'The weather's looking very nasty, sir,' he said. 'I was thinking that if Captain Hornblower wishes to rejoin his ship –'

'Yes, of course,' said Leighton, rising.

From the deck they could see black clouds to leeward, rising rapidly against the wind.

'You'll only just have time,' said Elliott, looking at the sky as Hornblower prepared to go down into his barge.

'Yes indeed,' said Hornblower. His main anxiety was to get away from the *Pluto* before anyone noticed that he was leaving Villena behind – the latter, with no understanding of the English conversation, was hanging back on the quarterdeck, and Hornblower was able to scramble down into the boat without anyone thinking of him.

'Give way,' said Hornblower, before he was fairly seated, and the barge shot away from the *Pluto*'s side.

With an admiral and his staff on board, the accommodation, three-decker though she was, must already be strained. The presence of a Spanish colonel would mean that some unfortunate lieutenant would be rendered extremely uncomfortable. But Hornblower could harden his heart to the troubles of the unknown lieutenant.

16

The thunder was already rolling on the horizon when Hornblower set foot on the *Sutherland*'s deck again, although the heat showed no signs of diminishing at present and the wind had dropped away almost to nothing. The black clouds had stretched over the sky nearly overhead, and what blue was left was of a hard metallic tint.

'It'll be coming soon, sir,' said Bush. He looked complacently upwards; the *Sutherland*'s sail had already been reduced by his orders to topsails only, and now the crew were busy taking a reef in them. 'But where it'll come from, God only knows.'

He mopped his sweating forehead; the heat was frightful, and the ship, with no wind to steady her, was heaving painfully on the uneasy sea. The blocks were chattering loudly as she rolled.

'Oh, come *on*, blast you,' grumbled Bush.

A breath of air, hot as though from a brick kiln, stole upon them, and the *Sutherland* steadied for a moment. Then came another, hotter and stronger.

'There it comes!' said Bush pointing.

The black sky was suddenly split by dazzling lightning, followed almost instantaneously by a tremendous crash of thunder, and the squall came racing down upon them; they could see its hard, metallic line on the surface of the grey sea. Almost taken aback, the *Sutherland* shuddered and plunged. Hornblower bellowed orders to the helmsman, and she paid off before it, steadying again. The shrieking wind brought hail with it – hailstones as big as cherries, which bit and blinded and stung, rattling with an infernal din on the decks, and whipping the sea into a yeasty foam whose hiss was audible even through the other noises. Bush held the big collar of his tarpaulin coat up round his face, and tried to shield his eyes with the brim of his sou'wester, but Hornblower found the keen wind so delicious that he was unconscious of the pain the hailstones caused him. Polwheal, who came running up on deck with his tarpaulin and sou'wester, had positively to jog his elbow to attract his attention and get him to put them on.

The *Pluto*, hove to, came drifting down two cables' lengths clear of the *Sutherland*'s starboard bow; the big three-decker was even more unhandy and made more leeway than the *Sutherland* herself. Hornblower watched her and wondered how Villena was feeling now, battened down below with the timbers groaning round him. He was commending himself to the saints, presumably. The *Caligula* was still up to windward under reefed topsails, her man o' war pendant blown out stiff and as straight as a pole. She was the most weatherly of the three ships, for her British designers had had in mind as principal object the building of a ship to contend with storms – not, as in the case of the *Pluto*, of cramming the utmost artillery into a given length and beam, nor, as the Dutch designers had been compelled to do in the case of the *Sutherland*, to give the minimum of draught compatible with a minimum of seaworthiness.

Almost without warning the wind whipped round

four whole points, and the *Sutherland* lurched and plunged, her storm canvas slatting like a discharge of guns, before she paid off again. The hail had given place to torrential rain now, driven along almost horizontally by the howling wind, and the sudden change in the wind called up a short, lumpy sea over which the *Sutherland* bucked and plunged in ungainly fashion. He looked over to the *Pluto* – she had been caught nearly aback, but Elliott was handling her well and she had paid off in time. Hornblower felt that he would rather command the flat-bottomed old *Sutherland* than a clumsy three-decker, ninety-eight guns and thirty-two pounders and first-rate's pay notwithstanding.

The wind shrieked at him again, nearly tearing his tarpaulin from his back. The *Sutherland* trying to lie over on her side in a gale like this was like a cow trying to waltz. Bush was yelling something at him. Hornblower caught the words 'relieving tackles' and nodded, and Bush vanished below. Four men at the wheel, aided by the powerful leverage of the barrel of the wheel, might possibly manage to control it despite the *Sutherland*'s frantic behaviour, but the strain thrown on the tiller ropes would be enormous, and as precautionary measure it would be better to place six or eight men at relieving tackles in the gun-room, to share the strain both on the men at the wheel and on the tiller ropes. A petty officer would have to be posted at the grating nearest the wheel to shout down instructions to the men at the relieving tackles – all highly skilled work, the thought of which made Hornblower bless his own resolution in stripping the East India convoy of seamen.

To windward the horizon was concealed in a pearly

mistiness of rare beauty, but to leeward it was clearer, and reaching up to the sky in that direction there was a bar of blue – the mountains of Spain. In that direction there was Rosas Bay, poor shelter with the present south-easterly gale blowing, and closed to British ships in any case because of the French guns mounted there; Rosas was a fortress whose siege and capture by the French had provided Cochrane with opportunities for distinguishing himself a year ago. The northern extremity of Rosas Bay was Cape Creux – the *Sutherland* had captured the *Amélie* while the latter was endeavouring to weather this point. Beyond Cape Creux the coast trended away again north-westerly, giving them ample sea room in which to ride out the gale, for those summer storms in the Mediterranean never lasted long, violent though they were.

'Flagship's signalling, sir,' yelled the midshipman of the watch. 'No. Thirty-five, make all sail conformable with the weather.'

The *Pluto* was showing storm-staysails as well as her close-reefed topsails; apparently the admiral had decided that Cape Creux was dangerously near, and wished to claw out a little farther to windward in case of emergencies. It was a sensible precaution; Hornblower gave the necessary orders to set the *Sutherland* on the same course, although it was all that the men at the wheel and relieving tackles could do to keep her from coming up into the wind. The guns' crews were busy double-breeching the guns lest the heavings of the ship should cause any to break loose, and there was already a party of men at work on the two chain pumps. The working of the ship was not causing her to take in much water as yet, but Hornblower believed in keeping the well as clear as possible in case the time should come when pumping would be urgently necessary. The *Caligula* was far to windward already – Bolton was making the fullest use of the weatherly qualities of his ship and was keeping, very properly, as far as possible out of harm's way. But the *Sutherland* and the *Pluto* were safe enough, always excepting accidents. The loss of a spar, a gun breaking loose, a sudden leak developing, and the situation might be dramatically changed, but at present they were safe enough.

Overhead the thunder was rolling so unceasingly that Hornblower noticed it no longer. The play of the lightning among the black clouds was dazzling and beautiful. At this rate the storm could not last much longer; equilibrium was restoring itself fast. But there would be some flurries yet, and the wind had already kicked up a heavy sea, here in this shallow corner of the Mediterranean; there was plenty of water washing over the maindeck as the *Sutherland* rolled. The air, even the deluges of rain and spray, were exhilarating after the stifling heat of the past few days, and the wind screaming in the rigging made a music which even Hornblower's tone-deaf ear could appreciate. He was surprised that so much time had passed when Polwheal came to tell him his dinner was ready – what dinner there was, with the galley fire extinguished.

When he came on deck again the wind had sensibly diminished, and over to windward there were patches of clear sky to be seen, of a steely green-blue, and the rain had ceased, although the sea was wilder than ever.

'It's blown itself out quick enough, sir,' said Bush.

'Yes,' answered Hornblower, but with mental reservation. That steely sky was not the blue of returning calm, and he never yet had known one of these Mediterranean storms die away without at least one expiring effort. And he was still very conscious of Cape Creux on the horizon to leeward. He looked keenly round him, at the *Pluto* to leeward, veiled in spray, and the *Caligula* far to windward and her canvas only rarely visible across the tossing grey water.

Then it happened – a sudden howling squall, which laid the *Sutherland* over and then veered round with astonishing quickness. Hornblower clung to the mizzen weather rigging, bellowing orders. It was wild while it lasted; for a moment it felt as if the *Sutherland* would never rise again, and then as if she might be driven under stern-foremost as the wind took her aback. It howled and shrieked round them with a violence which it had not yet displayed. Only after a long struggle was the ship brought to the wind again and hove to; the shift in the wind had made the sea lumpier and more erratic than ever, so that she was bucking and plunging in a senseless fashion which made it hard even for those who had spent a lifetime at sea to keep their footing. But not a spar had carried away, and not a rope had parted – clear proof of the efficient work of Plymouth Dockyard and of the seamanship of Bush and Harrison.

Bush was shouting something now, and pointing away over the quarter, and Hornblower followed the gesture with his eyes. The *Pluto* had vanished, and for a moment Hornblower thought she must have sunk with all hands. Then a breaking wave revealed her, right over on her beam ends, the grey waves breaking clean over her exposed bottom, her yards pointing to the sky, sails and rigging showing momentarily black through the white foam in the lee of her.

'Jesus Christ!' yelled Bush. 'The poor devils have gone!'

'Set the main topmaststays'l again!' yelled Hornblower back.

She had not sunk yet; there might possibly be some survivors, who might live long enough in the wild sea to grab a rope's end from the *Sutherland*'s deck and who might be hauled on board without being beaten to death; it had to be tried even though it was a hundred to one against one of the thousand men on board being saved. Hornblower worked the *Sutherland* slowly over towards the *Pluto*. Still the latter lived, with the waves breaking over her as if she were a half-tide rock. Hornblower's imagination pictured what was happening on board – the decks nearly vertical, with everything carrying away and smashing which could. On the weather side the guns would be hanging by their breechings; the least unsoundness there and they would fall straight down the decks, to smash holes on the opposite side which would sink her in a flash. Men would be crawling about in the darkness below decks; on the main deck the men who had not been washed away would be clinging on like flies on a windowpane, soused under as the waves broke.

Through his levelled glass he caught sight of a speck on the exposed upper side of the *Pluto*, a speck that moved, a speck which survived the breach of a wave over it. There were other specks, too, and there was a gleam of something in swift regular movement. Some gallant soul had got a party together to hack at the weather shrouds of the mainmast, and as the *Sutherland* closed he saw the shrouds part, and the foremast shrouds as well. With a shuddering roll the *Pluto* heaved herself out of the water like a whale, water cascading from her scuppers, and as she rolled towards the *Sutherland* her mizzenmast went as well, on the opposite side. Freed from the overpowering leverage of her top hamper she had managed to recover – naval discipline and courage had won her a further chance of life during the few seconds which had been granted her while she lay on her beam ends. Hornblower could see men still hard at work, hacking madly at the uncut shrouds to free the ship from the wreckage thrashing alongside.

But she was in poor case. Her mast had gone, a few feet from the deck; even her bowsprit had disappeared. And with the loss of their steadying weight the bare hull was rolling insanely, heaving right over until her bottom copper was exposed on one side, and then rolling equally far back again, taking only a few seconds to accomplish a roll which extended through far more than a right angle. The wonder was that she did not roll over and over, as a wooden ninepin might do, floating on one side. Inside the ship it must be like an inferno, like a madman's nightmare; and yet she lived, she floated, with some at least of her crew alive on her decks. Overhead the thunder pealed a final roll. Even westward, to leeward, there was a gap visible through the clouds, and the Spanish sun was trying to break through. The wind was no more now than a strong gale. It was the last hurricane effort of the storm which had done the damage.

And yet that last effort must have endured longer than Hornblower could have guessed. He was suddenly conscious of Cape Creux large upon the horizon, and the wind was driving nearly straight from the ship towards it. It would only be a matter of an hour or two before the dismantled hulk was in the shallows at the foot of the cape where certain destruction awaited her – and to make it doubly certain there were French guns on Cape Creux ready to pound a helpless target.

'Mr Vincent,' said Hornblower. 'Make this signal. "*Sutherland* to flagship. Am about to give assistance."'

That made Bush jump. In that boiling sea, on a lee shore, the *Sutherland* would find it difficult to give assistance to a mastless hulk twice her size. Hornblower turned upon him.

'Mr Bush, I want the bower cable got out through a stern port. As quickly as you can, if you please. I am going to tow the flagship off.'

Bush could only look his expostulations – he knew his captain too well to demur openly. But anyone could see that for the *Sutherland* to attempt the task was to take her into danger probably uselessly. The scheme would be practically impossible from the start, owing to the difficulty of getting the cable to the *Pluto* as she rolled and lunged, wildly and aimlessly, in the trough. Nevertheless, Bush was gone before Hornblower could do more than read his expression. With that wind steadily thrusting them towards the land every second was of value.

With her flat bottom and with all her top hamper exposed to the wind the *Sutherland* was going off to leeward a good deal faster than the *Pluto*. Hornblower had to work his ship with the utmost care, fighting his way to windward close-hauled before heaving-to and allowing her to drop back again; there was only the smallest margin to spare. The gale was still blowing strongly, and the least clumsiness in handling, the slightest accident to sail, or spar, meant danger. Despite the chill of the wind and the steady rain the *Sutherland*'s topmen were sweating freely soon, thanks to the constant active exertion demanded of them by their captain, as he backed and filled, worked up to windward and went about, keeping his ship hovering round the dismasted *Pluto* like a seagull round a bit of wreckage. And Cape Creux was growing nearer and nearer. From below came a steady tramp and thumps and dragging noises as Bush's party slaved away to haul the ponderous twenty-inch cable aft along the lower gun deck.

Now Hornblower was measuring distances with his eye, and gauging the direction of the wind with the utmost care. He could not hope to haul the *Pluto* bodily out to sea – it was as much as the *Sutherland* could do to work herself to windward – and all he intended was to tow her aside a trifle to gain advantage of the respite, the additional sea room which would be afforded by avoiding the cape. Postponement of disaster was always a gain. The wind might drop – probably would – or change, and given time the *Pluto*'s crew would be able to set up jury masts and get their ship under some sort of control. Cape Creux was nearly due west, and the wind was a little north of east, the tiniest trifle north. It would be best from that point of view to drag the *Pluto* away southerly; in that case they stood a better chance of weathering the cape. But southwards from Cape Creux stretched Rosas Bay, limited southward by Cape Bugar, and such a course might drift them under the guns of Rosas, expose them to the annoyance of the gunboats which were probably stationed there, and end in worse disaster than before. Northwards there would be no such danger, the guns at Llanza could not be remounted yet, and there were twenty miles of clear water from the tip of the cape to Llanza anyway. Northwards was safer – if only he could be sure of weathering the cape. Hornblower's imagination was hard at work trying to calculate, on quite insufficient data, the rate of drift he could expect and the possible distance the *Sutherland* would be able to tow the dismasted three-decker in the time granted. With the data insufficient, imagination was all he had to go upon. He had decided on a northward course when a young seaman came running breathless up to the quarterdeck.

'Mr Bush says the cable'll be ready in five minutes, sir,' he said.

'Right,' answered Hornblower. 'Mr Vincent, signal to the flagship "Stand by to receive a line." Mr Morkell, pass the word for my coxswain.'

A line! The quarterdeck officers stared at each other. The *Pluto* was plunging and lunging quite irrationally in the trough of the sea. She was still heeling over so as to show her copper before rolling back to bury the white streaks between her gun-ports, but in addition in the irregular sea, she was lunging now forward, now aft, as incalculable whim took her. She was as dangerous to approach as a gun loose on a rolling deck. Any sort of collision between the ships might well, in that sea, send them both incontinently to the bottom.

Hornblower ran his eyes over Brown's bulging muscles as he stood before him.

'Brown,' he said. 'I've selected you to heave a line to the flagship as we go down past her. D'you know anyone in the ship who could do it better? Frankly, now.'

'No, sir. I can't say as I do, sir.'

Brown's cheerful self-confidence was like a tonic.

'What are you going to use, then?'

'One o' them belayin' pins, sir, an' a lead line, if I can have one, sir.'

Brown was a man of instant decision – Hornblower's heart warmed to him, not for the first time.

'Make ready, then. I shall lay our stern as close to the flagship's bows as is safe.'

At the moment the *Sutherland* was forging slowly ahead under storm jib and close-reefed topsails, two hundred yards to windward of the *Pluto*. Hornblower's mind became a calculating machine again, estimating the *Sutherland*'s relative drift down upon the *Pluto*, the latter's drunken reelings and plungings, the *Sutherland*'s present headway, the send of the waves and the chances of a cross-wave intervening. He had to wait for two long minutes before the moment for which he was waiting should arrive, his eyes glued upon the *Pluto* until their relative positions should be exactly what he wanted.

'Mr Gerard,' said Hornblower – his mind was too busy for him to be afraid. 'Back the main tops'l.'

The *Sutherland*'s way was checked. At once the gap between the two ships began to narrow, as the *Sutherland* drifted down upon the *Pluto* – a gap of grey angry water with bearded waves. Fortunately the *Pluto* was lying fairly constantly in the trough without yawing, only surging forward or back as some unexpected sea struck her. Brown was standing statuesquely on the taffrail, balancing superbly. The lead line was coiled on the deck at his side, attached to the belaying pin which he swung pendulum fashion, idly, from his fist. He made a magnificent picture there against the sky, with no hint of nervousness as he watched the distance dwindle. Even at that moment Hornblower felt a hint of envy of Brown's physique and robust self-confidence. The *Sutherland* was coming down fast upon the *Pluto* – upon the latter's wave-swept forecastle Hornblower could see a group of men waiting anxiously to catch the line. He looked to make sure that Brown's assistants were ready with the stouter line to bend on the lead line.

'We'll do it, by God!' said Gerard to Crystal.

Gerard was wrong – at the present relative rate of drift the ships would pass at least ten yards farther apart than Brown could be expected to throw the belaying pin and its hampering trailer of line.

'Mr Gerard,' said Hornblower coldly. 'Back the mizzen tops'l.'

The hands were ready at the braces; the order was hardly given before it was executed. The *Sutherland* was making a tiny trifle of sternway now, and the gap was closing farther still. The *Pluto*'s towering bow, lifting to a wave, seemed right upon them. Gerard and Crystal were swearing softly in unison, without the slightest idea of what they were saying, as they watched, fascinated. Hornblower felt the wind blowing cold about his shoulders. He wanted to call to Brown to throw, and with difficulty checked himself. Brown was the better judge of what he could do. Then he threw, with the *Sutherland*'s stern lifting to a wave. The belaying pin flew with the line wavering behind it in the wind. It just reached the *Pluto*'s beak-head bows and caught round a remnant of the standing rigging of the bowsprit, where a ragged sailor astride the spar seized it with a wave of his arm. Next moment a wave broke clean over him, but he held on, and they saw him pass the end of the line up to the waiting group on the forecastle.

'Done it!' shrieked Gerard. 'Done it, done it, done it!'

'Mr Gerard,' said Hornblower. 'Brace the mizzen tops'l sharp up.'

The line was uncoiling fast from the deck as the *Pluto* hauled it in; soon the heavier line was on its way out to the dismasted ship. But they had not long to spare; with their different rates of drift it was impossible for Hornblower in that gale to keep the two ships that same distance apart – impossible and dangerous. The *Sutherland* hove-to went to leeward faster than the *Pluto*; close-hauled she forged ahead, and it was Hornblower's task to combine these two factors so that the increasing distance between the ships was kept down to a minimum – a nice algebraic problem in convergent series which Hornblower had to convert into mental arithmetic and solve in his head.

When suddenly the *Pluto* decided irrationally to rush forward upon the *Sutherland* he found himself recasting his estimates at the very moment when everyone else was holding their breath and waiting for the collision. Gerard had a couple of parties standing by with spars to try to bear the *Pluto* off – not that they could have achieved much against her three thousand tons dead-weight – and the bight of an old sail filled with hammocks as a fend-off, and there was wild activity on the forecastle of the *Pluto* as well, but at the very last moment, with blasphemy crackling all round, the dismasted ship suddenly sheered off and everyone breathed again more freely, except Hornblower. If the *Pluto* could surge in that fashion towards the *Sutherland*, she could surge away from her also, and if she were to do so while the line was hauling in the twenty-three inch cable she would part the line for certain and leave the whole business to be done again – and Cape Creux was looming very near now.

'*Caligula* signalling, sir,' said Vincent. '"How can I help?"'

'Reply "Wait",' said Hornblower over his shoulder to him; he had actually forgotten the *Caligula*'s existence. Bolton would be a fool if he came down unnecessarily to leeward, towards a hostile lee shore.

A mighty splash over the stern indicated that Bush down below was paying out some of the hawser through the after-port so as to provide some slack if the *Pluto* surged away, but the process might be overdone – it was a hemp cable, which sank in water, and to have out too much would imperil the line which was drawing it in. Hornblower leaned over the heaving stern.

'Mr Bush!' he bellowed.

'Sir!' said Bush's voice from below through the open port.

'Avast there, now!'

'Aye aye, sir.'

The line was taking the strain now, and the cable was

creeping slowly out towards the *Pluto* like some sea worm. Hornblower watched as it straightened – this was a business demanding calculation as close as any so far. He had to shout his orders for Bush to pay out more cable, or to wait, his eyes on the ships, on the sea, on the wind. The cable was two hundred yards long, but fifty of these lay in the *Sutherland* herself – the job had to be completed before the ships were a hundred and fifty yards apart. Hornblower only began to feel relieved when he saw the end of the cable curve up out of the sea on to the *Pluto*'s bows, and the waving of flags told him that the end had been taken inboard and made fast.

Hornblower looked at the nearing land, felt the wind on his cheek. His earlier calculations were proving correct, and if they held on this tack they would be drifted into Rosas Bay even if they cleared the land.

'Mr Vincent,' he said. 'Signal to the Flagship "I am preparing to go about on the other tack".'

Gerard looked his amazement. It appeared to him that Hornblower was going to unnecessary trouble and imperilling both ships by this manoeuvre – he could see no farther than Cape Creux, only the friendly sea and the dangerous land. With a seaman's instinct he wanted to get both ships comfortably under control with sea room under their lee, and he did not stop to consider beyond that. He could see the land and feel the wind, and his reaction to those circumstances was instinctive.

'Mr Gerard,' said Hornblower. 'Go to the wheel. When the strain comes on the hawser –'

Gerard did not need to be told about that. With three thousand tons trailing on her stern the *Sutherland* would behave unlike any ship the quartermasters had ever steered, and extraordinary and unexpected measures would have to be taken to keep her from flying up into the wind. The hawser was tightening already. The bight of it rose slowly out of the sea, straightening like a bar, the water spouting out of it in fountains, while a thunderous creaking below told how the bits were feeling the strain. Then the cable slackened a trifle, the creaking diminished, and the *Sutherland* had got the *Pluto* under way. With every yard they went, and every bit of way the *Pluto* received, the latter sagged less and less to leeward. As soon as she could answer the helm the strain on the *Sutherland*'s quartermasters would be eased.

Bush came up on the quarterdeck again, his task below completed.

'I want you to work the ship, Mr Bush, when we go about.'

'Aye aye, sir,' said Bush. He looked at the land, and felt the wind, and his thoughts followed an exact parallel to Gerard's, but Bush by now never dreamed of doubting his captain's judgement in a matter of seamanship. His mental state was now that if Hornblower thought it right, it must be so, and there was no need to wonder about it.

'Send the hands to the braces. It must be like lightning when I give the word.'

'Aye aye, sir.'

The *Pluto* was gathering way, and every yard after this that they made in a southerly direction would be a dead loss when they turned northerly.

'Back the mizzen tops'l,' said Hornblower.

The *Sutherland* lost way, and the *Pluto* came steadily forging down upon her. Hornblower could actually see

Captain Elliott come running forward to see for himself what was happening. He could not guess what Hornblower was intending.

'Have the signal "Tack" bent and ready to send up, Mr Vincent.'

The *Pluto* was very near now.

'Brace the mizzen tops'l up, Mr Bush.'

The *Sutherland* gathered speed again – she had just the distance allowed by the slackening of the hawser in which to gather way and go about before the two began to interfere. Hornblower watched the cable and estimated the speed of the ship through the water.

'Now, Mr Bush! That signal, Mr Vincent!'

The helm was put down, the yards braced up, with Rayner forward attending to the foretopmast staysail. She was coming round, her canvas volleying as she came into the wind; on board the *Pluto* as they read the signal they had the sense to put their own helm down too, and with steerage way upon her she began to come round a little and allow Hornblower a little more room for his manoeuvres. Now the *Sutherland* was over on the opposite tack, and gathering way, but the *Pluto* was only half-way round. There would be a terrific jerk in a moment. Hornblower watched the tightening cable rising from the sea.

'Stand by, Mr Gerard!'

The jerk came, and the *Sutherland* shuddered. The drag of the cable across her stern was doing the most fantastic things to her – Hornblower could hear Gerard volleying orders to the quartermasters at the wheel and down the grating to the men at the relieving tackles below. For one palpitating second it seemed as if she must be dragged back and thrown in irons, but Gerard at the wheel and Bush at the braces and Rayner forward fought her tooth and nail. Shuddering, she paid off again, and the *Pluto* followed her round. They were over on the other tack at least heading northwards towards the comparative safety of the Gulf of the Lion.

Hornblower looked at the green-topped Cape Creux, close in now, and a little forward of the port beam. It was going to be a very near-run thing, for besides her own natural leeway the *Sutherland* was being dragged to leeward by the dead weight of the *Pluto*, and her speed through the water towards safety was diminished by the same dead weight. It was going to be a very near thing indeed. Hornblower stood with the wind howling round him, his busy mind plunged into calculations of drift and distance again. He looked back at the *Pluto*, not rolling so badly now that she had way on her. The towrope was at an angle to the length of the *Sutherland*, and the *Pluto* was at a further angle to the towrope. He could rely on Elliott to make the most economical use of his helm, but the drag on the *Sutherland* must be tremendous. He ought to try to get a little more speed out of the *Sutherland*, but with a full gale blowing it was dangerous to spread any more canvas. If a sail were to split or a spar carry away they would be on the shore in no time.

He looked towards the land again, to measure the diminishing distance, and as he looked a warning rose out of the sea a cable's length away like a ghost. It was a pillar of water six feet high, which rose from the breast of a wave and vanished as quickly and as mysteriously as it had risen. Hornblower could hardly believe he had seen it, but a glance at Crystal's and Bush's faces, intentionally immobile, assured him that he had. A cannon ball had plunged into the water there, calling up that splash, although in the high wind he had neither heard the shot nor seen the smoke from the land. The battery on Cape Creux was firing at him, and he was nearly in range. Soon there would be forty-two pounder balls coming about his ears.

'Flagship's signalling, sir,' said Vincent.

On board the *Pluto* they had managed to attach a block to the top of the stump of the foremast and sent up a signal; the fluttering flags could be seen clearly from the *Sutherland*'s quarterdeck.

'"Flag to *Sutherland*,"' read Vincent. '"Cast off – tow – if necessary."'

'Reply "Submit not necessary".'

They must make more speed through the water, there was no doubt about that. It was an interesting problem in chances, but more of the sort to appeal to a player of hazard than a whist player. To set more sail increased the danger to both ships at the same time as it gave them a greater chance of reaching safety. Yet if he set more sail and lost a spar he still might possibly struggle with the *Sutherland* out of danger, and the *Pluto* would be no more lost than she would be if he cast her off ignominiously now.

'Mr Bush, I'll have the reefs shaken out of the foretops'l.'

'Aye aye, sir,' said Bush. He had anticipated the necessity for it, and he had guessed that his captain would choose the bolder course – he was learning fast, even at his age, was Bush.

The topmen went running up the rigging and out along the foretopsail yard; standing on the swaying foot ropes with the gale howling round them, holding on by their elbows over the yard, they struggled with the reef points. The sail shook itself out with a loud flap, and the *Sutherland* heeled sharply over under the increased pressure. Hornblower noticed the flat catenary curve of the heavy cable astern flatten itself a trifle more, but the rope gave no sign of breaking under the strain. Despite the increased heel of the ship the men at the wheel were actually finding their task a little easier, for the leverage of the big foretopsail forward tended to balance the ternal drag of the tow aft.

He glanced at the land just in time to see a puff of smoke from the summit of Cape Creux, blown instantly into invisibility by the gale. Where the shots fell he could not tell at all, for he neither saw nor heard them; the sea was too rough for the splashes to be easily seen. But the fact that the battery was firing showed that they must at least be almost in range – they were circling on the very edge of ruin. Nevertheless, the *Sutherland* was making better speed through the water, and looking aft he could see preparations advancing on the *Pluto*'s deck for setting up a jury mainmast. Any fragment of sail which the *Pluto* could carry would ease the *Sutherland*'s task enormously, and in an hour they might have the work completed. Yet in an hour darkness would be come to shield them from the fire of the battery; in an hour their fate would be decided one way or another. Everything depended on the occurrences of the next hour.

The sun had broken through the westerly clouds

now, changing the hills and mountains of Spain from grey to gold. Hornblower nerved himself to endure the waiting during the next hour, and the *Sutherland* and the *Pluto* came through that hour successfully. At the end of that time they had weathered Cape Creux, and had drawn so far to the northward that the land under their lee had dropped away abruptly from a mile and a half distant to fifteen miles. Night found them safe, and Hornblower very weary.

17

'Captain Hornblower will command the landing party,' said Admiral Leighton, finally.

Elliott and Bolton both nodded in entire agreement as they sat round the council table in the *Pluto*'s cabin. A landing party six hundred strong, contributed by three ships of the line, was certainly a captain's command, and Hornblower was equally certainly the best captain to command it. They had been expecting some such move as this ever since the *Pluto* had returned refitted from Port Mahon, and Leighton had shifted his flag back into her from the *Caligula*. The coming and going of Colonel Villena from the shore had heralded it, too. For three weeks the *Caligula* and the *Sutherland* had ranged along the coast of Catalonia, and the *Pluto* returning had brought back welcome fresh provisions, the *Sutherland*'s prize crews, and even a dozen new hands for each ship. With the crews at full strength they might well strike a heavy blow, and the capture of Rosas, if it could be effected, would undoubtedly throw the whole of the French arrangements for the subjection of Catalonia into confusion.

'Now, are there any comments?' asked the admiral. 'Captain Hornblower?'

Hornblower looked round the big cabin, the cushioned lockers, the silver on the table, Elliott and Bolton gorged with the vast dinner they had consumed,

Sylvester with paper and ink before him, Villena in his gaudy yellow uniform staring idly about him while the English conversation which he did not understand went on round him. On the bulkhead opposite him hung a portrait of Lady Barbara, a likeness so good as to be startling – Hornblower felt as if he might hear her voice at any moment. He caught himself wondering what they did with it when they cleared for action, tore his thoughts away from Lady Barbara with an effort, and tried as tactfully as he could to show his distaste for the whole scheme.

'I think,' he said at length, 'that it might be unwise to trust so entirely to the cooperation of the Spanish army.'

'There are seven thousand men ready to march,' said Leighton. 'From Olot to Rosas is no more than thirty miles.'

'But Gerona lies between.'

'Colonel Villena assures me that there are by-roads round the town passable to an army without cannon. He himself, as you know, has made the journey four times.'

'Yes,' said Hornblower. Sending a single horseman was a different proposition entirely from marching seven thousand men by mountain paths. 'But can we be certain of seven thousand men? And can we be sure that they will come?'

'Four thousand men would suffice for the siege,' said Leighton. 'And I have General Rovira's definite promise to march.'

'Still they might not come,' said Hornblower. He realized it was hopeless to try to argue with a man who had not had personal experience of Spanish promises, and who had not imagination enough to visualize the difficulties of arranging combined action between forces separated by thirty miles of mountainous country. The telltale groove had appeared between Leighton's eyebrows.

'What alternative do you suggest then, Captain Hornblower?' he asked, impatience evident at having thus to reopen the whole question.

'I should suggest that the squadron confines itself to actions within its own strength, without having to depend on Spanish help. The coast battery at Llanza has been re-established. Why not try that? Six hundred men ought to be able to storm it.'

'My instructions,' said Leighton ponderously, 'are to the effect that I must act in the closest cooperation with the Spanish forces. Rosas has a garrison of no more than two thousand men, and Rovira has seven thousand only thirty miles away. The main body of the French Seventh Corps is to the southward of Barcelona – we have a week at least in which to effect something against Rosas. From the squadron we can supply heavy guns, men to work them, and more men to head a storming column when we have effected a breach. It appears to me to be an eminently suitable opportunity for combined action, and I quite fail to understand your objections, Captain Hornblower. But perhaps they are not so cogent, now?'

'I did no more than to state them at your request, sir.'

'I did not ask for objections, but for comments, or helpful suggestions. I looked for more loyalty from you, Captain Hornblower.'

That made the whole argument pointless. If Leighton only wanted servile agreement there was no sense in continuing. He had clearly made up his mind, and on the face of it he had a very strong case. Hornblower knew that his objections were more instinctive than reasoned, and a captain could not very well put forward a plea of greater experience to an admiral.

'I can assure you of my loyalty, sir.'

'Very well. Captain Bolton? Captain Elliott? No comments? Then we can start work at once. Mr Sylvester will let you have your orders in writing. I trust that we are on the eve of the most resounding success the east coast of Spain has seen since this Spanish war began.'

The fall of Rosas would indeed be a resounding success if it could be achieved. As a town with practicable communication with the sea it could hardly be retaken by the French now that there was a strong English squadron on the spot to sustain it. It would be a constant threat to the French communications, a base where Spanish armies from anywhere in the Peninsula could be thrown on shore, of such importance that the Seventh Corps would be bound to cease their attempts at the conquest of Catalonia and concentrate all their strength on the task of retaking it or observing it. But it was Spanish information that there was no French field army within reach. It was a Spanish promise to bring Rovira down from Olot to effect a siege, and a Spanish promise to have transport animals ready to drag the siege train from the landing point.

But with Leighton set upon it, there was nothing for it but to go through with the affair wholeheartedly. If everything went right, they would win a great success, and although Hornblower had never yet heard of a combined operation of war in which everything went right, he could still hope for one, and draft his arrangements for the landing of the siege train from the fleet in accordance with that hope.

Two nights later the squadron came gliding in the early darkness, with the hills and cliffs of the Cape Creux peninsula looming faintly in the distance, to drop anchor together off the sandy cove beside Selva de Mar which had been agreed upon as the best place for landing. Four miles to the westward was the battery at Llanza; five miles to the east was the battery on the end of Cape Creux, and six miles due southward, across the root of the long peninsula of which Cape Creux forms the tip, lay the town of Rosas.

'Good luck, sir,' said Bush, looming up in the darkness of the quarterdeck as Hornblower made ready to go down into his barge.

'Thank you, Bush,' answered Hornblower. The punctilious 'Mr' could be dropped occasionally in unofficial speeches of this sort. But the fact that he found his hand sought and gripped by Bush's large horny one was an indication that Bush took the most serious view of the impending operation.

The barge took him quickly over the placid water which reflected the numberless stars overhead; soon the noise of the gentle waves breaking on the sandy beach was louder than the subdued rumbling of the landing force in process of embarkation. A sharp challenge came from the beach to the approaching boat; it was pleasant to hear that it was worded in Spanish, which made it appear much less likely that it was a French force posted there to oppose a landing, and probable that it was the party of guerilleros who had been promised. Hornblower stepped ashore, and a group of cloaked figures, just visible in the starlight, came down the beach towards them.

'The English captain?' asked one of them in Spanish.

'Captain Horatio Hornblower, at your service.'

'I am Colonel Juan Claros, of the third tercio of Catalan migueletes. I bid you welcome in the name of Colonel Rovira.'

'Thank you. How many men have you here?'

'My tercio. That is to say a thousand men.'

'How many animals?'

'Fifty horses and a hundred mules.'

Villena had promised that all northern Catalonia would be swept for draught animals for the siege train. There were four miles of hill paths and a mile of flat plain to be covered between here and Rosas – it would take fifty horses to drag one of the two-and-a-half-ton twenty-four pounders over rough country. Had there been fewer animals than this Hornblower would have refused to move, but the Spaniards had provided the barest minimum necessary.

'Take the barge back,' said Hornblower to Longley. 'The landing can proceed.'

Then he turned again to Claros.

'Where is Colonel Rovira?'

'He is over beyond Castellón, closing in on Rosas.'

'What is his force?'

'He has every Spaniard able to carry arms in northern Catalonia, Captain, except for my tercio. Seven thousand men at least.'

'H'm.'

That was exactly according to plan. The army was to be under the walls at dawn, and to be joined as quickly as possible by the siege train, so that the battering could start without delay immediately upon the alarm being given. There was only the barest minimum of time available to reduce Rosas before the main French army could come up from Barcelona. Hornblower felt that he must make every effort to carry out his part of the programme, since the Spaniards were adhering so closely to theirs.

'Have you any patrol watching Rosas?' asked Hornblower.

'A squadron of regular cavalry. They will give the alarm if any sortie comes from the fortress.'

'Excellent.'

He would not be able to get the guns far from the beach before dawn, and by that time Rovira would have hemmed Rosas in, while any hitch would be reported by the cavalry. It was a good piece of organization. Hornblower felt he had misjudged the Spaniards, or perhaps these Catalan irregulars were better soldiers than the ordinary Spanish army – which was not unlikely.

The steady splash of oars heralded the approach of the boats of the squadron; the leading ones were up to the beach and the men in them came tumbling out, stirring up a faint phosphorescence in the water. The white crossbelts of the marines showed up in startling contrast with their red coats, which appeared black in the faint light.

'Major Laird!'

'Sir!'

'Take a party to the top of the cliff. Post your pickets where you think best, but remember your orders. Allow nobody out of earshot.'

Hornblower wanted to have a solid disciplined force out as a screen in front of him, not trusting Spanish precautions against surprise, but in darkness, and with three languages – Spanish, Catalan, and English – in use, he did not want to risk any muddle or misunderstanding. It was the sort of minor technical difficulty which could not be appreciated by an admiral without experience. The longboats with the guns were grounding far out in the shallows. Men were already hauling into position the rough landing pontoon of spars lashed into rafts, the outer sections buoyed up by casks, which Hornblower had had prepared. Cavendish, the first lieutenant of the *Pluto*, was doing this part of the work thoroughly well and without troubling Hornblower for orders.

'Where are the horses and mules, Colonel?'

'Up above.'

'I shall want them down here shortly.'

It was only a matter of minutes for most of the material to be brought ashore, even though a thousand rounds of shot for the twenty-four pounders – a hundred rounds per gun, one day's consumption – weighed over ten tons. Three hundred seamen and three hundred marines, working under naval discipline, could land ten tons of shot, and the necessary powder barrels, and the beef and bread for one day's rations, in no time worth mentioning. It was the guns which presented the greatest difficulty. The first of the ten twenty-four pounders was only now being coaxed on to the pontoon, for it was a desperate business to run it up the brief ramp from the platform built on the thwarts, where it had been precariously perched during its passage from the ship, over the boat's gunwale. The pontoon sank under its ponderous weight until its surface was awash. Two hundred men, thigh deep in water, toiled on the drag-ropes which were attached to the gun, and, floundering and splashing, their feet seeking footholds in the soft sand below and finding none, they gradually hauled the thing towards the beach.

Like all guns Hornblower had ever seen, it behaved with a pigheaded obstinacy that might have been instigated by infernal powers with a perverted sense of humour. Although it had been fitted, by Hornblower's orders, with specially large trucks to make it more easy to surmount inequalities of surface, it caught and stuck, over and over again, in its passage over the spars. Handspikes and crowbars were handled diligently in the dark by Cavendish and his men to coax it over the inequalities. And then it would slew round, with Cavendish bellowing to the men to avast, for fear lest the maddening thing should run clean off the platform in the water alongside; only when it had been pushed and heaved straight again could the men tail on to the drag-ropes once more. There were ten of these guns, Hornblower reflected, and four miles of paths, uphill and down, over which they had to be dragged.

He had had the base of the pier prolonged over the sand by further rafts of timber laid out there, right up to where the sand gave place to the rock bottom of the steep combe which seamed the cliff here and led to the summit. The horses and mules, each with a man at its head whose rags were obvious in the darkness, were waiting here in a great herd, but of course the Spaniards, although they knew they had come to drag guns, had provided no sort of harness for the operation.

'Here, you men,' said Hornblower, turning to a waiting group of sailors. 'There's plenty of line over there. Harness up these horses to the gun. You can find some spare canvas if you look for it.'

'Aye aye, sir.'

It was quite fantastic to see what seamen could turn their hands to. They fell to work with a will, knotting and tying. The English words they used may have sounded strange to the Spanish horses' ears as they wheeled the animals into position, but they seemed to be effective enough. Even the horse-holders, gabbling Catalan, pushed and shoved until they were more help than hindrance. Whinnying and clattering in the darkness – barely relieved by the light of a dozen lanterns – the puzzled brutes were got into line. Rope collars padded with canvas were slipped over their heads, rope traces were passed back to the eyebolts in the gun carriage.

'Avast!' roared one of the sailors just as the strain was beginning to come on. 'This beggar's got his starboard leg over the line.'

By the time the second gun had reached the water's edge they were ready to start hauling up the first. Whips cracked and sailors shouted. The horses plunged as they sought footholds in the sand, but the gun began to move, with a vast creaking and crackling of timber under the trucks. The movement was spasmodic and jerky, and when they began to breast the steep slope of the combe it died away altogether. Twenty Spanish horses, underfed and undersized, could not haul that gun up the slope.

'Mr Moore,' said Hornblower, irritably. 'See that that gun is hauled up.'

'Aye aye, sir.'

A hundred men on drag-ropes as well as twenty horses managed it, aided by a party behind with crowbars to help over the worst inequalities and to sprag the wheels with rocks at moments when neither men nor horses could pull for another second. Hornblower felt he had really accomplished a great deal when he stood on the summit, with dawn creeping out of the sea, and looked at the line of ten guns, and the mountain of stores, which had been all dragged up in the course of the night.

The gradual coming of the light enabled him to look about him. Down below was the golden beach, dotted with details of the landing party, and beyond that the blue sea, with the ships of the squadron rolling to their anchors. On his own level the summit of the peninsula stretched in a rocky, uneven expanse before him. Over to his right the rock broke completely through in a vast table-topped hill, but southward, in the direction of Rosas which he would have to follow, a narrow goat path wound through the low scrub of arbutus bushes. Claros beside him was revealed as a lean man, sunburnt to the colour of tobacco, with a long black moustache above an excellent set of white teeth, which he displayed in a smile.

'I have a horse for you, Captain.'

'Thank you, Colonel. That is very kind of you.'

There were a few brown figures creeping dispiritedly about the rocks; in the dips between the low crests there were brown masses which were just beginning to disintegrate in the sunlight from huddles of sleeping men into sleepy groups, who, still clutching their blankets about them, moved aimlessly here and there. Hornblower regarded his allies with a disfavour which was not diminished by the fact that it was exactly what he had anticipated, and which was intensified by his sleepless night.

'Would you be so kind,' he said, 'as to send a message to Colonel Rovira, telling him that we are about to march on Rosas, and that I hope to reach there with at least some of the guns at noon?'

'Certainly, Captain.'

'And I must ask you for the help of your men in the transport of my guns and stores.'

Claros looked more dubious at that, and more dubious still when he was told that of his men four hundred would be needed to help with the guns while another four hundred would have to carry a twenty-four pound cannon ball each all the way to Rosas. Hornblower overrode his objections a little crossly.

'And after that, Colonel,' he said, 'they will have to return here for more. I was promised a sufficiency of pack animals; if you do not supply me with four-legged ones, I must use those with two. Now, if you please, I want to get the column started.'

Ten horses or mules to every gun, with a hundred men at the drag-ropes. A hundred men ahead to labour on the task of improving the path, rolling rocks out of the way and filling up holes. Four hundred men carrying cannonballs, some of them leading the packmules with gunpowder kegs slung over their backs. Claros looked still more askance when it became apparent that every man of his tercio would be at work, while Hornblower proposed to leave two hundred of his marines free of any labouring duty.

'That is how I wish it arranged, Colonel. If you do not like it, you can try to find a Spanish battering train.'

Hornblower was determined upon keeping a substantial portion of his disciplined force closed up and ready for an emergency, and his determination was obvious enough to silence Claros' protests.

There was already an outcry behind them where the mules were being loaded up. Hornblower strode over with Claros at his heels, to find a Spanish officer threatening Gray with a drawn sword, his ragged guerilleros behind him handling their muskets.

'What's all this? What is happening here?' demanded Hornblower, first in English and then in Spanish. Everybody turned to him all speaking at once, like schoolboys in a playground dispute. The officer's explosive Catalan was almost incomprehensible to him, and he turned to listen to Gray.

'It's like this, sir,' said the master's mate, displaying a lighted cigar in his hand. 'This Dago lieutenant here, sir, he was a-smoking this while he was loading up the mules. I says to him, very respectful, sir, "No smoking in the magazine, sir," but he didn't take no notice, not understanding, maybe. So I says to him, I says, "No smokingo, magazino, señor," an' he just blew out a puff of smoke and turned his back on me. So I took away his cigar, an' he drew his sword, sir.' Claros had at the same time heard his officer's explanation, and Claros and Hornblower faced each other.

'Your sailor has insulted my officer,' said Claros.

'Your officer has been very foolish,' said Hornblower.

It seemed like an impasse.

'Look, sir,' said Gray, suddenly. He pointed to one of the barrels swinging against the ribs of the patient mule who bore it. It was slightly stove, and a thin black trickle of powder had run from it. There was powder on the mule's flank, powder on the ground. The danger of fire was obvious, must be obvious even to a Catalan. Claros could not suppress a half smile as he looked.

'My sailor acted hastily,' said Hornblower, 'but I think you will admit, Colonel, that he was in part justified. He will tender a profound apology, and then, perhaps, you will issue strict orders against smoking near the powder.'

'Very well,' said Claros.

Hornblower turned to Gray.

'Say to the officer "God save our gracious king, señor." Say it humbly.'

Gray looked startled.

'Go on, man,' said Hornblower testily. 'Do what I say.'

'God save our gracious king, señor,' said Gray, in a tone that was at least unnatural, if not humble.

'The man wishes to express to you his profound regret for his rudeness,' explained Hornblower to the officer, and Claros nodded approvingly, spat out a couple of brief orders, and turned away. The crisis was over, and no feelings hurt on either side. The sailors were grinning and cheerful, while the Catalans looked proudly down upon the lighthearted barbarians.

18

Captain Hornblower checked his horse on the top of the last of the hitherto interminable rocky undulations. The August sun was blazing overhead, and innumerable flies plagued him and his horse and his companions. At his side rode Claros; behind them Longley and Brown sat uneasily their raw-boned Rosinantes along with the three Spanish staff officers. Far back along the path was a solid block of scarlet. Major Laird had his marines formed up as an advance guard, while here and there on the grey-green hills scarlet dots showed where he had posted pickets as a precaution against surprise. Farther back still could be seen a caterpillar of men, naked to the waist, labouring at their task of improving the path for the guns, and beyond that a sort of multiple caterpillar with a black dot at the end showed where the first gun had reached. In five hours it had travelled little more than three miles. Hornblower, looking up at the sun, saw that he had an hour and a half left in which to keep his appointment – in which to haul his guns over a mile of rock and over a mile of the plain which lay below him. He felt a twinge of conscience at the thought that he would probably be a little late with the first of the guns, and he certainly would not be able to open fire against the walls before five or six o'clock in the evening.

There below him, a mile away but seemingly much

nearer in the clear air, lay the town of Rosas. Hornblower could recognize all the features of the place which his map indicated. To the right was the citadel – from his elevated position Hornblower could see the pentagonal outline of its grey ramparts, with the blue sea behind. In the centre was the town itself, a single long street lying close to the shore, with a line of earthworks guarding it on the landward side. To the left was the high tower of Fort Trinidad on the other flank. The weakest point was undoubtedly the centre, but it would be of little use assailing that, as the citadel and the Trinidad could hold out independently. The best course would be to take the bull by the horns and breach and storm the citadel by an attack delivered from close by the water's edge. The town could not be held if the citadel fell, although the Trinidad might cause further trouble.

Hornblower had allowed his thoughts to run away with him. He had been so busy planning the reduction of Rosas that he had not even noticed the general peacefulness of the scene. The tricoloured flags flapped idly from the flagstaffs in the citadel and the Trinidad, and they were the most warlike things in sight. There was no sign of the bare plain of any besieging army. Meanwhile it could only be a question of hours before the garrison discovered how near to them lay a valuable convoy, and how weak was the force guarding it.

'Where is the army of Catalonia?' Hornblower demanded angrily of Claros. He received a deprecatory shrug of the shoulders.

'I do not know, Captain.'

To Hornblower it meant that his precious convoy, and his far more precious landing party, were strung out over three miles of country within easy reach of any column which the governor of Rosas might send out.

'You told me Colonel Rovira was marching on Rosas last night!'

'He seems to have been delayed.'

'The messenger – the one you said you would send at dawn – has he returned?'

Claros, by a raising of his eyebrows and a jerk of the head, passed this question on to the chief of staff.

'He did not go,' said the officer.

'*What?*' said Hornblower in English. He had to fight down his bewilderment and struggle with his dazed senses in order to speak Spanish again. 'Why not?'

'It would have put the officer to unnecessary trouble,' said the chief of staff. 'If Colonel Rovira comes, he comes. If he cannot, no message of ours will bring him.'

Hornblower pointed over to the right. In a fold of the hills a line of some fifty picketed horses and a few groups of seated men indicated the position of the squadron of cavalry which had been watching the town since yesterday.

'Why did they not report that Colonel Rovira had not arrived?' he demanded.

'The officer commanding had my orders to report when he *did* arrive,' answered Claros.

He was showing no signs of indignation at the barely concealed contempt in Hornblower's expression, but Hornblower kept his rage in hand for a little longer in his endeavour to keep the enterprise alive.

'We are in a very considerable danger here,' he said.

Claros shrugged his shoulders again at the Englishman's timidity.

'My men are used to the mountains. If the garrison comes out to attack us we can get away by goat paths over there,' he answered, pointing away to the precipitous sides of the mesa in the distance. 'They will never dare to follow us there, and if they did they would never catch us.'

'But my guns? My men?'

'In war there is always danger,' said Claros loftily.

Hornblower's answer was to turn to Longley.

'Ride back at once,' he said to the boy. 'Halt the guns. Halt the convoy. Halt every man on the path. Nothing is to move a yard farther without orders from me.'

'Aye aye, sir.'

Longley wheeled his horse round and clattered off; the boy had somewhere learned to ride well before coming to sea. Claros and his staff, Hornblower and Brown, all watched him go, and then turned back to face each other. The Spaniards could guess what were the orders that had been given him.

'Not a gun or a man of mine will stir,' said Hornblower, 'until I see Colonel Rovira's army on the plain there. Will you be good enough to send a message to him now?'

Claros tugged at his long moustache and then gave the order to his staff; his junior officers argued sulkily with each other before one of them took the note written by the chief of staff and set off with it. Clearly no one relished the prospects of a ride of perhaps twenty miles under a hot sun in search of Rovira's column.

'It is nearly the hour for dinner,' said Claros. 'Will you have my men's food served out to them, Captain?'

Hornblower's jaw dropped at that. He had thought

nothing more could surprise him, and he was proved wrong. Claros' tobacco-brown face gave no indication that he thought there was anything other than what was strictly ordinary in his assumption that his thousand men were to feed on the stores laboriously landed from the squadron. It was on the tip of Hornblower's tongue to refuse point-blank, but he stopped to consider. He guessed that if they were not fed, Claros' men would simply melt away in search of food, and there was still a faint chance that Rovira might arrive and the siege be taken in hand. For the sake of that chance, it was as well to make this concession and make the most of the few hours granted them before their presence should be discovered.

'I will give orders for it,' he said, and the dignified colonel's expression showed no change at either demanding or receiving favours from the Englishman with whom he had just been on the verge of quarrelling.

Soon sailors and Catalans were all of them eating heartily. Even the squadron of cavalry smelt food from afar, like vultures, and rode hastily back to join in the feast, leaving only an unhappy half dozen to continue the watch over Rosas. Claros and his staff seated themselves in a group ministered to by orderlies. And as was to be expected, comida was followed by siesta – after a vast meal every Spaniard stretched himself in the shade which the scrub afforded, and snored, flat on his back, with a Peninsular disregard for the flies which buzzed over his open mouth.

Hornblower neither ate nor slept. He dismounted and gave his horse over into Brown's charge, and then hobbled up and down on his hilltop looking down at

Rosas, with his heart full of bitterness. He had written carefully to the admiral to explain the reason of his halt – carefully, because he did not want to belong to the type of officer who sees difficulties at every turn – and the answer had simply enraged him. Was it not possible, Leighton had asked in his reply, to attempt something against the fortress with the fifteen hundred men he had in hand? Where was Colonel Rovira? The tone of that question indicated that Hornblower was somehow at fault regarding Rovira's non-arrival. Captain Hornblower must remember the need to work in the closest and most cordial cooperation with England's allies. The squadron could not possibly continue to supply Rovira's force with food for long; Hornblower must tactfully call Colonel Rovira's attention to the need of drawing upon his own sources of supplies. It was highly important that the arrival of the British squadron should be signalized by a great success, but on no account was any operation to be undertaken which might imperil the safety of the landing party. Leighton's letter was a completely futile piece of writing, having regard to the present facts, but a Court of Inquiry who knew none of them would consider it eminently sane and sensible.

'Begging your pardon, sir,' said Brown, suddenly. 'The Froggies down there is on the move.'

Startled, Hornblower looked down at Rosas. There were three serpents issuing out of the fortress – three long narrow columns of troops creeping out on to the plain, one each from the citadel, the village, and the Trinidad. A hoarse shout from the Spanish cavalry picket proclaimed that they had seen the same phenomenon; the little party left their post and rode headlong back to the scattered Spanish army. Hornblower went on staring for two more minutes; the columns showed no sign of ending, but wound on interminably out of the fortifications. Two were heading towards him, while the one from the citadel was taking a different route, off to his right, with the clear intention of cutting off the Spanish retreat to the mainland. Hornblower's eye caught the flash of musket barrels in the sunlight; still the columns were winding out – there must be a thousand men at least in each. The Spanish information which had estimated the garrison's strength at two thousand as a maximum must be as faulty as all the rest.

Claros came clattering up with his staff to gaze out over the plain. He paused only for an instant to take in the significance of what he saw – every man with him pointed simultaneously to the outflanking column – and then he wheeled about and spurred back again. As he wheeled his eyes met Hornblower's; they were expressionless as ever, but Hornblower knew what he intended. If he abandoned the convoy and marched his men with all haste for the mesa, he could just get away in time, and he was set upon it. Hornblower knew in that instant that there was not the least use appealing to him to cover the retreat of the convoy, even if the Catalans were steady enough to fight a rearguard action against greatly superior numbers.

The safety of the landing party was dependent solely on its own exertions, and there was not a moment to be lost. Hornblower scrambled on to his horse – the heads of the French columns were well out on to the plain now, and some would be soon ascending the steep escarpment of the plateau – and dashed back after

Claros. Then, as he neared the place where Major Laird had his marines already drawn up into line, he checked the pace of his weary horse to a sober trot. It would never do to display too much haste or anxiety. That would only unsteady the men.

And he had a difficult problem to decide, too. The obvious best course was to abandon everything, guns, stores, and all, and march his men back to the ship headlong. The lives of trained seamen were too valuable to be lightly thrown away, and if he did as common sense directed he would have every man safely on board before the French column caught them up; in any matter-of-fact scale of relative values even a few seamen were worth more than ten twenty-four pounders, and their ammunition and whatever foodstuffs had been landed. Yet in war the matter-of-fact frequently held only second place. A headlong flight to the ships, and abandonment of guns and stores, would depress the spirits of the men inordinately; a fighting retreat with next to no loss would raise them. He made up his mind as he halted his horse beside Major Laird.

'We'll have three thousand French on us in an hour, Laird,' he said quietly. 'You'll have to hold them back while we get the stores on board again.'

Laird nodded. He was a tall red-faced Scot, red-haired and inclined to stoutness; his cocked hat was tilted back off his forehead and he mopped his face with a lilac-coloured silk handkerchief which clashed dreadfully in the sunlight with his red coat and sash.

'Aye,' he said. 'We'll do that.'

Hornblower spared a second to glance down the double line of marines, the homely brown faces under the shakos, and the white cross-belts in Euclidean line. The disciplined composure the marines displayed was comforting and reassuring. He kicked his heels into the shaggy sides of his horse and trotted down the path. Here came Longley, tearing back on his pony.

'Ride to the beach, Longley. Tell the admiral it is necessary to re-embark the men and stores, and ask that all the boats of the squadron should be ready to take us off.'

A column of Spaniards was already hurrying off in disorderly fashion up a cross path towards the mainland. A Spanish petty officer was collecting the remainder of his men; a British petty officer was looking on in puzzled fashion as they unhitched a team of horses from one of the guns and began to lead them away.

'Stop!' shouted Hornblower, riding up in the nick of time and delving hurriedly into his mind for adequate Spanish. 'We shall keep those horses. Here, Sheldon, Drake, bring those horses back. Brown, ride on. Tell every officer that the Spaniards can go, but they're not to take a mule or horse with them.'

There were sullen looks among the Spaniards. In a country in whose every corner war had raged bitterly for two years, draught and pack animals were of the utmost imaginable value. The meanest Spanish peasant in the ranks knew it, knew that the loss of those animals would mean an empty belly for him in some new campaign a month off. But the British sailors were equally determined. They handled their pistols and cutlasses with every intention of using them if necessary, and the Spaniards remembered the French column which was marching to cut off their retreat. All down the path they abandoned the animals and drew off, sulkily, while Hornblower kicked his weary horse into renewed activity, as he rode along, turning back towards the beach all the guns and material which had been dragged so far with such exertion. He reached the head of the steep gully and rode down it to the beach. On that tranquil afternoon the sea was blue and smooth like enamel; far out the squadron rode peacefully at anchor, and below him lay the golden sand of the beach, while over the enamelled surface plied the boats of the squadron like huge beetles. All round him grasshoppers were singing deafeningly. The beach party was already hard at work re-embarking the beef barrels and bread bags piled there. He could safely leave this part of the work to Cavendish, and he turned back again and rode up the gully. At the top a party of seamen arrived with the first of the mule train. He left orders for the animals to be brought back to the guns as soon as their loads were taken off, and rode on.

The nearest gun was within half a mile of the gully, men and horses labouring to drag it up the path – for this half mile the land sloped away fairly steeply inland from the top of the cliffs. The men gave him a cheer, and he waved his hand and tried to sit his horse as if he were an accomplished rider; it was comforting to think that Brown behind him was an even worse horseman, so that the contrast might help. Then a distant pop-pop-popping, its tone unnatural in the heated air, told him that Laird's rearguard was in action.

He rode hastily along the path, Brown and Longley at his heels, past the other gun teams labouring on the steep hillsides, towards the firing. At one point along the path there was a long line of cannonballs, lying where the Spanish carrying party had dropped them when the alarm came. Those would have to be lost – there was no chance at all of getting them back to the ship. He arrived unexpectedly at the scene of the firing. Here the country was a succession of short steep ups and downs, the rocky soil covered with a dense undergrowth, amid which grasshoppers were still singing loudly through the musketry. Laird had his men strung out along the summit of one of the major ridges; Hornblower came upon him standing on a lump of rock overlooking the path, the lilac hand-kerchief still in one hand and his sword in the other, and muskets banging away all along the ridge on either side of him. He had the air of a man completely enjoying himself, and he looked down at Hornblower with the irritation of a man disturbed while compo-sing a work of art.

'All well?' said Hornblower.

'Aye,' said Laird, and then, grudgingly, 'come up and see for yourself.'

Hornblower got off his horse and scrambled up the rock, balancing precariously on its slippery summit beside the major.

'Ye'll observe,' said Laird, academically, and rolling his r's, 'the formed troops must keep to the paths in this terrain. Moreover, detached skirmishers lose their sense of direction rapidly, and this thorny vegetation is admirably adapted to hinder free movement.'

From the rock Hornblower looked down upon a sea of green – the nearly impenetrable maquis which clothes the stony hillside of Mediterranean Spain –

through which the red coats of the marines, shoulder deep in the scrub, were hardly visible. Here and there puffs of white smoke, drifting over the surface, marked where recently there had been firing. On the opposite hillside there were other puffs of smoke and faint stirrings among the undergrowth. Hornblower saw white faces, and blue coats, and sometimes even white breeches over there where the French struggled through the thorny scrub. Much farther back he could see part of a column of troops waiting on a section of the path. Two or three musket bullets came whizzing through the air close over his head.

'We are quite safe here,' said Laird, 'until the enemy turns our flank. If ye look over there to the right, ye'll observe a French regiment advancing along a path roughly parallel to this one. As soon as it reaches that thorn tree there, we shall have to retreat and take up a fresh position and leave them all their work to do again. Fortunately that path is only a sheep track of uncertain direction. It may never reach that thorn tree.'

Hornblower could see a long line of French shakos bobbing along above the maquis as he followed Laird's pointing finger; its loops and winds showed that the path must be, as Laird had suggested, a mere chance sheep track. Another bullet buzzed past them.

'The French standard of musketry,' said Laird, 'is lower now even than it was at Maida, where I had the honour of being engaged as an officer on Sir John Stuart's staff. Those fellows have been firing at me for half an hour now without hitting me, nor even with the remotest chance of hitting me. But with two of us up here the possibility is doubled. I would recommend you, sir, to descend and devote your attention to accelerating the march of the convoy.'

They looked at each other keenly. Hornblower knew quite well that the command of the rearguard was Laird's duty, in which he should not interfere as long as it was properly performed. It was the fear of being thought afraid which made him hesitate to descend. As he stood, he felt his cocked hat struck a violent blow which twisted it on his head so that it toppled off; with an instinctive grab he caught it as it fell.

'That outflanking column,' said Laird, steadily, 'is about to reach that thorn tree. I must ask you officially, sir' – he dragged out the long word into 'offeecially' – 'to go back before I call on my men to retreat. Our retirement will necessarily be hurried.'

'Very well, Major,' said Hornblower, grinning despite himself, and slipping down from the rock with all the dignity he could muster. He got on his horse and trotted down the path again; he examined his hat with a little thrill of pride to see that the bullet had hit the gold loop at the front, passing within two inches of his head, and he had felt no fear. Where the path crossed the summit of the next ridge he drew rein again; the musketry in the rear had suddenly become more intense. He waited, and then a detachment of marines came running along the path with Captain Morris at their head. They had no attention to spare for him as they turned aside and plunged into the undergrowth on either side of the path seeking points of vantage from which their fire would cover the retreat of their comrades. The musketry fire spluttered out abruptly, and then up the path they came, Laird at their head, half a dozen men under a young lieutenant bringing up the rear and turning to keep back the nearest enemy with warning shots.

Confident that the rearguard was under efficient direction, Hornblower was able to ride on to where the rearmost gun was standing stubbornly at the foot of a slope. The weary horses were plunging and slipping on the rocky surface as they strove to drag the thing up under the urgings of the sailors, but now there were only half a dozen seamen in place of the fifty Spaniards who had helped to drag it from the beach. They were reduced to heaving the gun up the slope foot by foot with crowbars; their naked ribs – most of them had thrown off their shirts – were glistening with sweat. Hornblower racked his brains for the appropriate thing to say.

'Heave away, my lads. Boney hasn't any guns as good as these. Don't let the Dagoes give him a birthday present.'

The column of Spaniards could now be seen like a long worm ascending the precipitous sides of the mesa. They had made their escape. Hornblower, looking after them, felt a sudden feeling of hatred for them and the race they represented. They were a proud nation, yet never so proud as to disdain favours from others, hating foreigners only a little more than they hated each other, ignorant, misgoverned, misusing the wealth with which nature had endowed their country; Spain was a natural prey to any stronger nation. France had made this attempt at conquest, and it was only England's jealousy which was defeating it. Some time in the future the country would be torn to pieces in the strife between Liberals and Conservatives, and at some period in that struggle the European powers would find sufficient accord to seize upon the fragments. Civil war and foreign aggression, centuries of them, perhaps constituted the future of Spain unless the Spaniards set their house in order.

He brought back his mind with an effort from profitless speculation on the future to deal with the petty problems in hand – detailing the returning mule teams to assist in dragging the guns, portioning out the failing strength of his men so as to make the best speed with the mass of material yet remaining; the spluttering musketry to the rear told how men were suffering wounds and death for the sake of preserving it from the enemy. He sternly cast out the doubt which assailed him as to whether the gesture were worth the price, and kicked his exhausted horse into a last effort as he clattered along the path.

Half the guns were on the beach at last – for the final run down the steep gully to the sand little exertion was needed – and the remainder were fast nearing the head of the gully. The beach was cleared of all the stores that had been landed, and the first gun was even now being dragged along the landing pier for transfer to the ships. Cavendish, in command at the beach, came up to Hornblower.

'What about the horses and mules, sir?'

Shipping a hundred and fifty animals would be as difficult a task as shipping the guns, and they would be an intolerable nuisance on board. Certainly they must not be allowed to fall into the hands of the French; in Spain at the present time they were the most valuable form of booty. The sensible thing to do would be to cut the brutes' throats on the beach. Yet they were enormously valuable. If only they could be got away, and kept alive on board for a few days, they might be landed again and handed back to the Spaniards. To slaughter the wretched beasts would have as bad a moral effect on the men as losing the guns. Crushed biscuit would feed them on board – from the look of them it would be better fare than they had experienced for some time – and the fresh water problem was hardly insurmountable. In the rear Laird was still fighting his successful rearguard action, and the sun was fast setting over the mesa.

'Send them on board with the other stores,' said Hornblower, at last.

'Aye aye, sir,' said Cavendish, allowing no shade of expression in his face to hint at his conviction that mules were far more trouble than guns to coax into small boats and to heave up into ships.

The work went on. One of the guns, with the malicious ingenuity of all its tribe, fell over and dismounted itself during its passage down the gully, but the men did not allow the accident to delay them long. With crowbars they heaved the huge mass of iron down the slope and over the sand, rolling it, like a barrel, along the pier and into the longboat awaiting it. The ships had tackle which would make light of its weight and would remount it in no time. Hornblower gave up his horse to be led to the water's edge and to be coaxed into a boat, while he walked away along the summit of the cliff to take his stand on a high point from which he could overlook both the beach and the head of the gully where Laird would make his final stand.

'Run to Major Laird,' he said to Brown. 'Tell him everything is on the beach now.'

Ten minutes later events suddenly moved with a rush. Brown must have met the marines in their final movement of retreat, for the scarlet uniforms came pouring back up the path, to take up their position along the summit of the cliff, their line reaching nearly to where Hornblower was standing. The French were hard on their heels; Hornblower could see their uniforms moving through the scrub, and the musketry popped furiously along the line.

'Look out, sir!' called Longley, suddenly. He pushed his captain violently in the ribs, jostled him off the flat rock on which he was standing. Hornblower heard two or three bullets pass over his head as he struggled to keep his footing, and at the same moment a group of French infantry, fifty or more, came bursting out of the bush, running hard for them. They were between Hornblower and the nearest marines; the only way of escape was down the steep face of the cliff, and he had no more than a second in which to make up his mind to take it.

'This way, sir!' squeaked Longley. 'Down here!'

Longley dropped like a monkey to a narrow ledge below, beckoning him down with waving arms. Two blue-coated infantry men were close upon him, their bayonets levelled; one of them was shouting something which Hornblower could not understand. He turned and jumped after Longley, his feet just reaching the ledge a dozen feet below; and he swayed there with a vertical drop of over a hundred feet below him. Longley caught his arm, and, leaning outwards, scanned the descent keenly and yet with a nightmare coolness.

'That is the best way, sir. You see that bush? If we can reach that, we ought to get over there. There's a bit of a gully there joining the big one. Shall I go first, sir?'

'Yes,' said Hornblower.

A musket banged over his head and he felt the wind of the bullet – the French were leaning over the top of the cliff firing down at them. Longley braced himself, and then leaped wildly along the face of the cliff, slid down it in a cloud of dust and fragments, and caught the stout bush he had pointed out to Hornblower. Then, moving cautiously away from it, he found an inequality on which to rest, and from there beckoned again to his captain. Hornblower tried to nerve himself for the leap, and then drew back. Another bullet – it actually struck the ledge close to his feet. Hornblower plunged heavily from the end of the ledge, turning his face to the cliff. He felt the rock tearing at his clothes as he slid. Then he crashed into the bush and grasped it madly, his feet seeking foothold.

'Now, over here, sir. Catch hold of that lump with your hands. Put your foot into that crack, sir. No! Not that foot! T'other one!'

Longley's voice went up into a squeak like a bat's in the excitement as he edged himself along the cliff and at the same time instructed his captain where to put his hands and feet. Hornblower clung to the cliff face like a fly on a window pane. His hands and arms were aching already – the activities of two days and a night had already drained his strength. A bullet whacked into the rock between him and the midshipman, a chip which it displaced struck his knee a sharp tap. He looked down, and his head swam at the sight of the drop below him. In his exhausted state he felt he would gladly loose his hold and drop down to the quick death awaiting him.

'Come on, sir!' said Longley. 'Not much more now, sir. Don't look down!'

He recalled himself to sanity. Changing foothold and handhold inch by inch, he shuffled along in accordance with Longley's instructions.

'Just a minute,' said Longley. 'Are you all right, sir? Wait here while I go and have a look.'

Hornblower clung on with aching arms and legs. He kept his face against the cliff, stupid with fatigue and fear. Then he heard Longley beside him again.

'It's all right, sir. There's only one nasty bit. Get your feet down on to that knob, there. Where that bit of grass is.'

They had to get past a projecting boss in the face of the cliff; there was one awful second when Hornblower had no foothold, and with his legs dangling had to stretch to a new handhold.

'They can't see us here, sir. You can rest a bit, if you'd like to,' said Longley solicitously.

Hornblower lay on his face in the shallow depression which grooved the cliff, conscious for a space of nothing save the cessation of strain. Then with a rush he remembered everything – his dignity, the work on the beach, the fighting on the summit. He sat up and looked down; with a solid lump of the cliff under him his head would stand that. The beach was clear of guns now, in the darkening evening, and only a few animals stood waiting their turn to be coaxed into the boats. Up above the firing seemed to have died down for a space; either the French had begun to despair of achieving anything further or they were gathering for a last effort.

'Come on,' said Hornblower, abruptly.

The rest of the descent was easy; they could slide and scramble all the way until he felt the welcome sand under his feet. A worried-looking Brown materialized here, his face clearing as he caught sight of his captain. Cavendish was standing supervising the dispatch of the last cutter.

'Very good, Mr Cavendish. The seamen can go next. Are the armed boats ready?'

'Yes, sir.'

It was nearly dark now, and the sky gave only a faint light when the marines began to pour down the gully and over the sand. The last shots in the long retreat were fired by the four-pounders mounted in the bows of the two longboats which lay nosing the sand while the final section of marines splashed out into the water to them. The long red tongues of flame lit up the dark masses of Frenchmen swarming down on to the beach, and the blast of grape which they had hurled was followed by a gratifying chorus of screams and cries from the stricken masses.

'A very handsome operation indeed,' said Major Laird from his seat in the stern of the longboat beside Hornblower.

Hornblower drooping in weariness was inclined to agree with him, although he was shivering with the chill of his soaked breeches, and his hands smarted from cuts and abrasions, and other parts of him pained him with saddlesoreness as if they were being held before a fierce fire. They rowed out over the silent sea to a ship strange with the whinnying of horses and smelling stable-like already.

Hornblower staggered on board; he saw the boatswain's mate who held the lantern for him glance curiously at his ragged clothes and white face. He walked blindly past the dark line of horses and mules, picketed head and heel to the deck ringbolts, to the security of his cabin. He ought to make his report to the admiral – surely he could leave that until daylight. The deck seemed to be heaving under him rhythmically. Polwheal was there, and food was laid on the candle-lighted table, but Hornblower later could never remember eating any. Faintly he could remember Polwheal helping him into bed, and a vivid, clearcut memory always abode with him of hearing Polwheal, through the closed cabin door, arguing with the sentry outside.

'Twarn't Horny's fault,' said Polwheal, didactically.

Then sleep swooped down upon Hornblower, sleep which held him fast, even though he was conscious through it of the aches and pains which assailed him, of the perils he had encountered that day, of the fear which had tortured him on the cliff.

19

The *Sutherland* was wallowing through the stormy waters of the Gulf of the Lion, under a grey sky, with flecked wave-tops all round her, while her captain stood on his heaving quarterdeck enjoying the cold blast of the mistral round his ears. The nightmare adventure on the Spanish mainland was three weeks past now, for over a fortnight the ship had been clear of horses and mules, and the stable-smell had nearly disappeared, and the decks were white once again. Much more important, the *Sutherland* had been sent away on detached duty with orders to examine the French coastline all the way along to Toulon; he was free from the clogging authority of the admiral again, and he breathed the keen air with the delight of someone released from slavery. Barbara's husband was not a man whom it was a pleasure to serve.

The whole ship seemed to be infected with this feeling of freedom – unless it was pleasure in the contrast between the present weather and the tranquil skies and calm seas which had prevailed so long. Here came Bush, rubbing his hands and grinning like a gargoyle.

'Blowing a little, sir,' said Bush, 'and it'll blow harder than this before it's over.'

'Very likely,' said Hornblower.

He grinned back, light-heartedly, with a bubbling of

high spirits within him. It was quite fantastic how stimulating it was to be thrashing to windward again against a stiff breeze, especially with the nearest admiral a hundred miles away. In Southern France that same wind would be causing grumbling and complaints, and the French would be going about hugging their cloaks to them, but here at sea it was perfectly delightful.

'You can put the hands to any work you please, Mr Bush,' said Hornblower magnanimously, as discretion returned to him and he evaded the tempting snares of falling into idle conversation.

'Aye aye, sir.'

Young Longley came aft with the sand glass to attend to the hourly heaving of the log, and Hornblower watched him from the corner of his eye. The boy was carrying himself with assurance now, and gave his orders easily. He was the only one of all the midshipmen whose calculations of the day's work made any pretence at accuracy, and the incident on the cliff had shown him to be a lad of quick decision. Towards the end of this commission, and at a suitable opportunity, Hornblower decided, he would appoint him acting lieutenant; he watched him bending over the traverse board marking up the hour's run, with a queer wonder as to whether he was observing a future Nelson, an admiral who would some day rule forty ships of the line.

He was an ugly little fellow, with this stubby hair and monkey face, yet it was hard not to feel a surge of affection for him. If little Horatio, the child whom smallpox had killed on the third day in those Southsea lodgings, had grown up in this fashion Hornblower would have been proud of him. Perhaps he might have done – but it was not a good thing to think himself into gloom on a fresh morning like this about the little boy he had loved. There would be another child by the time he reached home. Hornblower hoped it might be a boy; and he was nearly sure that Maria hoped the same. Not that any little boy could quite take the place of Horatio – Hornblower felt a new flood of depression when he remembered how Horatio had said 'Papa! Want papa!' and had rested his face against his shoulder that evening when the first malaise of the illness was creeping over him. He shook his depression off; if his return to England was at the earliest moment he could hope for, the child would be crawling about the floor with all a baby's misdirected zeal. He might even be talking a little, and would hang his head in shyness when his strange papa arrived, so that Hornblower would have the task of winning his confidence and affection. It would be a pleasant task.

Maria was going to ask Lady Barbara to be godmother to the child – it would be delightful if Lady Barbara agreed. Any child with the influence of the Wellesley family behind it could contemplate a secure future. Without a doubt it was the Wellesley influence which had put Leighton in command of the squadron he was mismanaging. And by this time Hornblower was sure that it was the Wellesley influence which had put him in command of one of the ships of that squadron and retained him in employment without a single day of half pay. He was still in doubt about what had been Lady Barbara's motive, but on a stimulating morning like this he could almost venture to believe that it was because she loved him; he would far rather it were that than it should merely be because she admired his professional ability. Or it might be just an amused and tolerant kindliness towards an inferior whom she knew to love her.

That thought called up a surge of revolt. She had been his for the asking, once. He had kissed her, clasped her. No matter that he had been afraid to take her – he slurred that memory over in his present indignation – she had offered, and he had declined. As a suppliant once, she had no right to pose to herself now as his patroness. He stamped his feet with mortification as he paced the deck.

But his clairvoyance was instantly blurred by his idealism. His memory of a cool and self-collected Lady Barbara, the perfect hostess, the dignified wife of an admiral, was overlaid by mental pictures of a tender Lady Barbara, a loving Lady Barbara, with a beauty which would take a man's breath away. His heart was torn with longing for her; he felt sick and sad and lonely in his rush of desire for her, for the angel of goodness and sweetness and kindliness he thought her to be. His pulse beat faster as he remembered her white bosom with the sapphire pendant resting on it, and animal desire came to reinforce the boyish affection he bore her.

'Sail ho!' bellowed the masthead lookout, and Hornblower's dreaminess was stripped from him in a flash, like the straw wrapping from a bottle.

'Where away?'

'Right in the wind's eye, sir, an' comin' up fast.'

A brisk nor'easterly wind like the present meant ideal weather conditions for French ships which wished to escape from the blockade of Marseille and Toulon. It was a fair wind for the escaping ship, enabling her to get out of harbour and cover a long distance during the first night, while at the same time it pushed the blockading squadron away to leeward. This might well be a ship engaged in breaking the blockade, and if such were the case she would have small chance of escape with the *Sutherland* right to leeward of her. It would be consistent with the good fortune he had enjoyed on detached service during the present commission if this were to be another prize for him.

'Keep her steady as she goes,' said Hornblower, in reply to Bush's look of inquiry. 'And turn the hands up, if you please, Mr Bush.'

'Deck, there!' hailed the lookout. 'She's a frigate, and British by the look of her.'

That was a disappointment. There were fifty possible explanations of a British frigate's presence here and on her present course which offered no chance of action as opposed to one which might involve the proximity of an enemy. Her topsails were in sight already, white against the grey sky.

'Begging your pardon, sir,' said the gunlayer of one of the port side quarterdeck carronades. 'Stebbings here thinks he knows who she is.'

Stebbings was one of the hands taken from the East India convoy, a middle-aged man with grey hairs in his beard.

'*Cassandra*, sir, thirty-two, seems to me. She convoyed us last v'yage.'

'Captain Frederick Cooke, sir,' added Vincent, flipping hastily over the pages of the printed list.

'Ask her number and make sure,' ordered Hornblower.

Cooke had been posted six months later than he had; in the event of any combined operations he would be the senior officer.

'Yes, she's the *Cassandra*, sir,' said Vincent, his eye to his telescope, as a hoist of flags went up to the frigate's foretopsail yardarm.

'She's letting fly her sheets,' said Bush, with a hint of excitement in his voice. 'Queer, that is, sir.'

From time immemorial, dating back long before a practical flag-signalling system had been devised, letting fly the sheets had been a conventional warning all the world over of the approach of a fleet.

'She's signalling again, sir,' said Vincent. 'It's hard to read with the flags blowing straight towards us.'

'Damn it, sir,' blazed Bush. 'Use your eyes, or I'll know the reason why not.'

'Numeral. Four. Literal. Seventeen – astern – to windward – source – sou'west,' translated Longley with the signal book.

'Beat to quarters, if you please, Mr Bush. And wear the ship directly.'

It was not the *Sutherland*'s task to fight odds of four to one. If there were any British ships in pursuit he could throw himself in the enemy's path and rely on crippling at least two Frenchmen so as to ensure their capture, but until he knew more about the situation he must keep as clear as was possible.

'Ask "Are any British ships at hand?"' he said to Vincent while the *Sutherland* first lay over on her side and then rose to an even keel as Bush brought her before the wind.

'Reply negative, sir,' said Vincent, a minute later, through the din of clearing for action.

It was as he expected, then. The four French ships of the line had broken out of Toulon during the darkness, and while the blockading squadron had been blown away to leeward. Only the *Cassandra*, the inshore lookout, had caught sight of them, and had run before them so as to keep them under observation.

'Ask "Where is the enemy?"' said Hornblower. It was an interesting exercise, calling for familiarity with the signal book, to frame a message so as to use the fewest number of flags.

'Six – miles – astern – bearing – nor'east,' translated Longley from the code book as Vincent read out the numbers.

So the French were lying right before the wind. That might merely be because they wanted to put as great a distance as possible between them and the blockading squadron off Toulon, but it was not likely that the officer in command would run wastefully direct to leeward unless that was the course most suited to his plan. It ruled out completely any thought of Sicily or the Adriatic or the Eastern Mediterranean as objective, and it pointed directly to the Spanish coast near Barcelona and beyond that to the Straits of Gibraltar.

Hornblower on his quarterdeck set himself to try to think the thoughts of Bonaparte at the Tuileries. Beyond the Straits lay the Atlantic and the whole world. Yet it was hard to imagine any useful objective for four French ships of the line out there; the French West Indies had been nearly all reduced by English expeditions, the Cape of Good Hope was in English hands, Mauritius was about to fall. The French squadron might be intended for a mere commerce-destroying raid, but in that case an equal number of frigates would be both cheaper and more effective. That was not like Bonaparte. And on the other hand exactly enough time had elapsed for the appearance of Leighton's squadron on the Catalan coast and the resultant dearth of supplies to have been reported to the Tuileries, and for orders to have been transmitted thence to Toulon. Those orders would bear the Bonaparte stamp. Three British ships on the Catalan coast? Then send four French ones against them. Man them with crews picked from all the ships rotting in Toulon Harbour. Load them with all the stores for which the Barcelona garrison is clamouring. Let them slip out one dark night, hack their way through to Barcelona, crush the British squadron if they can, and return if they are lucky. In a week they might be safe and sound, and if not – every omelette demands the breaking of eggs.

That must be the French plan, and he would gladly bet all he had that he was right. It only remained to decide how to defeat the French aims, and the opening moves were obvious. First, he must keep between the French and their objective, and second, it would be desirable to keep out of sight of the French, over their horizon, as long as possible – it would be a surprise to them to find a ship of considerable force, and not a mere frigate, in their path; and surprise was half a battle. In that case his first instinctive move had been correct, and the *Sutherland* was on the right course to achieve both these ends – Hornblower wondered uneasily whether his unthinking mind had jumped at once to the conclusions which his thinking mind had only just reached. All that remained to be done was to call down the *Pluto* and the *Caligula*. Three British ships of the line and a frigate could fight four French ships, picked crews or not, and Bonaparte's opinion notwithstanding.

'Cleared for action, sir,' said Bush, touching his hat. His eyes were bright with the anticipation of action. Hornblower saw in him a fighting man of the type to which he regretted he did not belong – a man who relished the prospect of a battle for its own sake, who loved physical danger, who would never stop to count the odds against him.

'Dismiss the watch below, if you please,' said Hornblower. There was no object in keeping every man at his station when action was far distant, and Hornblower saw Bush's expression alter when he heard the words. They meant that the *Sutherland* was not going to plunge immediately into action against odds of four to one.

'Aye aye, sir,' he said, reluctantly.

There was something to be said for Bush's point of view, for the *Sutherland* well handled might knock away so many French spars as to leave two or three at least of the French so crippled as to fall a certain prey into British hands sooner or later. It would be at the cost of her own destruction, however, and he could think about it again later. A fair wind today might still mean a foul wind tomorrow; there might still be time for the *Pluto* and the *Caligula* to come up if only they could be informed of the proximity of their prey.

'Give me that signal book,' said Hornblower to Longley.

He turned its pages, refreshed his memory regarding the wording of some of the arbitrary signals. In sending a long message there was always danger of misunderstanding. And he pulled his chin while he composed his message. Like every British officer retreating, he was running the risk of having his motives misunderstood, even though, as he told himself petulantly, not even the mad British public, gorged with past victories, could condemn him for refusing action against odds of four to one. But if anything went wrong the Wellesley faction might seek a scapegoat; and the order he was about to transmit might mean the difference between success and failure, between a court of inquiry and the thanks of Parliament.

'Send this message,' he said abruptly to Vincent.

Hoist after hoist the flags crept up the mast. The *Cassandra* was to set all sail she could carry, and to make use of her frigate's turn of speed to turn westward, seek out the *Pluto* and *Caligula* – Hornblower could not be exact in his description of their position – and bring them down to Barcelona. Phrase by phrase the *Cassandra* acknowledged the signal. Then there was a pause after its completion, before Vincent, glass to eye, reported.

'*Cassandra* signalling, sir. "Submit –."'

It was the first time Hornblower had ever had that word addressed to him. He had used it so often in signals to admirals and senior captains, had included it so often in reports, and now another officer was beginning a signal to him with the word 'Submit'. It was a clear, definite proof of his growing seniority, and gave him a thrill keener even than he had known when a ship had first piped the side for him on his being posted. Yet naturally the word 'submit' ushered in a protest. Cooke of the *Cassandra* was not in the least anxious to be thus summarily dismissed from the scene of a promising action. He submitted that it would be better for the *Cassandra* to stay in sight of the French.

'Signal "Carry out orders acknowledged",' said Hornblower, tersely.

Cooke was wrong and he was right – Cooke's protest helped his decision to crystallize. A frigate's whole function, what she was built for, was to enable the ships of the line to come into action. The *Cassandra* could not face a single broadside from one of the ships rolling along after her; if she could bring the *Pluto* and the *Caligula* into action she would have multiplied her own value an infinity of times. It was heart-warming to Hornblower to be not only convinced that he was right, but to be able to enforce the course of action he had decided upon. That six months' difference in seniority made Cooke obedient to him, and would make him obedient all their lives – if ever Cooke and he flew their flags together as admirals, he would still be the senior and Cooke the junior. He watched the *Cassandra* shake out the reefs from her topsails and bear away westwards, with all her five knots' superiority of speed being put to its best use now.

'Shorten sail, Mr Bush,' said Hornblower.

The French would see the *Cassandra* vanish over their horizon; there was a chance that the *Sutherland* might keep them under observation without being seen. He stuck his telescope into his pocket and set himself to climb the mizzen rigging, sedately – even a little laboriously; it was imperilling his dignity to do so, when every hand in the ship could climb the mast quicker than he, but he had to see with his own eyes the enemy astern of him. The ship was plunging heavily in the following sea, and the wind blew keenly about his ears. It called for resolution to continue his ascent without undignified pauses, so as to appear merely as leisurely as a captain had a right to be, and yet neither timid nor awkward.

At last he found a secure perch on the mizzen topmast crosstrees, and could train his glass on the heaving horizon. With her main topsail taken in the *Sutherland*'s speed was considerably reduced, and it could not be long before the French appeared. He saw them soon enough – a tiny rectangle of white just lifting over the horizon, then another beside it, and another, and another.

'Mr Bush!' he roared. 'Set the main tops'l again, if you please. And send Mr Savage up here.'

The four French ships were rolling along in lubberly French fashion in a wide line abreast, half a mile apart – presumably their captains were afraid of collision if they drew closer – and it was a hundred to one that their lookouts would never notice the tiny dot which would be all they could see of the *Sutherland*. Savage came tumbling up beside him, hardly out of breath after his lightning scramble up the ratlines.

'Take this glass,' said Hornblower. 'You see the French squadron? I want to hear instantly if they alter course, or if they headreach upon us, or we on them.'

'Aye aye, sir,' said Savage.

He had done all he could do now, when he reached the deck again. It only remained to wait, patiently, until tomorrow. Tomorrow would see some sort of battle, hopeless or even – or if there were no battle it would mean that the French had disappeared and he would go before a court martial. He was careful to keep his expression quite composed, and to try and appear as if he did not feel the tension of waiting in the least. It would be in the old tradition if he invited his officers to dinner and whist tonight.

20

The situation was one likely to disturb any captain's sleep, with four hostile ships of the line to windward needing to be kept under observation, and with calculations continually bobbing up from the subconscious to the conscious regarding the chances of the *Cassandra* bringing down Admiral Leighton in time to cut off the enemy. The weather conditions were unsettling, too – the wind, having worked up nearly to a gale force towards evening, diminished until midnight, increased again, and then, with the inconsequence of Mediterranean winds, began to die away steadily.

Certainly Hornblower never expected sleep. He was too excited, and his mind was too active. He lay down on his cot when the watch was changed in the evening to have a rest, and, being quite convinced that he had no chance of sleeping he naturally fell into a heavy dreamless sleep so heavy that Polwheal had to shake him by the shoulder at midnight to awaken him. He came on deck to find Bush standing by the binnacle.

'Too dark for anything to be seen, sir,' said Bush, and then, excitement and exasperation getting the better of his formality, he growled, 'Black as Newgate Knocker.'

'Have you seen anything of the enemy?'

'I thought I did, sir, half an hour back, but nothing to be sure of. Wind's dropped a lot, too.'

'Yes,' said Hornblower.

As so often was the case at sea, there was nothing to do but wait. Two screened lanterns swayed down on the maindeck, where the watch lay at their stations by the guns; the keen wind harped in the rigging, and the ship rose and plunged in the following sea with a lightness and grace no one would expect of her who had only seen her with the wind abeam. Nothing to do but to wait; if he stayed on deck he would only fidget and display his nervousness, so that he might as well go and conceal his nervousness in his screened-off cot.

'Send for me at once if you catch sight of the enemy,' he said, with elaborate carelessness, and went back again below.

He lay on his cot with his mind busy, for he knew that having slept once there was no chance whatever of sleeping again. So perfect was this conviction that sleep ambushed him once more, leaped upon him unawares, as he lay thinking about the *Cassandra*, so that it only seemed two minutes later that he heard Polwheal speaking to him as if from another world.

'Mr Gerard's compliments, sir, an' it's beginnin' to get lighter, sir.'

It called for quite an effort to rouse himself and get up from his cot; only when he was drowsily on his feet did he begin to feel pleased at having been genuinely asleep each time that Polwheal came to call him. He could picture Polwheal telling his cronies about the iron nerves of the captain, who could sleep like a child on a night when the ship was aboil with the prospect of action.

'Anything to report, Mr Gerard?' he said, as he reached the quarterdeck.

'No, sir. I had to reef down for an hour at two bells, it blew so hard. But it's dropping fast now, sir, and backing sou'easterly.'

'H'm,' said Hornblower.

The faintest hint of light was beginning to tinge the gloomy sky, but nothing could be seen yet more than a cable's length away. A south-easterly wind would be nearly foul for the French on their course to Barcelona; it would be dead foul for the *Pluto* and *Caligula*.

'Thought I felt the loom o' the land, sir, before the light came,' said Gerard.

'Yes,' said Hornblower. Their course during the night would bring them close into Cape Creux of hated memory; he picked up the slate beside the binnacle, and, calculating from the hourly readings of the log, he made their position to be some fifteen miles off the cape. If the French had held the same course during the night they would soon have Rosas Bay and comparative security under their lee – of course, if they had not, if they had evaded him in the darkness, the consequence to him did not bear thinking about.

The light was broadening fast. Eastwards the watery clouds seemed to be thinning just above the horizon. Undoubtedly they were thinning; for a second they parted, and a speck of gold could be seen through them, just where the white-flecked sea met the sky, and a long beam of sunlight shone level over the sea.

'Land-ho!' yelled the masthead lookout, and westward they could see a bluish smudge on the horizon where the mountains of Spain loomed faintly over the curve of the world.

And Gerard glanced anxiously at his captain, took a

turn or two up and down the deck, gnawed at his knuckles, and then could restrain his impatience no longer.

'Masthead, there! What do you see of the enemy?'

The pause that followed seemed ages long before the reply came.

'Northin', sir. Northin' in sight barrin' the land to looard.'

Gerard renewed his anxious glance at his captain, but Hornblower, during that pause, had set his face sternly so that his expression was unmoved. Bush was coming on to the quarterdeck now; anyone could see that he was wild with anxiety. If four French ships of the line had evaded action it would mean half pay for Hornblower for life, if nothing worse. Hornblower retained his stony expression; he was proud of being able to do so.

'Put the ship about, Mr Gerard, if you please, and lay her on the starboard tack.'

The French might perhaps have altered course in the darkness, and might now be lost in the centre of the Western Mediterranean, but Hornblower still did not think it likely. His officers had made insufficient allowance for the lubberliness of the unpractised French. If Gerard had had to reef topsails in the night they might well have had to heave to; and both Bush and Gerard were over-eager – during the night the *Sutherland* might have gained twenty miles on the French. By retracing his course he was confident that he would sight them again.

Confident as far as the whist-playing part of his mind was concerned, that is to say. He could not control the sick despair in his breast, nor the acceleration of his heartbeats; he could only conceal them, keeping his face a mask and forcing himself to stand still instead of pacing about in his anxiety. Then he thought of an activity which would help to occupy his mind and yet not betray his nervousness.

'Pass the word for my steward,' he said.

His hands were just steady enough to permit him to shave, and a chill bath under the washdeck pump gave him new vigour. He put on clean clothes and parted his lessening hair with elaborate exactitude, for under the washdeck pump he had told himself that they would sight the French again before he had completed his toilet. It was with a sense of acute disappointment that he laid down the comb when he had no more smallest excuse to continue its use, and turned to put on his coat, with no news of the French. And then, with his foot on the companion, there came a wild yell from Midshipman Parker at the masthead.

'Sail in sight! Two – three of 'em, sir. Four! It's the enemy!'

Hornblower continued his progress up the companion without faltering in his step, and he hoped people noticed it. Bush was half-way up the rigging with his glass, and Gerard was pacing – almost prancing – about the quarterdeck in his delight. Observing them, Hornblower was glad he had had no childish doubts about the correctness of his actions.

'Wear the ship, if you please, Mr Bush. Lay her on the port tack.'

A talkative captain might supplement the order with a brief explanation of the necessity for keeping the ship between the French and Spain, but Hornblower bit off the explanation as it rose to his lips. No unnecessary words would escape him.

'The wind's still working round southerly, sir,' said Gerard.

'Yes,' said Hornblower.

And it would drop a good deal, too, as the day progressed, he decided. The sun was fast breaking through the clouds, with every prospect of a warm day – a Mediterranean autumn day, with a rising barometer and only the faintest of breezes. The hammocks had been piled in the netting, and the watch not at their stations were clattering on to the deck with buckets and holystones. The routine of the navy had to be maintained, even though there was every chance that the decks they were swabbing would be running with blood before the day was over. The men were skylarking and joking – Hornblower felt a little thrill of pride as he looked at them and remembered the sullen despondent crowd with which he had sailed. Consciousness of real achievement was some compensation for the thankless service which employed him; and it helped him to forget, too, the uneasy feeling that today or tomorrow – soon, anyway – he would know again, as the whirl of battle eddied round him, the physical fear of which he was so intolerably ashamed.

As the sun climbed up the sky the wind dropped steadily, moving round even more southerly, and the mountains of Spain came nearer and nearer and grew more and more defined as their course brought them closer to the land. Hornblower held on as long as he could, bracing up his yards as the wind veered, and then finally heaving-to while the French squadron crept up over the horizon. The shift in the wind had deprived them of the windward position; if they moved down to attack him he could escape northward so that if they pursued him they would be running towards the *Pluto* and *Caligula*, but he had no hope that they would. French ships of the line who had evaded the blockading squadron would race to accomplish their mission first, and would only fight afterwards, however tempting the bait dangled before them. If the wind shifted no farther round they could just hold their course for Barcelona, and he had not the least doubt that they would do so if not prevented. He would hang on to them and try to attack some isolated ship during the night if no help arrived.

'They're signalling a lot, sir,' said Bush, his glass to his eye. They had been signalling all day, for that matter – the first flurry of bunting, Hornblower shrewdly surmised, had been occasioned by their catching sight of the *Sutherland*, unaware that she had been keeping company with them for fifteen hours. Frenchmen retained their talkative habits at sea, and no French captain was happy without messages passing back and forth along the squadron.

The *Sutherland* was clear of the Cape Creux peninsula now, and Rosas Bay was opening out on her beam. It was in these very waters, but in very different weather conditions, that the *Pluto* had lost her masts and had been towed to safety by the *Sutherland*; over there, on those green-grey slopes, had occurred the fiasco of the attack on Rosas; through his glass Hornblower thought he could discern the precipitous face of the mesa up which Colonel Claros had led his fugitive Catalans. If the wind came farther round now, the French had a refuge open to them under the guns of Rosas, where they would be safe until the British could bring up fireships and explosion vessels to drive them out again; actually it would be a more secure refuge for them than the anchorage at Barcelona.

He looked up at the pendant flapping at the masthead – the wind was certainly more southerly. It was growing doubtful whether the French would weather Palamos Point on their present tack, while he would certainly have to go about soon and stand out into the Frenchmen's wake, with all his advantages of position lost by the inconstancy of the weather. And the wind was beginning to come in irregular puffs now – a sure sign of its diminishing force. He turned his glass on the French squadron again to see how they were behaving. There was a fresh series of signals fluttering at their yardarms.

'Deck, there!' yelled Savage from the masthead.

Then there was a pause. Savage was not too sure of what he could see.

'What is it, Mr Savage?'

'I think – I'm not quite sure, sir – there's another sail, right on the horizon, sir, abaft the enemy's beam.'

Another sail! It might be a stray merchant ship. Otherwise it could only be Leighton's ships or the *Cassandra*.

'Keep your eye on her, Mr Savage.'

It was impossible to wait for news. Hornblower swung himself up into the shrouds and climbed upwards. At Savage's side he trained his glass in the direction indicated. For a second the French squadron danced in the object glass, disregarded, as he searched.

'A bit farther round, sir. About there, I think, sir.'

It was the tiniest flash of white, too permanent for a wave crest, of a different shade from the few clouds against the blue. Hornblower nearly spoke, but succeeded in limiting himself to 'Ha – h'm.'

'It's nearer now, sir,' said Savage, telescope to eye. 'I should say, sir, it's a ship's fore-royal.'

There could be no doubt about it. Some ship under full sail was out there beyond the Frenchmen, and standing in to cross their wake.

'Ha – h'm,' said Hornblower. He said no more, but snapped his telescope shut and addressed himself to the descent.

Bush dropped to the deck to meet him from the shrouds he had ascended; Gerard, Crystal, they were all on the quarterdeck eyeing him anxiously.

'The *Cassandra*,' said Hornblower, 'standing in towards us.'

By saying that, he was risking his dignity to demonstrate his good sight. No one could guess the new arrival to be the *Cassandra* from just that glimpse of her royals. But it could only be the *Cassandra* who would be on that course, unless his judgement were sadly at fault. Should she be revealed not to be, he would appear ridiculous – but the temptation to appear to recognize her when Savage was not even sure whether she was a ship or a cloud was too strong.

All the implications of the *Cassandra*'s appearance were evident to the officers' minds at once.

'Where's the flagship and *Caligula*?' demanded Bush, of no one in particular.

'May be coming up, too,' said Gerard.

'The Frogs are cut off if they are,' said Crystal.

With the *Pluto* and *Caligula* to seaward of them, and the *Sutherland* to landward, Palamos Point to windward, and a fluky wind veering foul, it would be only by good fortune they could escape a battle. Every eye turned towards the French squadron; they were nearly hull-up now, heading south-by-west close-hauled, a three-decker in the van followed by three two-deckers, admiral's flags flying at the foremasts of the first and third ships. The broad white stripes which decorated their sides stood out sharp and clear in the pure air. If the *Pluto* and *Caligula* were far astern of the *Cassandra* the Frenchmen would still be as much in ignorance of their proximity as was the *Sutherland*, which would explain why they were still holding their course.

'Deck there!' hailed Savage. 'The strange sail's *Cassandra*. I can see her tops'l now, sir.'

Bush and Gerard and Crystal looked at Hornblower with a strange respect for his penetrating vision; it had been well worth risking his dignity for that.

The sails suddenly flapped loudly; a puff of wind had followed a comparative lull, and from a more southerly point than before. Bush turned to shout orders for the trimming of the sails, and the others turned instantly to watch the French reaction.

'They're going about!' said Gerard, loudly.

Undoubtedly they were doing so; on the new tack they would weather Palamos Point but would be standing out to sea nearer to the British squadron – if the British were there.

'Mr Bush,' said Hornblower. 'Put the ship about, if you please.'

'*Cassandra*'s signalling, sir,' yelled Savage.

'Up with you!' snapped Hornblower to Vincent and Longley. Telescope and signal book in hand, they raced for the masthead; everyone on the quarterdeck watched their progress anxiously.

'*Cassandra*'s signalling to the flagship, sir!' yelled Vincent.

So Leighton was out there over the horizon – over the Frenchman's horizon, too, judging from their actions. Bonaparte might send out four French ships to fight three English ones, but no French admiral safely at sea and knowing the capacity of his crews far better than his emperor, would obey those orders if he could help it.

'What's she saying, boy?' hailed Hornblower.

'She's too far off to be sure, sir, but I think she's reporting the enemy's new course.'

Let the Frenchmen hold that course for an hour, and they were lost, cut off from Rosas and certain to be over-hauled before they reached Barcelona.

'They're going about again, by God!' said Gerard, suddenly.

Wordless, they watched the four French ships come up into the wind, and come over on to the other tack. Then they came round, farther and farther still, until in all four ships their three masts were in line; every one of them was heading straight for the *Sutherland*.

'Ha – h'm,' said Hornblower, watching his fate bearing down upon him: and again, 'Ha – h'm.'

The French lookouts must have glimpsed Leighton's mastheads. With Rosas Bay six miles under his lee and Barcelona a hundred miles almost to the windward the

French admiral could have taken little time to reach a decision in face of those strange sails on the horizon. He was dashing instantly for shelter; the single ship of the line which lay directly in his path must be destroyed if she could not be evaded.

The sick wave of excitement and apprehension which Hornblower experienced did not prevent calculations pouring into his mind. The French had six miles to go with a fair wind. He still did not know whereabouts on the circumference of the possible circle whose centre was the French flagship Leighton was at the moment. But he would have twenty miles, perhaps a little more, to sail for certain, and with the wind – such wind as there was – abeam, if he were in the most advantageous position, and on his port bow if he were far astern. And shifting as it was, it would be dead foul for him in two hours. Twenty to one, Hornblower estimated the odds against the admiral being able to catch the French before they reached the protection of the guns of Rosas. Only unheard-of flukes of wind would do it, and only then if the *Sutherland* were able to knock away a good many spars before she was beaten into helplessness. So keenly had Hornblower been calculating that it was only then that he remembered, with a gulp of excitement, that the *Sutherland* was his ship, and the responsibility his, as well.

Longley came sliding down the backstay, the whole height from topmast head to the deck, his face white with excitement.

'Vincent sent me, sir. *Cassandra*'s signalling, and he thinks it's "Flag to *Sutherland*, No. Twenty-one". Twenty-one's "Engage the enemy", sir. But it's hard to read the flags.'

'Very good. Acknowledge.'

So Leighton at least had the moral courage to assume the responsibility for sending one ship against four. In that respect he was worthy of being Barbara's husband.

'Mr Bush,' he said. 'We've a quarter of an hour. See that the men get a bite to eat in that time.'

'Aye aye, sir.'

He looked again at the four ships all steering slowly down upon him. He could not hope to turn them back, but he could only hope to accompany them in their race to Rosas Bay. Any ship that he could totally dismast would fall a prey to Leighton; the others he must damage so sorely that they could not repair themselves in Rosas, which had the smallest dockyard facilities. Then they would stay there until fireships, or a large scale cutting out expedition, or a properly organized attack by land on the fortress, should result in their destruction. He thought he ought to succeed in that, but he could not bring himself to visualize what would happen to the *Sutherland* meanwhile. He swallowed hard, and set himself to plan the manoeuvres of the first encounter. The leading French ship had eighty guns mounted – they were run out and grinning at him through her open ports, while each of the Frenchmen had, as though in bravado, at least four tricolour flags floating in the rigging. He looked up at the battered red ensign hanging from the peak against the blue of the sky, and then he plunged into realities.

'Hands to the braces, Mr Bush. I want the ship handled like lightning when the time comes. Mr Gerard! I'll have every gun captain flogged tomorrow who fires before his gun bears.'

The men at the guns grinned; they would give of their best for him without any threat of flogging, and they knew he knew it.

Bow to bow the *Sutherland* was approaching the eighty-gun ship, unwavering; if both captains held their courses steadily there would be a collision which might sink both ships. Hornblower kept his eye on the Frenchmen to detect the first signs of irresolution; the *Sutherland* was lying as near to the wind as she could, with her sails on the point of flapping. If the French captain had the sense to bring his ship to the wind the *Sutherland* could do nothing decisive against her, but the chances were he would leave his decision to the last moment and then instinctively put his ship before the wind as the easiest course with an unhandy crew. At half a mile smoke suddenly eddied round the Frenchman's bows, and a shot came humming overhead. She was firing her bow chasers, but there was no need to warn Gerard not to reply – he knew the value of that first unhurried broadside too well. With the distance halved two holes appeared in the *Sutherland*'s main topsail; Hornblower did not hear the passing of the shot, so intent was he on noting the Frenchman's actions.

'Which way will he go?' said Bush, beating one hand with the other. 'Which way? He's holding on farther than I thought.'

The farther the better; the more hurried the Frenchman's manoeuvre the more helpless he would be. The bowsprits were only a hundred yards apart now, and Hornblower set his teeth so as not to give the instinctive order to up-helm. Then he saw a flurry on the Frenchman's decks, and her bow swung away from him – to leeward.

'Hold your fire!' Hornblower shouted to Gerard, fearful lest a premature broadside should waste the opportunity. Gerard waved his hat in reply, with a flash of white teeth in his brown face. The two ships were overlapping now, not thirty yards apart, and the Frenchman's guns were beginning to bear. In the bright sunlight Hornblower could see the flash of the epaulettes of the officers on the quarterdeck, the men at the forecastle cannonades stooping to look along the sights. This was the moment.

'Helm a-weather, slow,' he said to the helmsman. A glance at Bush was enough – he was anticipating this order. The *Sutherland* began to wear round slowly, beginning her turn to cross the Frenchman's stern before the two ships were alongside. Bush began to bellow the orders to the men at the braces and the headsail sheets, and as he did so the Frenchman's broadside burst into thunder and flame and smoke. The *Sutherland* shook and jarred with the impact of the shot; one of the mizzen shrouds above Hornblower's head parted with a twang at the same moment as a hole appeared in the quarterdeck bulwark near him amid a shower of splinters. But the *Sutherland*'s bow was already almost touching the Frenchman's stern. Hornblower could see an eddy of panic on her quarterdeck.

'Keep her at that!' he shouted to the helmsman.

Then with a series of heavy crashes, one following another as the *Sutherland* crossed her enemy's stern and each section of guns bore in turn, she fired her broadside into her, heeling slightly at each discharge, with every shot tearing its destructive course from end to end of the ship. Gerard came leaping on to the quarterdeck, having run down the whole length of the maindeck, keeping pace with the firing. He bent eagerly over the nearest carronade, altered its elevation with a quick twist of the screw, and jerked the lanyard, with a wave of the hand to the other gun captains to do the same. The carronades roared out, sweeping the Frenchman's quarterdeck with grape on top of the roundshot. Hornblower saw the officers there dashed to the deck like lead soldiers, saw rigging parting, and the big stern windows of the French ship disappear like a curtain jerked from its pole.

'That's given him a bellyful,' said Bush.

That was the sort of broadside which won battles. That single discharge had probably knocked half the fight out of the Frenchman, killing and wounding a hundred men or more, dismounting half a dozen guns. In a single ship duel she would strike her flag in less than half an hour. But now she had drawn ahead while the *Sutherland* was completing her turn, and the second Frenchman, the one with the rear admiral's flag, was close on the weather quarter. She had all plain sail set, and was overhauling them fast; in a moment she would be able to rake the *Sutherland* as the *Sutherland* had raked her consort.

'Starboard!' said Hornblower to the helmsman. 'Stand to your guns on the port side!' His voice rang uncannily loud in the stillness following the firing.

The Frenchman came on undeviating, not disdaining a broadside to broadside duel, but not attempting to manoeuvre, especially against an enemy who had proved himself alert, at a time when manoeuvring meant delay in gaining the shelter of Rosas. The ships inclined together, growing nearer and nearer as the Frenchman headreached upon the *Sutherland* and the *Sutherland*'s course approached hers. From the *Sutherland*'s deck they could hear the excited orders which the French officers were shouting to their men, trying to restrain their eagerness until the decisive moment.

They were not entirely successful all the same, as first one gun and then another went off as excitable gunners let fly – where the shots went Heaven alone knew. A word from Hornblower swung the *Sutherland* round till she lay parallel to her opponent, and as she steadied on her new course Hornblower waved his hand to Gerard as a signal to open fire. There was not more than half a second between the two broadsides; the *Sutherland*, heaving up her side to the recoil of her guns, heaved over farther still to the impact of the shot. As the smoke came billowing up round her the air was filled with the splintering crash of the shot striking her sides; there were screams and cries from below in proof of the damage received.

'Keep at it now, lads! Fire as you will!' shouted Gerard.

Those hours of drill bore fruit now. The sponges were thrust into the reeking gun muzzles, and the moment they were withdrawn the powder and the rammer and the shot were ready for insertion. Almost simultaneously the gun trucks rumbled as the crews flung themselves on the tackles and ran the guns up; almost simultaneously the guns roared out. This time there was a perceptible and measurable interval before the Frenchman replied in a straggling and irregular salvo. The gentle wind blowing on the engaged quarter kept the ship engulfed in the smoke; the gunners labouring on the maindeck were as vague as in a dense fog to Hornblower, but the masts and sails of the Frenchman still stood out clear against the blue sky. The *Sutherland*'s third broadside followed close on the heels of the Frenchman's second.

'Three to her two, as usual,' said Bush, coolly. A shot struck the mizzenmast bitts and sprayed the deck with splinters. 'She's still drawing ahead, sir.'

It was hard to think clearly in this frightful din, with death all round. Captain Morris had his marines all along the port side gangway firing away at everyone visible on the other ship's decks; the two ships were within easy musket shot. The *Sutherland*'s broadside were growing irregular now, as the most efficient crews worked their guns faster than the others, while the Frenchman was delivering a running fire in which there were occasional louder explosions to be heard when several guns went off together. It was like the clattering of the hoofs of four coach horses on a hard road, sometimes in unison for a space, and then spreading out again.

'I fancy his fire's slackening, sir,' said Bush. 'It doesn't surprise me.'

The *Sutherland* had not suffered mortally yet, judging by the number of dead on the maindeck. She could still fight for a long time yet.

'See his mainmast, sir!' yelled Bush.

His maintopmast was bowing forward, slow and dignified, with the topgallantmast bowing further forward still. Through the smoke they could see the mainmast inclining aft. Then all dignity left the soaring mass of spars and canvas. It hung s-shaped in the air for a breathless second, and then tumbled down with a rush, fore- and mizzentopmasts falling with it. Hornblower felt a grim satisfaction at the sight – there were no spare mainmasts to be had in Rosas. The *Sutherland*'s crew cheered piercingly, and hastened to fire in a few last shots as their ship drew ahead of her crippled opponent. A minute later the din of the firing ceased, the tiny breeze blew away the smoke, and the sun came shining through upon the littered deck again.

Aft lay their late antagonist, a great mass of wreckage trailing alongside, the second lower deck gun from the bow pointing out of its port at an impossible angle of elevation to show she had one gun at least knocked useless. A quarter of a mile ahead was the first ship they had fired into; she had paid no attention to the duel behind her but had continued under all sail for the safety of Rosas Bay, just like a Frenchman. And beyond her, sweeping round the horizon, were the cruel mountains of Spain, and the white roofs of Rosas were clearly visible above the golden shore. The *Sutherland* was close to the wide mouth of the bay; half-way between her and Rosas lay two gigantic beetles on the flat blue surface – gunboats coming out of Rosas under sweeps.

And close astern of the crippled ship came the other two ships of the French squadron, the three-decker with the vice-admiral's flag and a two-decker in her wake. It was the moment for decision.

'Masthead there!' hailed Hornblower. 'Can you see anything of the flagship?'

'No, sir. Nothing but *Cassandra*.'

Hornblower could see the *Cassandra*'s royals himself, from the deck, pearly white on the horizon; the *Pluto* and *Caligula* must still be nearly twenty miles away – possibly becalmed. The tiny breeze which was urging the *Sutherland* into the bay was probably a sea breeze; the day was hot enough for that. Leighton would hardly arrive in time to take part in this battle. Hornblower could put his ship about now, and tack into safety, beating off the two enemies if they interfered with him, or he could throw himself into their path; and with every second carrying him a yard nearer Rosas he must decide quickly. If he fought, there was the faintest possible chance that Leighton might be brought up in time to pick up the cripples, but so faint a chance as to be negligible.

The *Sutherland* would be destroyed, but her enemies would be so knocked about as to be detained in Rosas for days or even weeks. And that was desirable, because it would be several days before preparations could be made to attack them in their anchorage, and during those days there would always be the chance of their escaping – three of them, at least – from Rosas, as they had escaped from Toulon.

Hornblower balanced in his mind the loss of a seventy-four to England against the certain loss of four ships of the line to France. And then he knew, suddenly, that his cogitation had been wasted. If he withdrew, he would all the rest of his life suspect himself of having done so out of cowardice, and he foresaw with clarity the years of mental uneasiness it would bring. He would fight whether it was the right thing or not and as he reached that decision he realized with relief that it was the correct course as well. One more second he wasted, looking up at the blue sky which he loved, and then he gulped down his muddled emotions.

'Lay the ship on the port tack, if you please, Mr Bush,' he said.

The crew cheered again, the poor fools, when they saw that they were about to face the rest of the French, even though it meant the certain death of half of them at least. Hornblower felt pity – or was it contempt? – for them and their fighting madness or thirst for glory. Bush was as bad as any of them, judging by the way his face had lit up at the order. He wanted the Frenchmen's blood just because they were Frenchmen, and thought nothing of the chance of being a legless cripple if he were granted the chance of smashing a few French legs first.

The crippled two-decker with the rear admiral's flag came drifting down on them – this sea breeze would push all wrecks into Rosas Bay under the guns of the fortress – and the men working lackadaisically at clearing the wreckage ran from their work when they looked up and saw the *Sutherland*'s guns swinging around towards them. The *Sutherland* fired three broadsides into her with hardly a gun in reply before she drifted clear – another fifty or so dead Frenchmen for Bush, thought Hornblower, viciously, as the rumble of the gun trucks died away and the men stood waiting once more, silent now, beside their guns. Here came the three-decker, now, beautiful with her towering canvas, hideous with her grinning guns. Even at that moment Hornblower marked, with professional interest, the decided tumble-home of her sides, much greater than English shipwrights allowed.

'Let her pay off slowly, Mr Bush,' he said. He was going to set his teeth into the three-decker like a bulldog.

Round came the *Sutherland*, slowly, slowly. Hornblower saw that his last manoeuvre with the *Sutherland* was going to be as well timed as ever he could wish. She was on the same course as the three-decker at exactly the moment the latter drew up opposite to her; the guns of both ships bore simultaneously, a hundred yards apart, and burst simultaneously into thunder and smoke.

In the earlier encounters time had seemed to pass slowly. Now it seemed to be passing fast, the infernal din of the broadsides seeming almost unintermitting, the figures hurrying about in the smoke seeming to be moving twice as fast as normally.

'Edge in closer on her,' said Hornblower to the helmsman, and then, his last order given, he could abandon himself to the mad inconsequence of it all. Shots seemed to be tearing up the deck all around him, smashing great gashes in the planking. With the clear unreality of a nightmare he saw Bush fall, with blood running from the stump of one leg where a foot was missing. Two men of the surgeon's crew bent over him to carry him below.

'Leave me on deck,' said Bush. 'Let go of me, you dogs.'

'Take him away,' said Hornblower. The harshness of his voice was a piece with the madness of everything else, for he was glad to be able to order Bush into a place of safety where he might yet live.

The mizzentopmast fell, and spars and blocks and tackle came raining all round him – death falling from the heavens as well as hurtling in from overside, but still he lived. Now the foretopsail yard was shot through in the slings; dimly through the smoke he could see Hooker leading a party aloft to repair it. Out of the tail of his eye he saw something new and strange looming through the smoke – it was the fourth French ship, coming up on the *Sutherland*'s disengaged side. He found himself waving his hat and shrieking some nonsense or other to his men, who cheered him back as they brought the starboard side guns into action. The smoke was thicker, and the din more tremendous, and the whole ship throbbing with every gun in action.

Little Longley was at his side now, white faced, miraculously alive after the fall of the mizzentopmast. 'I'm *not* frightened. I'm *not* frightened,' the boy said; his jacket was torn clean across the breast and he was trying to hold it together as he denied the evidence of the tears in his eyes.

'No, sonny, of course you're not,' said Hornblower.

Then Longley was dead, hands and breast smashed into pulp. There was a maindeck gun not run out, he saw as he looked away from Longley's body. He was about to call attention to the abandoned gun, when he noticed its slaughtered crew lying in fragments round it, and he saw that there were no longer any men to spare to get it into action again. Soon there would be more guns than one out of action. The very carronade beside him had but three men to man it – so had the next one, and the next. Down on the maindeck there were marines carrying powder and shot; Gerard must have set them to that work, and the powder boys must be mostly dead. If only this din would stop, and allow him to think!

It seemed to him as if at that the din redoubled. Foremast and mainmast came down together with a splintering crash audible high above the gunfire, the mass of wreckage tumbling over the starboard side. He ran forward, to find Hooker there already hard at work with a group of men drawn from the blinded guns hacking away at the rigging to cut it clear. The three-feet-thick end of the broken mainmast had smashed a gun carriage and killed the crew during its fall. Shots from the two-decker on that side were smashing through the men at work, and already smoke was pouring up from the canvas hanging over the side where the flame of the guns had set it on fire. Hornblower took an axe from the hand of a dead man and fell to work hacking and cutting along with the others. When the last rope was cut, and the flaring mass had dropped overside, and hasty inspection showed that the timber of the ship had not caught fire, he swept the sweat from his forehead and looked around the ship from his new point of view.

The whole deck was heaped and littered with dead men and fragments of dead men. The wheel was gone, the masts, the bulwarks were beaten flat, the very hatch coamings indicated by a mere fringe of splinters. But the guns which could still be worked were still firing, each manned by its attenuated crew. On either side the enemy loomed through the smoke, but the three-decker had lost two topmasts and the two-decker her mizzen-mast, and their sails were in shreds and their rigging hanging in festoons, seen dimly in the smoke. The firing was as fierce as ever. He wondered dully by what miracle he survived to walk through the tempest of shot back to his post on the quarterdeck.

Some puff of wind was altering the relative position of the ships. The three-decker was swinging round, coming closer; Hornblower was already running forward down the port side, with seeming feet of lead, when the three-decker's starboard bow came with a grinding bump against the *Sutherland*'s port bow. Frenchmen were gathering to leap down on to the *Sutherland*'s deck, and Hornblower drew his sword as he ran.

'Boarders,' he yelled. 'All hands repel boarders! Boom them off, there, Hooker, Crystal.'

High above his head towered the three-decker. Musketry was spattering along her bulwarks, and Hornblower heard bullets rapping into the deck round him. Men with swords and pikes in their hands were scrambling down the three-decker's sides, and more were spewing out of the middle-deck gun port on to the *Sutherland*'s gangway. Hornblower found himself caught up in a wave of British sailors with cutlasses and pikes, rammers and handspikes, men naked to the waist and grey with powder smoke. Everyone was jostling and slipping and struggling. He was flung up against a dapper little French lieutenant with his hat rakishly awry. For the moment his arms were pinned to his sides by the press, and the Frenchman was struggling to pull a pistol from his waistband.

'*Rends-toi,*' he spluttered, as the weapon came free, but Hornblower brought up his knee and the Frenchman's head went back in agony and he dropped the pistol.

And the three-decker was swinging away clear again, urged by the puff of wind and the thrust of the spar Crystal and Hooker and their party were pushing against her side. Some of the Frenchmen leaped back to the ship. Some leaped into the sea. A dozen who were left dropped their weapons – one of them too late to check the pike which was thrust into his stomach. The puff of wind was still blowing, drifting the French ships away from the dismasted *Sutherland* and rolling away the smoke. The sun came out and shone upon them and the hideous decks as though from behind a cloud, and the din of the firing ended magically as the guns ceased to bear.

Sword in hand, Hornblower stood while the men about him secured the prisoners. The cessation of the noise had not brought him the relief he had hoped for – on the contrary, he was amazed and stupid, and in his weariness he found it a desperate effort to think clearly. The wind had drifted the *Sutherland* well inside the bay, and there was no sign at all of the *Pluto* and *Caligula* – only the *Cassandra*, hull down over the horizon, a helpless spectator of the fight. The two battered French ships, almost as helpless as the *Sutherland*, thanks to the damage they had received aloft, were floating a short distance off; down the side of the three-decker, dribbling from the scuppers, Hornblower noticed a dark streak – human blood.

The two-decker was still swinging round; her shattered side was out of sight, now she was presenting her stern, and now her other side to the *Sutherland*'s bow. Hornblower watched her stupidly. And then – a bellowing roar, and her broadside came tearing into the

Sutherland. A cloud of splinters flew from the shattered stump of the foremast, and the gun beside Hornblower rang like a bell to a glancing shot.

'Oh, stop!' muttered Hornblower. 'For God's sake!'

The men on the *Sutherland*'s deck were dragging themselves to the guns again. Gerard was nowhere to be seen, but Hooker – a good boy, that – was walking along the main deck apportioning the men to the guns so that some at least might be worked. But the men were faint with fatigue, and at present no gun would bear, while the dismasted *Sutherland* could do nothing to save herself. Another broadside, ripping and tearing through the ship. Hornblower became conscious of a faint undercurrent of noise – the feeble chorus of the wounded men huddled in every corner of the ship. The gunboats were working round cautiously with their sweeps to take up a position under the *Sutherland*'s stern; soon they would be firing their forty-two pounders into her on the water line. Sun and blue sea and blue sky; the grey-green mountains of Spain, the golden beach and white houses of Rosas – Hornblower looked round at them all, despairingly, and it was agony to look.

Another broadside; Hornblower saw two men knocked into a bloody mess at Hooker's side.

'Strike,' he said to himself. 'We must strike.'

But the *Sutherland* had no colours flying that she could strike, and Hornblower's dazed mind wrestled with this problem as he walked aft. The forty-two pounder in one of the gunboats boomed out loudly, and Hornblower felt the jar as the shot smashed into the ship's side below him. Hooker was on the quarterdeck now, and Crystal, and Howell the carpenter.

'There's four feet of water in the well, sir,' said this last, 'an' no pump left.'

'Yes,' said Hornblower, dully. 'I shall surrender.'

He read agreement in the grey faces of his officers, but they said nothing. If only the *Sutherland* would sink under them the problem would solve itself but that would be too much to hope for. She would only grow more and more waterlogged, sinking as each deck in turn was submerged, while the pitiless cannonade would continue. It might be as much as twenty-four hours before she sank completely and in that time the little wind would have drifted her aground under the guns of Rosas. All he could do was to surrender. He thought of the other British captains who had found themselves in similar positions. Thompson of the *Leander* and the captain of the *Swiftsure* and the unfortunate man under Saumarez' command in Algeciras Bay; they, too, had hauled down their flags after a long fight against heavy odds.

Somebody was hailing from the two-decker; he could not understand what was said, but it must be a demand to surrender.

'*Oui*,' he shouted back, '*Oui*.'

For answer there came another broadside, smashing home with a splintering of timber and to the accompaniment of a shriek from below.

'Oh God!' said Hooker.

Hornblower realized that he must have misunderstood the question, and with the realization came a solution of the difficulty. He ran as fast as his stiff legs would carry him, down to the indescribable chaos which represented what was left of his cabin. Hurriedly he turned over the litter there, while the men at the guns watched him expressionless as animals. He found what he sought at last, and came up on the quarterdeck with his arms full of it.

'Here,' he said, giving it to Crystal and Howell. 'Hang that over the side.'

It was the tricolour flag he had had made to deceive the batteries at Llanza. At sight of it the men in the gunboats bent to their oars to propel their craft alongside, while Hornblower stood with the sun shining on his bare head waiting for them. They would take his sword of honour away from him. And the other sword of honour was still in pawn to Duddingstone the ship chandler, and he would never be able to redeem it now, with his career wrecked. And the shattered hull of the *Sutherland* would be towed in triumph under the guns of Rosas – how long would it be before the Mediterranean fleet came down to avenge her, to retake her from the captors, or burn her in one vast pyre along with her shattered conquerors? And Maria was going to bear him a child, whom he would never see during all the years of his captivity. And Lady Barbara would read of his capture in the newspapers – what would she think of his surrendering? But the sun was hot on his head, and he was very weary.

C. S. FORESTER

FLYING COLOURS

A humiliated and shipless captive of the French, Horatio Hornblower faces execution unless he can escape and make a triumphant return to England . . .

Forced to surrender his ship, *HMS Sutherland*, after a long and bloody battle, Captain Horatio Hornblower is held prisoner in a French fortress. Prospects turn bleaker when he learns that he and Lt. Bush are to be tried and executed in Paris as part of Napoleon's attempts to rally the war-weary Empire. Even if Hornblower can escape this fate and make it safe to England, he still faces court-martial for surrendering his ship. With little hope for the future and little left to lose, Hornblower throws caution to the wind once more.

This is the seventh of eleven books chronicling the adventures of C. S. Forester's inimitable nautical hero, Horatio Hornblower.

'I find Hornblower admirable, vastly entertaining' Sir Winston Churchill

C. S. FORESTER

THE COMMODORE

1812 and the fate of Europe lies in the hands of newly appointed Commodore Hornblower ...

Dispatched to northern waters to protect Britain's Baltic interests, Horatio Hornblower must halt the advance of Napoleon's empire into Sweden and Russia. But first he must battle the terrible Baltic weather: fog, snow and icebound waterways; overcome Russian political and commercial intrigues; avoid the seductive charms of royalty as well as the deadly reach of assassins in the imperial palace; and contend with hostile armies and French privateers. With the fate of Europe balanced on a knife edge, the responsibility lies heavy on a Commodore's shoulders ...

This is the eighth of eleven books chronicling the adventures of C. S. Forester's inimitable nautical hero, Horatio Hornblower.

'Hornblower is Hamlet in command of a battleship' *New York Times*

'I find Hornblower admirable, vastly entertaining' Sir Winston Churchill

---

C. S. FORESTER

LORD HORNBLOWER

1813, and Horatio Hornblower is propelled toward the heart of the French Empire and his old enemy, Napoleon . . .

Sir Horatio Hornblower has received strict and highly confidential orders from the highest rank: he must embark upon a grave and perilous mission to recapture the *Flame* in the Bay of Seine, where the brutal and foul-tempered Lieutenant Augustine Chadwick is being held prisoner by a mutinous crew. Rescuing the Lieutenant demands all of Horatio's spirit and seafaring prowess – for at the same time, he must contend with capturing two French cargo vessels and take part in negotiations to topple the faltering Napoleon once and for all . . .

This is the ninth of eleven books chronicling the adventures of C.S. Forester's inimitable nautical hero, Horatio Hornblower.

'I find Hornblower admirable, vastly entertaining' Sir Winston Churchill

C. S. FORESTER

HORNBLOWER IN THE WEST INDIES

1815, the Napoleonic Wars are over. Yet peace continues to elude Horatio Hornblower overseas . . .

As an admiral struggling to impose order in the chaotic aftermath of the French wars, Horatio Hornblower, Commander-in-chief of His Majesty's ships and vessels in the West Indies, must still face savage pirates, reckless revolutionaries and a violent hurricane.

And while his retirement at half-pay might well be in sight, Hornblower will need every ounce of his rapier wit and quick thinking – not to mention his courage and leadership – to ensure that the lasting peace in Europe reaches the turbulent seas of the West Indies.

This is the tenth of eleven books chronicling the adventures of C. S. Forester's inimitable nautical hero, Horatio Hornblower.

'I find Hornblower admirable, vastly entertaining' Sir Winston Churchill

C. S. FORESTER

HORNBLOWER AND THE CRISIS

The final Horatio Hornblower story tells of Napoleon's plans to invade England.

Set in 1805, *Hornblower and the Crisis* finds Horatio Hornblower in possession of confidential dispatches from Bonaparte after a vicious hand-to-hand encounter with a French brig. The admiralty rewards Hornblower by sending him on a dangerous espionage mission that will light the powder trail leading to the battle of Trafalgar . . .

Hornblower and the Crisis was unfinished at the time of Forester's death, but the author left notes – included here – telling us how the tale would end. Also included are two further stories – *Hornblower and the Widow McCool* and *The Last Encounter* – that tell of Hornblower as a very young and very old man, respectively.

This is the final book chronicling the adventures of C. S. Forester's inimitable nautical hero, Horatio Hornblower.

'I find Hornblower admirable, vastly entertaining' Sir Winston Churchill

C. S. FORESTER

LIEUTENANT HORNBLOWER

The nineteenth century dawns and the Napoleonic Wars rage as Horatio Hornblower faces the fury of the French and Spanish fleets combined.

Amidst the hissing of wet wads, the stifling heat of white-hot cannonshot and the clamour of a mutinous crew, new Lieutenant Hornblower will need all of his seafaring cunning to overcome his first challenge in independent command on the high seas. And while blood and violence flow thick and fast aboard a beleaguered *HMS Renown*, the aftermath of war promises intrigue of an entirely different order: Maria, a young señorita, who might just soften the steely resolve of a young lieutenant.

This is the second of eleven books chronicling the adventures of C. S. Forester's inimitable nautical hero, Horatio Hornblower.

'One of the best...Everyone interested in war, or in human nature, should read this fascinating tale' *The Times Literary Supplement*

'I recommend Forester to every literate I know' Ernest Hemingway

C. S. FORESTER

HORNBLOWER AND THE *HOTSPUR*

April 1803, and the Peace of Amiens is failing as Horatio Hornblower takes a three-master on a vital reconnaissance mission . . .

On the day of his marriage to Maria, Hornblower is ordered to take the *Hotspur* and head for Brest – war is coming and Napoleon will not catch His Majesty's navy with its britches round its ankles. With thoughts of his new life as a husband intruding on his duties, Hornblower must prove himself to be not only the most capable commander in the fleet, but also its most daring if he is to stop the French gaining the upper hand.

This is the third of eleven books chronicling the adventures of C. S. Forester's inimitable nautical hero, Horatio Hornblower.

'A master of the genre' *New York Times Book Review*

'I recommend Forester to every literate I know' Ernest Hemingway

C. S. FORESTER

HORNBLOWER AND THE *ATROPOS*

1805, and Hornblower is both humbled and honoured in quick succession . . .

After near disaster on board a canal barge, Horatio Hornblower is given his first assignment as Captain, taking charge of the *Atropos*, a 22-gun sloop that will act as flagship for the funeral procession of Lord Nelson. Soon the *Atropos* is part of the Mediterranean fleet's assault upon Napoleon, and Captain Hornblower must execute a bold and daring salvage operation for buried treasure lying deep in Turk waters. Under the guns of a suspicious port captain and the threat of a Spanish frigate more than double *Atropos*'s size, Hornblower must steer his ship unscathed and triumphant. . .

This is the fourth of eleven books chronicling the adventures of C.S. Forester's inimitable nautical hero, Horatio Hornblower.

'Hornblower is Hamlet in command of a battleship' *New York Times*

'I find Hornblower admirable, vastly entertaining' Sir Winston Churchill

C. S. FORESTER

THE HAPPY RETURN

June, 1808 – and off the Coast of Nicaragua Captain Horatio Hornblower has his hands full . . .

Now in command of HMS *Lydia*, a thirty-six-gun frigate, Hornblower has instructions to form an alliance against the Spanish colonies with a mad and messianic revolutionary, El Supremo; to find a water route across the Central American isthmus; and 'to take, sink, burn or destroy' the fifty-gun Spanish ship of the line *Natividad* – or face court-martial. And as if that wasn't hard enough, Hornblower must also contend with the charms of an unwanted passenger: Lady Barbara Wellesley . . .

This is the fifth of eleven books chronicling the adventures of C. S. Forester's inimitable nautical hero, Horatio Hornblower.

'I find Hornblower admirable, vastly entertaining' Sir Winston Churchill

C. S. FORESTER

A SHIP OF THE LINE

May, 1810 – and thirty-nine-year-old Captain Horatio Hornblower has been
handed his first ship of the line . . .

Though the seventy-four-gun *HMS Sutherland* is 'the ugliest and least desirable
two-decker in the Navy' and a crew shortage means he must recruit two hundred
and fifty landlubbers, Hornblower knows that by the time *Sutherland* and her
squadron reach the blockaded Catalonian coast every seaman will do his duty. But
with daring raids against the French army and navy to be made, it will take all
Hornblower's seamanship – and stewardship – to steer a steady course to victory
and home . . .

This is the sixth of eleven books chronicling the adventures of C. S. Forester's
inimitable nautical hero, Horatio Hornblower.

'I find Hornblower admirable, vastly entertaining' Sir Winston Churchill

He just wanted a decent book to read ...

Not too much to ask, is it? It was in 1935 when Allen Lane, Managing Director of Bodley Head Publishers, stood on a platform at Exeter railway station looking for something good to read on his journey back to London. His choice was limited to popular magazines and poor-quality paperbacks – the same choice faced every day by the vast majority of readers, few of whom could afford hardbacks. Lane's disappointment and subsequent anger at the range of books generally available led him to found a company – and change the world.

'We believed in the existence in this country of a vast reading public for intelligent books at a low price, and staked everything on it'
Sir Allen Lane, 1902–1970, founder of Penguin Books

The quality paperback had arrived – and not just in bookshops. Lane was adamant that his Penguins should appear in chain stores and tobacconists, and should cost no more than a packet of cigarettes.

Reading habits (and cigarette prices) have changed since 1935, but Penguin still believes in publishing the best books for everybody to enjoy. We still believe that good design costs no more than bad design, and we still believe that quality books published passionately and responsibly make the world a better place.

So wherever you see the little bird – whether it's on a piece of prize-winning literary fiction or a celebrity autobiography, political tour de force or historical masterpiece, a serial-killer thriller, reference book, world classic or a piece of pure escapism – you can bet that it represents the very best that the genre has to offer.

Whatever you like to read – trust Penguin.